GIRL

AT

WAR

Sara Nović

ABACUS

First published in the United States in 2015 by Random House
First published in Great Britain in 2015 by Little, Brown
This paperback edition published in 2016 by Abacus

1 3 4 5 7 9 10 8 6 4 2

Copyright © 2015 by Sara Nović
Maps © 2015 by David Lindroth, Inc.

The moral right of the author has been asserted.

A CIP catalogue record for this book
is available from the British Library.

ISBN 978-0-349-14098-8

Book design by Dana Leigh Blanchette
Title-page and part-title image: © iStockphoto.com

Printed and bound in Great Britain by
Clays Ltd, St Ives plc

Papers used by Abacus are from well-managed forests
and other responsible sources.

MIX
Paper from
responsible sources
FSC
www.fsc.org   FSC® C104740

Abacus
An imprint of
Little, Brown Book Group
Carmelite House
50 Victoria Embankment
London EC4Y 0DZ

An Hachette UK Company
www.hachette.co.uk

www.littlebrown.co.uk

Sara N̶... ...
States ... ...
MFA ... ...
fiction and translation. She is the ....ouss
Magazine and teaches writing at the Fashion Institute of
Technology and Columbia University. She lives in Queens,
New York.

www.sara-novic.com
@NovicSara

'This vivid debut recalls *Half of a Yellow Sun*. Ana's journey
from a ten-year-old tomboy to young woman will leave you
reeling' *Stylist*

'I read it in one night ... devastating ... Nović excels at
distilling visual poetry from action scenes ... [she] has
breathed f   and ice into these pages. Immersing herself in
the darkest materials, she has given us the real stuff dystopian
fantasies are made of' *Guardian*

'An outstanding first novel ... *Girl at War* performs the
miracle of making the stories of broken lives in a distant
country feel as large and universal as myth' *New York Times
Book Review* (Editor's Choice)

'*... at War* is an extraordinarily poised and ... novel, a story about grief and exile, memory ... identity, and the redemptive power of love' *Financial Times*

'A shattering debut ... The book begins with what deserves to become one of contemporary literature's more memorable opening lines. The sentences that follow are equally as lyrical as a folk lament and as taut as metal wire wrapped through an electrified fence' *USA Today*

'Heartfelt, in places harrowing, but ultimately redemptive' *Mail on Sunday*

'From its first sentence, Sara Nović's debut novel unfolds on both intimate and immense scales ... The first section ends with a brilliantly abrupt, devastating event that essentially ends Ana's childhood. It's a scene that haunts the rest of the book ... [Nović is] a writer whose own gravity and talent anchor this novel' *New York Times*

'The first third of this gripping debut novel depicts the start of the Yugoslavian civil war through the eyes of Ana Jurić, a ten-year-old girl residing with her family in Croatia's capital ... Through Ana's journey, Nović, in tender and eloquent prose, explores the challenge of how to live even after one has survived' *Oprah magazine*

'If we looked for and celebrated a "book of the summer" as we do that one song every year (what will it be this year?!), this novel would surely be this summer's star. This debut work from a rising author examines in painful, tender detail the cost of war on a young woman, many years after her simple life with her family in Croatia was interrupted by war. Ana, the main character, is haunted by the memories of what she thought her country once was, and how to deal with the secrets of what really happened to her and her family' *Vanity Fair*

'Powerful and vividly wrought ... Nović writes about horrors with an elegant understatement. In cool, accomplished sentences, we are met with the gravity, brutality and even the mundaneness of war and loss as well as the enduring capacity to live' *San Francisco Chronicle*

'A powerful and unforgettable novel that made me see Croatia in a whole new light' *Stylist*

'Sara Nović's powerful debut novel, *Girl at War*, is a superb exploration of conflict and its aftermath, and a stark reminder that while ceasefires and peace treaties may end the fighting, they don't always end the suffering' *The National*

For my family,
and for A

I had come to Yugoslavia to see what history meant in flesh and blood. I learned now that it might follow, because an empire passed, that a world full of strong men and women and rich food and heady wine might nevertheless seem like a shadow-show: that a man of every excellence might sit by a fire warming his hands in the vain hope of casting out a chill that lived not in the flesh.

—Rebecca West,
Black Lamb and Grey Falcon

I see pictures merging before my mind's eye—paths through the fields, river meadows, and mountain pastures mingling with images of destruction—and oddly enough, it is the latter, not the now entirely unreal idylls of my early childhood, that make me feel rather as if I were coming home.

—W. G. Sebald,
On the Natural History of Destruction

The Balkans, 1991

AUSTRIA
SLOVENIA
Ljubljana • Zagreb
C R O A T I A
Vukovar
Vojvodina
HUNGARY
Danube R.
Plitvice
Safe House
•Village
BOSNIA-
HERZEGOVINA
Knin
Šibenik•
Split•
Ana's
Tiska
Sarajevo
Belgrade
Danube R.
S E R B I A
A D R I A T I C S E A
I T A L Y
Dubrovnik•
MONTENEGRO
Kosovo
ALBANIA
MACEDONIA
ROMANIA
BULGARIA
GREECE

EUROPE
Yugoslavia
(1991)

0   MILES   100
0   KM   100

The Balkans, 2001

AUSTRIA
SLOVENIA
Ljubljana • Zagreb
C R O A T I A
Vukovar
VOJVODINA
HUNGARY
Danube R.
Plitvice
BOSNIA-
HERZEGOVINA
Knin
Šibenik•
Split•
Ana's
Tiska
Sarajevo
Belgrade
Danube R.
SERBIA
&
MONTENEGRO
A D R I A T I C S E A
I T A L Y
Dubrovnik•
KOSOVO
ALBANIA
FORMER YUGOSLAV
REPUBLIC OF
MACEDONIA
Skopje
ROMANIA
BULGARIA
GREECE

EUROPE
Croatia
(2001)

0   MILES   100
0   KM   100

I

They Both Fell

1

The war in Zagreb began over a pack of cigarettes. There had been tensions beforehand, rumors of disturbances in other towns whispered above my head, but no explosions, nothing outright. Caught between the mountains, Zagreb sweltered in the summer, and most people abandoned the city for the coast during the hottest months. For as long as I could remember my family had vacationed with my godparents in a fishing village down south. But the Serbs had blocked the roads to the sea, at least that's what everyone was saying, so for the first time in my life we spent the summer inland.

Everything in the city was clammy, doorknobs and train handrails slick with other people's sweat, the air heavy with the smell of yesterday's lunch. We took cold showers and walked around the flat in our underwear. Under the run of cool water I imagined my skin sizzling, steam rising from it. At night we lay atop our sheets, awaiting fitful sleep and fever dreams.

I turned ten in the last week of August, a celebration marked by a soggy cake and eclipsed by heat and disquiet. My parents invited their best friends—my godparents, Petar and Marina—over for dinner that weekend. The house where we usually stayed the summers belonged to Petar's grandfather. My mother's break from teaching allowed us three months of vacation—my father taking a train, meeting us later—and the five of us would live there together on the cliffs along the Adriatic. Now that we were landlocked, the weekend dinners had become an anxious charade of normalcy.

Before Petar and Marina arrived I argued with my mother about putting on clothes.

"You're not an animal, Ana. You'll wear shorts to dinner or you'll get nothing."

"In Tiska I only wear my swimsuit bottoms anyway," I said, but my mother gave me a look and I got dressed.

That night the adults were engaging in their regular debate about exactly how long they'd known each other. They had been friends since before they were my age, they liked to say, no matter how old I was, and after the better part of an hour and a bottle of FeraVino they'd usually leave it at that. Petar and Marina had no children for me to play with, so I sat at the table holding my baby sister and listening to them vie for the farthest-reaching memory. Rahela was only eight months old and had never seen the coast, so I talked to her about the sea and our little boat, and she smiled when I made fish faces at her.

After we ate, Petar called me over and handed me a fistful of dinar. "Let's see if you can beat your record," he said. It was a game between us—I would run to the store to buy his cigarettes and he would time me. If I beat my record he'd let me keep a few dinar from the change. I stuffed the money in the pocket of my cutoffs and took off down the nine flights of stairs.

I was sure I was about to set a new record. I'd perfected my route, knew when to hug the curves around buildings and avoid the bumps in the side streets. I passed the house with the big orange BEWARE OF DOG sign (though no dog ever lived there that I could remember), jumped over a set of cement steps, and veered away from the dumpsters. Under a concrete archway that always smelled like piss, I held my breath and sped into the open city. I skirted the biggest pothole in front of the bar frequented by the daytime drinkers, slowing only slightly as I came upon the old man at his folding table hawking stolen chocolates. The newsstand kiosk's red awning shifted in a rare breeze, signaling me like a finish line flag.

I put my elbows on the counter to get the clerk's attention. Mr. Petrović knew me and knew what I wanted, but today his smile looked more like a smirk.

"Do you want Serbian cigarettes or Croatian ones?" The way he stressed the two nationalities sounded unnatural. I had heard people on the news talking about Serbs and Croats this way because of the fighting in the villages, but no one had ever said anything to me directly. And I didn't want to buy the wrong kind of cigarettes.

"Can I have the ones I always get, please?"

"Serbian or Croatian?"

"You know. The gold wrapper?" I tried to see around his bulk, pointing to the shelf behind him. But he just laughed and waved to another customer, who sneered at me.

"Hey!" I tried to get the clerk's attention back. He ignored me and made change for the next man in line. I'd already lost the game, but I ran home as fast as I could anyway.

"Mr. Petrović wanted me to pick Serbian or Croatian cigarettes," I told Petar. "I didn't know the answer and he wouldn't give me any. I'm sorry."

My parents exchanged looks and Petar motioned for me to sit on his lap. He was tall—taller than my father—and flushed from the heat and wine. I climbed up on his wide thigh.

"It's okay," he said, patting his stomach. "I'm too full for cigarettes anyway." I pulled the money from my shorts and relinquished it. He pressed a few dinar coins into my palm.

"But I didn't win."

"Yes," he said. "But today that's not your fault."

That night my father came into the living room, where I slept, and sat down on the bench of the old upright piano. We'd inherited the piano from an aunt of Petar's—he and Marina didn't have space for it—but we couldn't afford to have it tuned, and the first octave was so flat all the keys gave out the same tired tone. I heard my father pressing the foot pedals down in rhythm with the habitual nervous jiggle of his leg, but he didn't touch the keys. After a while he got up and came to sit on the armrest of the couch, where I lay. Soon we were going to buy a mattress.

"Ana? You awake?"

I tried to open my eyes, felt them flitting beneath the lids.

"Awake," I managed.

"Filter 160s. They're Croatian. So you know for next time."

"Filter 160s," I said, committing it to memory.

My father kissed my forehead and said good night, but I felt him in the doorway moments later, his body blocking out the kitchen lamplight.

"If I'd been there," he whispered, but I wasn't sure he was talking to me so I stayed quiet and he didn't say anything else.

———

In the morning Milošević was on TV giving a speech, and when I saw him, I laughed. He had big ears and a fat red face, jowls sagging like a dejected bulldog. His accent was nasal, nothing like the gentle, throaty voice of my father. Looking angry, he hammered his fist in rhythm with his speech. He was saying something about cleansing the land, repeating it over and over. I had no idea what he was talking about, but as he spoke and pounded he got redder and redder. So I laughed, and my mother poked her head around the corner to see what was so funny.

"Turn that off." I felt my cheeks go hot, thinking she was mad at me for laughing at what must have been an important speech. But her face softened quickly. "Go play," she said. "Bet Luka's already beat you to the Trg."

My best friend, Luka, and I spent the summer biking around the town square and meeting our classmates for pickup football games. We were freckled and tan and perpetually grass-stained, and now that we were down to just a few weeks of freedom before the start of school we met even earlier and stayed out later, determined not to let any vacation go to waste. I found him along our regular bike route. We cycled side by side, Luka occasionally swinging his front tire into mine so that we'd nearly crash. It was a favorite joke of his and he laughed the whole way, but I was still thinking about Petrović. In school we'd been taught to ignore distinguishing ethnic factors, though it was easy enough to discern someone's ancestry by their last name. Instead we were trained to regurgitate pan-Slavic slogans: *"Bratstvo i Jedinstvo!"* Brotherhood and Unity. But now it seemed the differences between us might be important after all. Luka's family was originally from Bosnia, a mixed state, a confusing third category. Serbs wrote in Cyrillic and Croats in the Latin alphabet, but in Bosnia they used both, the spoken differences even more minute. I wondered if there was a special brand of Bosnian cigarettes, too, and whether Luka's father smoked those.

When we arrived in the Trg it was crowded and I could tell something was wrong. In light of this new Serb-Croat divide, everything—including the statue of Ban Jelačić, sword drawn—now seemed a clue to the tensions I hadn't seen coming. During World War II the ban's sword was aimed toward the Hungarians in a defensive gesture, but afterward the Communists had removed the statue in a neutralization of nationalistic symbols. Luka and I had watched when, after the last elections, men with ropes and heavy machinery returned Jelačić to his post. Now he was facing south, toward Belgrade.

The Trg had always been a popular meeting place, but today people were swarming around the base of the statue looking frantic, milling through a snarl of trucks and tractors parked right in the cobblestoned Trg, where, on normal days, cars weren't even allowed to drive. Baggage, shipping crates, and an assortment of free-floating housewares brimmed over the backs of flatbeds and were splayed across the square.

I thought of the gypsy camp my parents and I once passed while driving to visit my grandparents' graves in Čakovec, caravans of wagons and trailers housing mysterious instruments and stolen children.

"They'll pour acid in your eyes," my mother warned when I wiggled in the pew while my father lit candles and prayed for his parents. "Little blind beggars earn three times as much as ones who can see." I held her hand and was quiet for the rest of the day.

Luka and I dismounted our bikes and moved cautiously toward the mass of people and their belongings. But there were no bonfires or circus sideshows; there was no music— these were not the migrant people I'd seen on the outskirts of the northern villages.

The settlement was made almost entirely out of string. Ropes, twine, shoelaces, and strips of fabric of various thicknesses were strung from cars to tractors to piles of luggage in an elaborate tangle. The strings supported the sheets and blankets and bigger articles of clothing that served as makeshift tents. Luka and I stared alternately at each other and at the strangers, not knowing the words for what we were seeing, but understanding that it wasn't good.

Candles circled the perimeter of the encampment, melting next to boxes on which someone had written "Contributions for the Refugees." Most people who passed added something to a box, some emptying their pockets.

"Who are they?" I whispered.

"I don't know," Luka said. "Should we give them something?"

I took Petar's dinar from my pocket and gave them to Luka, afraid to get too close myself. Luka had a few coins, too, and I held his bike while he put them in the box. As he leaned in I panicked, worrying that the city of string would swallow him up like the vines that come alive in horror movies. When he turned around I shoved his handlebars at him and he stumbled backward. As we rode away I felt my stomach twist into a knot I would only years later learn to call survivor's guilt.

My classmates and I often met for football matches on the east side of the park, where the grass had fewer lumps. I was the only girl who played football, but sometimes other girls would come down to the field to jump rope and gossip.

"Why do you dress like a boy?" a pigtailed girl asked me once.

"It's easier to play football in pants," I told her. The real reason was that they were my neighbor's clothes and we couldn't afford anything else.

We began collecting stories. They started out with strings of complex relationships—my best friend's second cousin, my uncle's boss—and whoever kicked the ball between improvised (and ever-negotiable) goal markers got to tell their story first. An unspoken contest of gore developed, honoring whoever could more creatively describe the blown-out brains of their distant acquaintances. Stjepan's cousins had seen a mine explode a kid's leg, little bits of skin clinging to grooves in the sidewalk for a week afterward. Tomislav had heard of a boy who was shot in the eye by a sniper in Zagora; his eyeball had turned to liquid like a runny egg right there in front of everyone.

At home my mother paced the kitchen talking on the phone to friends in other towns, then hung out the window, passing the news to the next apartment building over. I stood close while she discussed the mounting tensions on the banks of the Danube with the women on the other side of the clothesline, absorbing as much as I could before running off to find my friends. A citywide spy network, we passed on any information we overheard, relaying stories of victims whose links to us were becoming less and less remote.

On the first day of school, our teacher took attendance and found one of our classmates missing.

"Anyone hear from Zlatko?" she said.

"Maybe he went back to Serbia, where he belongs," said

Mate, a boy I'd always found obnoxious. A few people snick-ered and our teacher shushed them. Beside me, Stjepan raised his hand.

"He moved," Stjepan said.

"Moved?" Our teacher flipped through some papers on her clipboard. "Are you sure?"

"He lived in my building. Two nights ago I saw his family carrying big suitcases out to a truck. He said they had to leave before the air raids started. He said to tell everyone goodbye." The class erupted into high-strung chatter at this news:

"What's an air raid?"

"Who will be our goalie now?"

"Good riddance to him!"

"Shut up, Mate," I said.

"Enough!" said our teacher. We quieted.

An air raid, she explained, was when planes flew over cit-ies and tried to knock buildings down with bombs. She drew chalky maps denoting shelters, listed the necessities our families should bring underground with us: AM radio, water jug, flashlight, batteries for the flashlight. I didn't un-derstand whose planes wanted what buildings to explode, or how to tell a regular plane from a bad one, though I was happy for the reprieve from regular lessons. But soon she began to swipe at the board, inciting an angry cloud of eraser dust. She let out a sigh as if she were impatient with air raids, brushing the settling chalk away from the pleats in her skirt. We moved on to long division, and were not offered a time for asking questions.

It happened when I was running errands for my mother. I was supposed to get milk, which came in slippery plastic bags that wiggled during any attempt at pouring or gripping, and I'd rigged a cardboard box to my bike's handlebars to carry the uncooperative cargo. But all the stores nearest our flat had run out—stores were running out of everything now—and I commissioned Luka to join the quest. Expanding the search, we ventured deeper into the city.

The first plane flew so low Luka and I swore later to anyone who would listen that we'd seen the pilot's face. I ducked, my handlebars twisting beneath me, and fell from my bike. Luka, who'd been looking skyward but had forgotten to stop pedaling, crashed into my wreckage and landed facedown, cutting his chin on the cobblestone.

We scrambled to our feet, adrenaline overriding pain as we tried to right our bikes.

Then the alarm. The grained crackle of shoddy audio equipment. The howl of the siren, like a woman crying out through a megaphone. We ran. Across the street and through the side alleys.

"Which one's closest?" Luka called over the noise. I visualized the map on the blackboard at school, stars and arrows marking different paths.

"There's one underneath the kindergarten." Beneath the slide of our first playground, a set of cement steps led to a steel door, triple-thick, as fat as a dictionary. Two men held the door open and people funneled from all directions down into the shadows. Reluctant to leave our bicycles to fend for themselves in the impending doom, Luka and I dropped them as close to the entrance as possible.

The shelter smelled of mold and unwashed bodies. When my eyes adjusted I surveyed the room. There were bunk beds, a wooden bench near the door, and a generator bicycle in the far corner. My classmates and I would come to fight over the bike in subsequent raids, elbowing one another for a turn converting pedals into the electricity that powered the lights in the shelter. But the first time we barely noticed it. We were occupied with surveying the odd collection of people seized from their daily activities and smashed together in a Cold War lair. I studied the group closest to me: men in business suits, or coveralls and mechanics' jackets like my father's, women in pantyhose and pencil skirts. Others in aprons with babies at their hips. I wondered where my mother and Rahela were; there was no public shelter near our building. Then I heard Luka calling for me and realized we'd been separated by an influx of newcomers. I felt my way in his direction, identifying him by the outline of his unruly hair.

"You're bleeding," I said.

Luka wiped his chin with his arm, tried to make out the line of blood on his sleeve.

"I thought it would happen. I heard my dad talking about it last night." Luka's father worked for the police academy and was in charge of training new recruits. I was annoyed Luka hadn't mentioned the possibility of a raid earlier. He looked comfortable there in the dark, his arm draped on the rung of a bunk bed ladder.

"Why didn't you tell me?"

"I didn't want to scare you."

"I'm not scared," I said. I wasn't. Not yet.

The siren again, signaling an all-clear. The men pressed back the door and we ascended the stairs, unsure of what to expect. Aboveground it was still daylight and the sun obscured my vision as much as darkness had below. I saw spots. When they dissipated, the playground came into focus just as I'd remembered it. Nothing had happened.

At home I barged through the front door, announcing to my mother that there was no milk left in the entire city of Zagreb. She pushed her chair back from the kitchen table, where she'd been grading a pile of student assignments, and shifted Rahela closer up against her chest as she stood. Rahela cried.

"Are you okay?" my mother asked. She gathered me up in a forceful embrace.

"I'm fine. We went to the kindergarten. Where'd you and Rahela go?"

"In the basement. By the *šupe*."

The basement of our building had only two notable characteristics: filth and *šupe*. Every family had a *šupa*, a padlocked wooden storage unit. I loved to press my face against the gap between the door and the hinges to see inside, a private viewing of a family's lowliest possessions. We kept potatoes in ours, and they fared well in the darkness. The basement didn't seem very safe; there wasn't a big metal door or bunk beds or a generator. But my mother seemed sad when I asked about it later. "It's just as good a place as any," she said.

That night my father came home with a shoe box full of brown packing tape he'd pilfered from the tram office, where he worked some days. He pulled big sticky Xs diagonally across the windows and I followed behind him pressing the tape down, smoothing out the air bubbles. We put a double layer on the French doors that led to the little balcony off the living room. The balcony was my favorite part of our flat. If I ever felt a twinge of disappointment after coming home from Luka's house, where his mother did not have to work and he slept in a real bed, I would step outside and lie on my back, letting my feet swing over the ledge, and reason that no one who lived in a house could have a high-up balcony like mine.

Now, though, I worried that my father would tape the doors shut. "We'll still be able to go outside, right?"

"Of course, Ana. We're just shoring up the glass." The tape was supposed to hold the windows together if there was an explosion. "And anyway," my father said, sounding tired, "a little packing tape's not good for much."

"*Which* color are we again?" I stood behind my father, resting my chin on his shoulder as he read the newspaper, and pointed to a map of Croatia splashed with red and blue dots indicating the opposing armies. He'd already told me once but I couldn't keep it straight.

"Blue," my father said. "The Croatian National Guard. The police."

"And the red ones?"

"*Jugoslavenska Narodna Armija*. The JNA."

I didn't understand why the Yugoslav National Army would want to attack Croatia, which was full of Yugoslavian people, but when I asked my father he just sighed and closed the paper. In the process I glimpsed the front page, a photo of men waving chain saws and skull-emblazoned flags. They had felled a tree across a road, blocking passage in both directions; the headline TREE TRUNK REVOLUTION! ran across the bottom of the page in fat black type.

"Who are *they*?" I asked my father. The men were bearded and wearing mismatched uniforms. In all the military parades, I had never seen JNA soldiers carrying pirate flags.

"Četniks," he said, folding the paper and tucking it on a shelf above the television, out of my reach.

"What are they doing with the trees? And why do they have beards if they're in the army?"

I knew the beards were important because I'd noticed all the shaving. Across the city, men with more than two days' stubble were eyed suspiciously by their clean-shaven counterparts. The week before, Luka's father had shaved off the beard he'd worn since before Luka and I were born. Unable to part with it completely, he'd left his mustache, but the effect was mostly comical; the bushy whiskers atop his upper lip were a specter of the face we'd known, and left him looking perpetually forlorn.

"They're Orthodox. In their church men grow beards when they're in mourning."

"What are they sad about?"

"They're waiting for the Serb king to be returned to his throne."

"We don't even have a king."

"That's enough, Ana," my father said.

I wanted to know more—what a beard had to do with being sad, why the Serbs had both the JNA and the Četniks on their side and we only had the old police force, but my mother set a knife and a bowl of unpeeled potatoes in front of me before I could bring it up.

Amid the disorder, Luka analyzed. It had always been his habit to ask me questions I couldn't answer, hypotheticals that supplied our bike rides with endless conversation. We used to speak mostly of outer space, how it was possible that a star was already dead by the time we saw it shooting, why airplanes and birds stayed up and we stayed down, and whether or not, on the moon, you'd have to drink everything from a straw. But now his investigative attentions had turned exclusively to the war—what did Milošević mean when he said the country needed to be cleansed, and how was a war supposed to help when the explosions were making such a big mess? Why did the water keep running out if the pipes were underground, and if the bombings were breaking the pipes, were we any safer in the shelters than in our houses?

I'd always loved Luka's inquiries, and that he trusted my opinion. With other friends, the boys at school, he usually just kept quiet. And given the grown-ups' penchant for evading my questions, it was a relief to have someone who'd talk about it all. But the moon was far away, and now that he was dissecting issues so close to home I found my head aching with the idea that all the familiar faces and parts of the city were pieces of a puzzle I couldn't fit together.

"What if we die in an air raid?" he said one afternoon.

"Well they haven't actually blown any buildings up yet," I reasoned.

"But what if they do, and one of us dies?"

Somehow, the prospect of just *him* dying was a scarier place than I'd allowed my imagination to go thus far. I felt sweaty and nervous, unzipped my jacket. I was so rarely angry with him I almost didn't recognize the feeling.

"You're not going to die," I said. "So you can just forget about it." I took a sharp turn and left him there alone in the Trg, where the refugees were untangling their belongings and getting ready to make their next move.

We entered an era of false alarms. Air raid warnings and pre–air raid warnings. Whenever police reconnaissance spotted Serb planes approaching the city, a strip of alert text ribboned its way across the top of the television screen. No siren sounded, no one ran to the shelters, but those who'd seen the warning would poke their heads out into the hallway and begin the Call: *"Zamračenje, zamračenje!"* It drifted down the stairwells, across clotheslines to neighboring buildings, through the streets, the air humming with the foreboding murmur—"darken it."

We pulled the blinds over our taped-up panes, secured strips of black cloth atop the shades. Sitting on the floor in the dark I wasn't afraid; the feeling was more like expectation during a particularly intense round of hide-and-seek.

"Something's wrong with her," my mother said, one night when we were squatting beneath the windowsill. Rahela cried, was still crying, it seemed, from a spell she'd begun a few days earlier.

"Maybe she's afraid of the dark," I said, though I knew that wasn't it.

"I'm taking her to the doctor."

"She's fine," my father said in a way that ended the discussion.

A Serbian man who lived in our building refused to pull down his shades. He turned on all the lights in his flat and, through the most impressive of boom boxes, blasted cassettes of garish orchestral music that had been popular during the height of communism. At night, families took turns begging him to turn out his lights. They asked him to have a heart and help them protect their children. When that didn't work they appealed to logic, reasoning that if the apartment building was bombed, he would surely die in the explosion as well. He seemed willing to make the sacrifice.

On weekends when he was in the car park working on his broken Jugo, we lurked around the lot and stole his tools when he wasn't looking. Some mornings before school we'd gather in the hallway outside his flat. We'd buzz his doorbell again and again, and run when we heard him pad toward the door.

The refugee kids showed up at school a few weeks after their arrival in the city. With no record of their academic skills, the teachers tried to divide them among the classes as evenly as possible. Our class got two boys who looked close enough to our age to blend in. They were from Vukovar and spoke with funny accents.

Vukovar was a small city a few hours away and had never meant much to me during peacetime, but now it was always in the news. In Vukovar people were disappearing. People were being forced at gunpoint to march east; people were becoming hemic vapor amid the nighttime explosions. The boys had walked all the way to Zagreb and they didn't like to talk about it. Even after they settled in they were always a little dirtier, the circles beneath their eyes a little darker than ours, and we treated them with a distant curiosity.

They were living in a warehouse we'd referred to before as Sahara because of its desertedness; it was where the older kids used to go to talk and smoke and kiss in the dark. Rumors swelled: people were sleeping on the floor and there was only one bathroom, or maybe not even any bathroom, and definitely no toilet paper. Luka and I tried to sneak in a few times, but a soldier was checking refugees' documents at the door.

Soon they were checking IDs at the front of my apartment building, too. Families in the building alternated sending an adult down in five-hour shifts to guard the door, an attempt to prevent some Četnik from coming in and blowing himself up. One night there was an argument; the men outside were yelling so loudly we could hear it through the window. The guard didn't want to let the Serbian man back in.

"You're an animal! You're trying to get our children killed!" the doorman screamed.

"I'm doing nothing of the sort."

"Then turn your fucking lights out during the blackout!"

"I'll turn your lights out, you filthy Muslim!" said the Serb, followed by more shouting and grunting.

My father opened our window and stuck his head out. "You're both animals!" he said. "We're trying to get some sleep up here!" The noise woke Rahela, who resumed her crying. My mother glared at my father and went into the bedroom to retrieve my sister from her cradle. My father pulled on his work boots and ran downstairs to keep the brawl from getting out of hand. All the policemen were away being soldiers, and there was no one else left to do it.

"Will you have to go to the army someday?" I asked my father.

"I'm not a policeman," he said.

"Stjepan's dad isn't either, and he had to go."

My father sighed and rubbed his forehead. "Let's get you back in bed." He scooped me up with a deft swing of his arm and plopped me on the couch.

"The truth is, I'm embarrassed. But I'm not allowed to be in the army. Because of my eye."

My father had a crooked eye and couldn't tell near from far. Even when driving he'd sometimes close the bad eye and squint the other, guessing his distance from cars and hoping for the best. He'd learned to make do this way, and liked to brag that he'd never had an accident. But the police-turned-army were harder to convince that hoping for the best was an effective methodology, particularly when grenades were involved.

"At least for now. Maybe, if forces are down, I could be a radio operator or a mechanic. Not a real soldier, though."

"That's not embarrassing," I said. "You can't help it."

"But it'd be better if I could protect the country, no?"

"I'm glad you can't go."

My father bent to kiss my forehead. "Well, I would miss you, I *suppose*." The lights flickered, then went out. "All right, all right, she's going to bed!" he said to the ceiling, and I giggled. He went into the kitchen and I heard him bumping around in search of matches.

"In the top drawer by the sink," I called. I switched off the lamp in case the electricity came back in the middle of the night, and willed myself to sleep amid the sudden silence of our flat.

As a side effect of modern warfare, we had the peculiar privilege of watching the destruction of our country on television. There were only two channels, and with tank and trench battles happening across the eastern counties and JNA ground troops within a hundred kilometers of Zagreb, both were devoted to public service announcements, news reports, or political satire, a burgeoning genre now that the secret police were no longer a concern. The anxiety that arose from being away from the television, the radio, our friends' latest updates, from not knowing, panged our stomachs like a physical hunger. The news became the backdrop to all our meals, so much so that televisions lingered in the kitchens of Croatian households long after the war was over.

My mother taught English at the technical high school, and she and I arrived home from our respective schools around the same time, I dirt-streaked and she fatigue-stricken and carrying Rahela, who spent the school days with the old woman across the hall. We'd turn on the news and my mother would hand Rahela off to me while she wielded her wooden spoon to create another meal from

water and carrots and chunks of chicken carcass. I'd sit at the
kitchen table with Rahela on my lap and tell them both
what I'd learned that day. My parents were strict about
school—my mother because she had been to college and my
father because he hadn't—and my mother would interject
questions about my times tables or spelling words, little
quizzes after which she sometimes rewarded me with a bit
of sweet bread she hid in the cabinet under the sink.

One afternoon an extra-large block of special report text
caught my attention and I let my account of the day's lessons trail off and turned up the television. The reporter,
pressing on her earpiece, announced there was breaking
news, uncut footage from the southern front in Šibenik. My
mother darted away from the stove and stood behind me to
watch:

An unsteady cameraman jumped a ledge to get a better
view as a Serbian plane spiraled toward the sea, its engine on
fire and blending with the late September sunset. Then to
the right, a second plane ignited in midair. The cameraman
spun around to reveal a Croatian antiaircraft soldier pointing incredulously at his handiwork saying, *"Oba dva! Oba su
pala!"* Both of them! They both fell!

The *oba su pala* footage played on both television channels for the remainder of the day, and continuously throughout the war. *"Oba su pala"* became a rallying cry, and whenever
it appeared on TV, or when someone yelled it on the street
or through the walls at the Serb upstairs, we were reminded

that we were outnumbered, outweaponed, and we were win-
ning.

That first time we saw it, my mother and I together, she
patted my shoulder because these men were protecting Croatia and the fighting didn't look too dangerous. She smiled
and the soup steamed, and even Rahela wasn't crying for
once, and I allowed myself to slide into the fantasy I recognized as such even while my mind was still spinning it—
that there in the flat, with my family, I was safe.

3

"There is no way a doctor is going to see us on a Saturday," my father said. My mother ignored him and continued filling her purse with bread and apples.

"Dr. Ković already called her. She knows we're coming." Rahela had been vomiting for two weeks, the second of which my mother had spent taking unpaid sick days from school to navigate the complex web of Communist healthcare—bouncing from doctor to doctor, receiving one referral, then the next, this doctor open only on Wednesdays, that one only Tuesdays and Thursdays, from one to four. They had run blood tests, taken X-rays (one doctor to take the X-rays, another to read them), tried bottle-feeding Rahela with a special formula that was expensive and nearly impossible to get. She'd only gotten skinnier, and my parents now stayed awake through the night, taking turns holding her upright so she wouldn't choke on her own vomit.

"But Slovenia, Dijana. How are we going to pay for it?"

"Our daughter is sick. I don't *care* how we are going to pay for it." I carried Rahela out to her car seat.

In Slovenia there'd been a ten-day war. They didn't share a border with Serbia or have full access to the sea; they weren't the wrong ethnicity. Now Slovenia was a free country. A separate country. We passed through the desolate fields of northern Croatia and my father slowed as a Slovenian police officer waved us toward a makeshift customs booth, hastily constructed to mark the new border. My father cranked down the window and my mother dug through her purse for our passports. In winters past we'd come to Slovenia to spend the day in Čatež, an indoor water park just over the border. Strange, I thought, to need a passport to go swimming. The policeman licked his thumb and flipped through our documents.

"What's the purpose of your visit?"

"We're visiting cousins," my father said. I wondered why he didn't just tell the truth.

"How long will you be staying?"

"Just for the day. A few hours."

"Right," said the officer, smirking. I remembered the inky square stamps we'd gotten when we'd driven to Austria once, but the man just scribbled something in pen in each of our passports and motioned us through.

Unsure of what to expect from a whole new country, I was disappointed to see that Slovenia looked the same as I remembered it, looked the same as Croatia did in the rural parts outside of Zagreb—flat and blank and grassy against a backdrop of mountains that never seemed to get any closer.

"You know I don't care about the money," my father said, cracking the silence he'd been keeping since we'd left the house.

"I know."

"I'm just worried."

"I know."

My father took my mother's hand and kissed the inside of her wrist. "I know," she said.

As we approached the capital, the population thickened, a dense buildup of houses clustered around the city. At its core, Ljubljana looked like a smaller, squatter version of Zagreb, except the river ran right through the town center rather than along the edge. The difference between Croatian and Slovenian was exasperatingly mild, the storefronts and street signs filled with words that looked familiar but not quite right, rendering comprehension just out of reach.

"This is not a doctor's office," my father said when my mother instructed him to turn down an unmarked alley. He was overarticulating the way he did when he was frustrated.

"That's it." My mother pointed to a second-floor flat with a red cross taped to the front door. My father parked the car in front of a fire hydrant.

———

"Good afternoon," a woman said in English, ushering us inside. "I'm Dr. Carson." I'd studied English since the first grade but considered it a murky language, one whose grammar seemed to have been made up on the fly. Still, I resolved to concentrate and pick up as much as I could. Dr. Carson shook my parents' hands, hard. The door of her flat opened directly into the living room, and she led us to her sofa, a fixture too big for the room and covered in pilling floral throw pillows. Black-and-white photos of sickly children being hugged by toothy American doctors hung poster-size on all walls. MEDIMISSION, said the posters in block lettering beneath the photos, followed by an assortment of uplifting slogans about children and miracles and the future.

Dr. Carson was thin and blond and had the same teeth as the people in the posters, and I resolved to dislike her based on these things, the perkiness in her face that reminded me of the way teachers spoke to students who they thought were stupid. But I knew she was Rahela's best chance at getting better; though Dr. Carson's uniform consisted of blue jeans, rubber gloves, and a stethoscope, she still had better equipment than all the real doctors' offices back home.

She drew blood in her kitchen. "It's sterile," she said over and over, as if we had other options. I didn't like seeing Rahela's tiny arm pinned against the woman's countertop, though Rahela wasn't crying, hadn't cried since we arrived.

She looked tired. I looked away, stared at an image of an Asian girl, half her face burned, contorted like gnarled tree bark. A doctor held her on his knee and applied a bandage.

Dr. Carson ran more tests. She and my parents conversed in broken languages, my mother translating for my father in semicoherent chunks. Rahela's kidneys weren't functioning properly, the ultrasound showed. It looked as if she might have only one, though the images were inconclusive even with the newer equipment.

"There are better machines for these tests, in other cities," Dr. Carson said. "But for now we can try medication. To stabilize." My mother barraged her with questions. The two switched completely to English, and my father and I stood back fidgeting. Dr. Carson disappeared into her kitchen, then returned with a stack of papers and a small glass bottle of red and blue capsules.

"Twice a day. We'll be in touch."

At border control my father cranked down the window and offered our passports to the approaching officer, whose eyes flitted between our faces and ID photos with increasing curiosity.

"Are you sure you want to go back over there?" He gestured with his head toward the border and spoke with something between condescension and genuine concern.

My father snatched at our papers and rolled the window up so fast I thought he might close the officer's hand inside.

He opened his mouth to say something through the glass, but seemed to think better of it and accelerated across the border into Croatia.

"What kind of question is that?" he asked after a while, his voice raw. "Of course we want to go back. Of course we're going home."

"You awake?" My father poked his head into the living room that night. "I have a story for you." I sat up on the couch with my back against the armrest. My father was holding my favorite book, *Tales from Long Ago*. The fairy tales inside were very old and very famous, and the copy we had was so worn we'd had to tape the middle pages back in.

"Which one?"

"One day," he read, "a young man stumbled into Stribor's Forest. He didn't know the forest was enchanted and that all kinds of magical creatures lived there. Some of the forest's magic was good and some was evil, and the whole place would stay enchanted until the right person entered it to break the spell—someone who preferred his own life, even with its sorrows, over all the ease and happiness in the world." My father snapped the book shut and I pretended to be patient, knowing he would continue, that he didn't need the words in front of him.

"The young man was headed home to his mother after

chopping wood when"—my father jumped up and feigned stumbling—"he crossed the threshold into Stribor's kingdom. Inside, everything seemed to glow with little flecks of gold, as if it were coated in fireflies."

I tried to think of a place in Zagreb where everything was clean and twinkling, but the city did not feel very magical of late.

"And the woman who appeared before him in the clearing was no exception. She was the most beautiful woman he had ever seen."

"She wasn't!" I said. "She was faking!"

"You're right. The woman was really a snake in disguise. But the young man didn't know it. He was willfully blinded by her beauty."

"His mother knew, though."

"When the young man brought her home, his mother saw right away that the woman had the forked tongue of a sssssssserpent!" My father stuck out his tongue in a reptilian hiss. "The young man's mother tried to warn him, but he ignored her. He was happy, he insisted. Soon, he and the serpent-woman were married.

"The new daughter-in-law treated the young man's mother very badly. The mother was old, but the daughter-in-law made her work hard, cooking and cleaning and tending the garden. At night, the mother sat in her room and cried, wishing for a way out of her predicament—"

"And?" I interrupted here, my favorite part. "The fairies!"

"The fairies had heard the cry of one desperate for help. So, in the middle of the night, they flew up the mountainside to the village and into the house through the kitchen window."

"What did they look like?"

"They were surrounded by a cloud of yellow light, and they each had two sets of paper-thin wings that fluttered so fast you could barely see them! Like a hummingbird's." I'd seen a hummingbird on TV once. He looked much too heavy to be hovering in midair like that.

"The fairies picked the old woman up by the sleeves of her nightgown and carried her out of the village, down the mountain, and through the tall white oaks, where Stribor, Lord of the Forest, was waiting for them. Now Stribor lived in a golden castle inside the hollow of the biggest, strongest oak tree—"

"How did he fit the castle in a tree?"

"*Magic,* Ana. When the fairies had delivered the mother to his tree, he stepped outside. 'I AM STRIBOR, LORD OF THE FOREST! WHO GOES THERE?'" my father bellowed in his best Stribor bass.

"'I am Brunhilda, and my son has married an evil serpent-woman!'" he squeaked.

"Brunhilda?" I said. I laughed at the silly name, one my father changed in each retelling.

"'Ah, yes, Brunhilda, I know of your situation and I can help you. As you know, I am very mighty and have many powers.'" My father stuck out his chest and put his hands on his hips. "'With my supermagical powers, I can return you to your youth. I'll subtract fifty years from your age, so you'll be young and beautiful again!'

"The woman was excited by the prospect of being young again, and out of the clutches of her evil daughter-in-law. She agreed.

"So Stribor stirred all the magic of the forest into motion." My father paused for dramatic stirring pantomime. "And a giant gate appeared before them. Stribor told the woman that when she passed through, she would go back in time. The woman had one foot over the threshold when she had a thought:

"'Wait! What will happen to my son?'

"Stribor scoffed at this question, which he thought was a stupid one. 'He won't be there, of course, in your new life, in your youth.'

"The woman shied away. 'I'd rather know my son than live happily as a young woman without him,' she said. And just like that"—my father snapped his fingers—"Stribor disappeared and the magic of the forest was gone. The evil daughter-in-law became a snake again. The one who preferred her own sorrows to all the joys in the world had entered the forest and broken the spell."

My father pulled the blanket up around my chin.

"Do you understand, Ana, that sometimes hard things are worth the trouble?"

"I think so." Suddenly I was very tired again.

"Good." My father kissed my forehead. *"Laku noć,"* he said. He reshelved the fairy tales and turned out the lamp as I shrank down into the creases of the couch.

4

The Presidential Palace was rocketed two days later. In the shelter my schoolmates and I waited for the all-clear to release us from the confines of mildew and shadows. This shelter had bunk beds stacked three high, and while waiting for our turn on the generator bike we'd made a game of clambering to the top level and jumping off, measuring our success by the volume of the smack our sneakers made against the cement floor. Our teacher, normally quick to snuff out such athletic outbursts, gave us a stern command not to break any bones but let us continue. Something was taking longer than usual. I glanced sidelong at the butcher, self-nominated guardian of the door, his flabby form swaddled in a bloody apron. A handheld police scanner protruded from his front pocket, and he whispered with the cashier from the shop next to his. Then, almost frantically, he spun around and fumbled with the door latches, his thick hands moving faster than I'd ever seen them work behind his counter.

"Did you hear the signal?" Luka asked. I hadn't, but the door was open and the push of the crowd toward the stairs overpowered the spindly legs of children. Besides, we didn't want to miss out on the excitement. My classmates and I pressed against one another as we mounted the steps toward daylight.

At first, the smell. The earthy scent of burning wood, the chemical stink of melted plastic, the stench of something sour and unfamiliar. Flesh, we'd learn.

Then the smoke: three burgeoning columns above the upper town, broad and dense and dark red.

It was not anxiety or excitement now, but real fear. I felt dizzy, as if someone had tied a rope around my middle and squeezed out all my air. Somewhere behind us our teacher was shouting instructions for us to go home. Still, everyone who'd emerged from the shelter moved as one toward the explosion. I grabbed for Luka's hand; a girl beside me clutched a clump of my T-shirt, and the others joined until our whole class had formed a disorderly human chain. It was scarier now to separate than to walk into a city on fire.

We reached the base of the stone steps that led to the upper town, toward Banski Dvori. The police had already blocked off the stairways, so we weaved through the adult

crowd, pushing ourselves up onto a cement ledge to get a
better view. My father worked in the transportation office in
the upper town some days, though now I couldn't remember
which. It wasn't close enough for him to have been hurt in
this explosion, was it? In the haze it was impossible to tell,
and I scanned the faces of all the broad-shouldered men in
sight, but did not find him.

Fragments of conflicting reports churned around us:

"Have you heard? The president exploded right at his
desk!"

"Come on, they've had him in a bunker since last week."

"Have you heard? His wife was inside, too!"

A voice from behind: "Are you kids up here alone?" My
classmates and I were startled to find someone talking to
rather than over us, the same shock of nerves firing as if we'd
been caught sharing answers to a math test. I spun around
to see a newsman wielding a large microphone and fiddling
with a wire in his ear. He wore a gray vest with a sheen of
nylon and metal.

"We're not alone," I said. "My dad just—"

"What's it to you?" Luka cut in, puffing out his chest to
mimic the man's bulky vest. The reporter, whose cameraman
had come over to get a shot with the children, now stuttered.

"You should be at home," he said, his apprehension ex-
posing a French accent. His revealed foreignness dissolved
any remaining authority.

"You should go home, *stranac*," I said, emboldened. My classmates giggled, and I reveled in the girls' acceptance, if only momentary. I was brave, powerful even.

"*Stranac, stranac,*" my classmates chanted. One of them threw an apple core, and it bounced off the newsman's padded shoulder.

"Oh, what do I care if you all blow up, you gypsy vermin!" he said. He motioned his cameraman to move a few feet over so we were out of the picture and began to refilm his report.

Another explosion rumbled near the palace, then rippled down the hill through the concrete. A crack, thin as a strand of hair, bloomed across the ledge beneath our feet. Home suddenly didn't sound like such a bad idea. We took off, Luka and I sprinting down Ilica Street before our paths diverged.

"Good luck!" I called as we split. It seemed afterward like a stupid thing to say, but another string of ambulances rounded the corner, sirens screaming as they passed, and if he replied I didn't hear.

I arrived home hyper and smelling of fire, swinging the door open with such force that I enlarged the dent, born of similar displays of overzealousness, in the opposite wall.

"Where were you?" my mother yelled from her bedroom, sounding frantic.

"At the shelter. Haven't you heard about Banski Dvori?"

I had expected her to hold me tightly like she had after the first air raid, but instead she looked me over and said, "You *stink*. God, Ana, why can't you play with girls?" then slipped back into her room. I followed her a few steps and leaned in her doorway. Though it seemed like an odd reaction, I recognized it as the bait to engage in a well-worn argument; she wanted me to chat and jump rope, bake things; I wanted to ride my bike, swim in the Sava, play football. I loved the feeling of dry mud cracking on my arms and the grass-stained knees of my jeans, felt important when my clothes carried the traces of my daily activities. Almost all my possessions, including my bicycle, were castoffs of a boy who lived one floor up in our building. If my mother was disappointed by my tomboyish tendencies, she may have found solace in the fact that nearly everything sustaining my existence was free.

The path of hand-me-downs was a complex web that connected neighbors and strangers across the city. I always wondered who it was that was buying everything in the first place, imagined some royal family at the top of the chain purchasing piles of clothes and spreading them throughout different family networks. In the streets we occasionally glimpsed familiar T-shirts within our circles of friends, though we had an unspoken agreement not to mention it. On the weekends we spent our mornings scrubbing the stains from our new old clothes, wringing out each other's memories.

"Girls were there," I said under my breath.

But my mother didn't fight back, continued flitting around her room looking busy. She moved a pile of student work from her nightstand to her desk, straightened the pencils standing at attention in a coffee mug nearby. This was a surefire indicator that something was wrong. I'd noticed Rahela lying on my mother's bed before, but now I took a closer look. She was propped against a stack of pillows, the bib at her neck stained slightly red.

"Mama? Is that blood?"

Rahela coughed, the dribble at her lip tinged a foreboding pink.

"It's the new medicine. Dr. Carson said it might happen."

"Does that mean it's working?" I said. My mother slammed her dresser drawer.

When my father got home my parents argued. They shouted about doctor bills and border crossings, about Banski Dvori and the shelters and America. They shouted about Rahela, then about me.

I held Rahela and paced the living room. The yelling seeped through our shared wall.

"I'm tired of waiting. I'm tired of you telling me to wait," my mother said.

"What do you want me to say? We have no other choice except to see if the medicine works."

"It's not working. We need to go."

"We can't get visas if we're a flight risk."

"We have steady jobs. We have a flat."

"The city is burning, Dijana. We're a flight risk."

One of them was banging things around on the desk. "Besides," my father said after a while. "I've already applied. For all of us." I only vaguely understood the rules of passports and visas, what an attempt at obtaining them implied, but I knew better than to interrupt an argument. Instead I wrapped Rahela in an extra blanket, tugged at the doors still fortified with a double layer of X tape, and escaped out onto the balcony. The view from nine stories up spanned most of the city. A cluster of skyscrapers on the far right was a representative sampling of Zagreb's more modern, uglier architecture. They were the Braća Domany towers, though no one seemed to know any Domany brothers or why they had apartment buildings named in their honor. The complex housed so many people it was a citywide joke that if you couldn't track down an acquaintance, sending a letter in the general direction of the towers would suffice.

On the left, the twin peaks of Zagreb Katedrala stretched taller than all the surrounding buildings. I couldn't remember a time when the cathedral wasn't at least partly swathed in scaffolding and tarps, but that only added to its sense of majesty, its wounds a physical manifestation of the sorrows and confessions of the city. In nights before the war, two spotlights lit the stone towers in dual rushes of warm gold. Now, with the lights quelled in anticipation of a blackout, it was difficult to pinpoint the boundary between the spires and the night sky.

The hint of smoke still hung in the air, but the cloud over the upper town was slowly receding. I lay down on my back, pushed my legs between the metal slats of the railing, and hugged Rahela to my chest. She was awake but quieter now. Being out on the balcony always made me feel better when I was upset, and I wondered if she felt that, too.

After a while my mother called me back inside, scolding me for taking Rahela out in the cold. I tried to think of my mother the way she was before my sister was born, whether she had always been annoyed with me, but found it difficult to remember a life that did not revolve around a crying baby. "You've gotta get better," I whispered to my sister. I wanted it as much for myself as for her, and felt guilty when I realized it.

I handed Rahela to my mother, and she shut the bedroom door. After a few minutes, my father came in and sat down at the piano. He played the first few bars of a Springsteen riff that had been popular before the war, then hit a wrong note and stopped. In happier times he'd played often; he'd take the pile of yellowing sheet music from inside the bench and let me pick a song. It was never perfect but always recognizable, and he'd never had a lesson.

Music, I'd heard him say, was like dessert. He could live without it, but life just wasn't as good. Some nights when I was supposed to be doing homework, my father and I would take the cassette player down from the shelf and put it in the middle of the living room floor. When a song we liked came on the radio, we'd stop whatever we were doing, rush back to the living room, and dive at the cassette player like football goalies, arms flailing. One of us would push the Record button as we landed in a mess of rug burn and overenthusiastic athleticism. Then, before I was sent to bed, we'd add the new songs to the label and put the stereo back on the shelf, carefully filing the tape into our collection of songs missing the first ten seconds. Sometimes if a tape broke we would pull out its filmy, iridescent insides and stretch them around the room, running and laughing, our shins knocking against furniture legs. My mother, who called to us impatiently throughout most of our other attempts at procrastination, never interrupted these giddy dissections.

But tonight when my father turned on the radio it was only static. "They bombed Sljeme, too," my father said. "Tried to take out the signal tower." He twisted the tuning knob all the way in both directions before switching it off. I heard his breathing fall into a rhythmic cycle and he began to hum, a new song that had been floating through Zagora's hills, the anthem of the Croatian soldiers in the east. *"Nećete u Čavoglave dok smo živi mi."* You'll never get to Čavoglave— not while we're alive.

"Nećete u Čavoglave dok smo živi mi!" I joined in.

"Be quiet," said my mother through the wall.

"Dok smo živi mi!" my father yelled back at the bookshelf. I giggled. My mother was in the kitchen now, banging dishes together, and my father's smile faded. "Time for bed, Ana," he said.

"Sing the rest first," I said as I stretched my sheet and blanket across the couch. He looked over his shoulder for my mother, then turned off the lamp and whispered it to me in the dark.

In the morning the police built the sandbag walls. I stood on the balcony before school and watched as they sealed off the roads into the city. They heaved the bags bucket-brigade-style into neat, crosshatched stacks, with men on stepladders straightening out the higher sections.

The sandbags were supposed to be strongholds we could stand behind and shoot from if the Serbs came to capture us. But instead of a sense of safety, the barricade imparted an air of naïveté. It was as if we believed a flood of tanks was like a flood of water and could be stopped by a pile of sacks. It was as if we'd never seen the footage of the tank plowing over the little red Fićo in the streets of Osijek, of an army truck crushing a passenger bus into a ditch on the side of the road. It was as if it never occurred to anyone that blocking the incoming roads was the same as blocking the escape routes.

But already yesterday's fear had grown stale, and my

friends and I decided to meet at the nearest blockade after school; it begged to be climbed, so tall and alluring it might as well have been a jungle gym. By the end of the week we'd absorbed the sandbags into our playscape. War quickly became our favorite game and soon we had given up the park altogether. We gathered near the sandbags because the lines were predrawn. If we could convince enough people to be Serbs we'd play teams, Četnici versus Hrvati, which meant you only got one life, and when you died you had to stay dead. The game was over when one team had killed the other in its entirety. Other times, we played every-man-for-himself war, in which you got three lives and everyone got to kill everybody else indiscriminately.

In both versions, the idea was to kill a person by shooting him with your imaginary gun; a block of wood or empty beer bottle served as a good stand-in. It was essential to make eye contact with the person you were killing, so as to avoid discrepancies. There were also two subcontests within each game. One was who could make the most realistic machine-gun sound effects; top players could distinguish between a Thompson, a Kalashnikov, and a Zbrojovka. Luka usually won. The second was who could act out the best death. If there had been points, players would have been awarded extra for a slow-motion fall. Postmortem twitching or delusional babbling was also a plus, if it wasn't too dramatic. Those who died with their limbs bent in unnatural angles and could hold their positions the longest were the winners.

Even if the sandbags might have been useful against an outside attack, they couldn't protect us from those already inside the blockade. There were stories that Serb civilians in Zagreb had taken matters into their own hands, mixing explosives in their kitchens. They booby-trapped household items and left them on sidewalks; Matchbox cars and ballpoint pens were their favored vessels. Mate swore they nearly got him with a beer can, which caught fire when he kicked it. It burned the cuff of his pants but sputtered out instead of exploding, he said, and we weren't sure whether to believe him. But our teacher seemed to take the stories seriously, reminding us each afternoon that we were never to pick anything up off the street, no matter how shiny. A hard lesson for an already frugal population under pressure of rations.

Our classmate Tomislav found his older brother in an alley a block from their house, his blood already congealing and caked into the sidewalk cracks. No one ever told us what had happened, not directly, but from the conversations that occurred above our heads, we knew.

I saw Tomislav underground during a raid two days later. The rest of us were shoving in line for the generator bike when he showed up. We stopped pushing and stared. The starkness in his eyes scared me much more than if he had been crying. The boy who was riding stopped without discussion. Tomislav passed us and mounted the bicycle.

For a moment I watched him as he pedaled furiously, turning his pain into power, something tangible and scientific. Then we dissolved the line and moved to another corner of the shelter to give him some privacy, which seemed like the right thing to do according to the code of wartime behavior we were making up as we went along.

5

Summer gave way to fall in the abrupt, unbeautiful way Zagreb always changed its seasons. The leaves turned only brown before falling, and the sky looked like it had been whitewashed with a dirty rag. Some days it felt cold enough to snow, but instead the clouds hung fat and heavy, releasing just enough drizzle to stop us from playing outside. My friends and I stayed in and grown-ups walked around donning frowns and black umbrellas.

After the bombing of the palace, Croatia had officially declared independence, inciting a flurry of modifications that called even the most mundane detail of our former lives into question. Pop singers famous across Yugoslavia recorded dual versions of their hits in both dialects; seemingly innocuous words like *coffee* had to be replaced with *kava* and *kafa* for Croatian and Serbian audiences. Even one's greeting habits could be analyzed—a kiss on each cheek for hello was acceptable, three kisses too many, a custom in the Orthodox Church and therefore traitorous.

Luka and I navigated the breakdown of our language with more questions. "You think we'll have to get new birth certificates now that Yugoslavia isn't Yugoslavia anymore?" he said.

"Probably not. It was still Yugoslavia when we were born."

"What about health cards? Passports?"

"Passports." I mulled it over. "I guess we'll need new passports when we win the war."

"Tram passes?"

"Tram—who cares? We never buy passes." I looked at him and he flashed a goofy smile.

"Gotcha."

After a while I said, "When we get married, will it say our kids are Croatian or Bosnian on their birth certificates?"

Luka braked abruptly. "What?"

"When we get married—"

"What makes you think we're getting married?"

I hadn't thought about it, really; I had just assumed. "Because we're best friends?"

"I don't think that's how it works."

"Why not?"

"You have to be in love and stuff. You know."

I considered it. "Well I love you," I said. "I've known you forever."

"You don't know whether you're in love until you're a teenager and you kiss," said Luka. "I mean we'll have to wait and see, to test it."

"Sure."

"But you can't say that kind of stuff at school. They make fun of me enough already."

I hadn't realized the boys were teasing Luka just like the girls were teasing me. "I won't," I said, embarrassed. I wished I hadn't mentioned it and thought about making up some excuse to go home, but Luka swung his leg back over his bicycle and started off again, so I followed. We passed by a roadblock where some of the boys from our class were climbing the sandbags. Luka waved.

"Let's talk about something else," he said. "Have you seen the money?"

The government had already started producing new currency, also called dinar, but with an image of Zagreb Katedrala stamped on the back of every note, regardless of denomination. It was thrilling at first, to hold money that said "Republic of Croatia" in the bland typeface of an official country, exciting that the featured illustration was a place I could see from the back of my flat. But no one even knew how much a dinar was worth; the value fluctuated wildly from day to day, and certain stores with Serb owners, or just thrifty businessmen, wouldn't accept it, worried the money might change again during the course of the war. A transaction of any substantial amount was carried out in deutsche marks.

My mother sent me to the butcher with a wad of new dinar and instructions to buy a bag of bones, and I watched as she made soup from the flavor of meat. She ladled out ever-shrinking portions, sometimes skipping meals completely herself, feigning headaches or student paperwork as excuses to leave the table. After dinner I was never full, but I was more adept at reading my parents' faces than they gave me credit for so I kept quiet.

Petar and Marina still came over every weekend, with my mother and Marina pooling supplies to feed everyone at once. There was no longer money for wine or cigarettes, so we drank water and Petar chewed bubble gum and, when that ran out, his fingernails.

One Sunday, Marina arrived looking pale. My mother handed Rahela to me and the two of them went into the bedroom, where they whispered behind the door. Trying to ignore the nervous atmosphere, I paced the flat with Rahela facing out so she could see everything, so she would be distracted from the fact that she was sick and probably hungry. I whispered jokes from the playground in her ear. *What's small and red and moves up and down? A tomato in an elevator. What do you get when you sit twelve Serbian women in a circle? One full set of teeth.* Sometimes I thought I saw her smile after I delivered the punch line. Rahela was skinnier but crying less, which I'd decided meant the medicine was working, despite the tiny wheeze that sounded each time she took in air.

Finally Marina and my mother emerged from the bedroom and Petar made his announcement: he was due at the training base in a week.

"Are you nervous?" said my father.

"No," Petar said. "Just out of shape!" He patted his stomach and grinned at me, hoping to get a laugh, but even I could see that he'd lost weight and his smile didn't match his eyes.

"Where are they going to send you?"

"I'll be close by. After training I'll be part of the Ring of Defense for Zagreb. Maybe even come home on weekends."

"You can stay with us, Marina, if you like," said my mother.

"Don't be silly. I'll be fine."

"She won't even notice I'm gone," he said. The four of them looked at each other and I felt that frustration so common to childhood, like when everyone laughs at a joke you don't understand, though it was silent in the flat save for the clinking of spoons against bowls, and Petar's heavy sighs when he swallowed.

I stayed awake as long as I could that night, listening to my parents in the kitchen.

"I should be out there. Everyone who can stand should be defending the city," my father said.

"There are plenty of soldiers. With your eyes—it's better this way."

"It'd be better if I could protect my family."

"Everything's going to be okay," my mother said. Usually he was the one reassuring her, and hearing the reversal made me feel guilty for eavesdropping. "Besides, I'm glad you're here with me. With us."

"Me, too," he said after a while, and I heard them kiss before I fell asleep.

The air raid siren was our alarm clock, one that in those first months we diligently obeyed. A siren at one in the morning meant a collective rolling out of bed and pulling on of boots, an outpouring of groggy neighbors into the fluorescent light (or, in an outage, the impermeable darkness) of the hallway. That night it seemed like I'd only been asleep for seconds when my father took me and my blanket from the couch, my mother with Rahela close behind. I bounced sleepily against his chest as he carried me down the stairs to the basement, our hearts beating out the quick, irregular rhythms of those abruptly pulled from their beds. The basement air cut cold through my pajamas, and I sat leaning against our *šupa* and pulled the blanket tighter around my shoulders, waiting for sleep.

Just as my mind was growing warm with unconsciousness the siren sounded, signaling an all-clear. I rubbed my eyes as my father carried me back up the stairs and returned me to the couch. But as soon as he'd gone from the room the siren began to howl. Again Rahela cried. I pulled the blanket over my head. My father appeared in the doorway, embracing a pile of blankets and pillows.

"Come here, Ana."

"I don't want to go again," I said, but I got up anyway.

He dropped the pile in the middle of the kitchen and led me to the pantry, clearing the floor inside and spreading my blanket as best he could in the small area. I looked at my father, read on his face a silent apology before stepping in and pulling my knees to my chest. My mother arranged Rahela on a pillow beside me, then she and my father lay down in front of the pantry door. I slept with a broom pressed to the back of my head, and my father held my hand, squeezing it tighter whenever the siren called out through the earliest hours of the morning.

6

I woke to an empty flat. Rahela was gone from the pillow, and I crawled out of the pantry on stiffened knees and pulled myself to my feet. The television blared at the empty kitchen chairs. The door to our flat was open in a display of carelessness uncharacteristic of either of my parents, and, panicked, I rushed out into the hallway. My neighbors' doors were ajar as well, televisions on and rooms vacant.

"*Tata!* Where are you?" I yelled down the hallway, hoping at the very least I could incite a neighbor to come out and chastise me for making a racket. No one appeared. I was beginning to think I was the only one left in the building when someone from the flat across the hall murmured my name.

"Psssssst. Jurić kid," the voice hissed. It was Rahela's ancient babysitter. Her door was open a crack and I pushed my way in. She was hunched over her kitchen counter, entwined in her phone cord, whispering. When I looked her way she covered the receiver with a hand so pallid and veined it looked green.

"They're all down there," she said to me. She tapped a bony index finger to her window. I took off for the stairs.

Outside, what looked like the residents of the entire building were huddled in tight conversational knots in the courtyard. Handkerchiefs, hugging, rivulets of mascara. I spotted my parents, Rahela wiggling in a tangle of blanket in my mother's arms, and felt relief, then an uprush of anger that they'd forgotten about me.

"*Tata!*" I slipped my arm around his leg. My father put his hand on my shoulder but remained immersed in a discussion with one of the main door guards.

I squirmed from my father's grip and pushed my way into the center of the circle my parents and neighbors had created. I tried my mother this time, tugging at the pocket of her apron. The fact that she was in her apron outside was indicative of the weightiness of the morning's events; she wouldn't have been caught dead wearing it in public otherwise. "Mama," I said, on tiptoe now. "Why'd you leave me upstairs?"

Again neither of my parents acknowledged me, but I

learned of the news through a collective murmur that floated through the court, at times so synchronized it seemed intentionally in unison.

"Vukovar je pao." The sound of such a large whisper was haunting, in keeping with the message it carried. Vukovar had fallen.

Vukovar had been under siege for months. The people from the string city now living in Sahara, the boys who'd joined our class mid-lessons, had gotten out early. We knew the stories of their families who were marched to displaced persons camps and never heard from again; we'd heard about the people who'd stayed behind, men and women with do-it-yourself weaponry gunning at the JNA from their bedroom windows. But I didn't understand what it meant, that Vukovar "had fallen," and tried to come up with a comparable image. First I thought of an earthquake, though I'd never experienced one. Next I pictured the cliffs of Tiska, where we had spent the summers, imagining the side of the mountain crumbling and dropping into the Adriatic. But Vukovar wasn't a tiny village and it wasn't near the sea. The rocket at Banski Dvori had collapsed part of the Upper Town, but that was only a little piece of Zagreb. I knew a fallen city must mean something much worse.

After a while it became clear that the clusters of people were not static, were instead moving in a circular crush toward something I wasn't tall enough to see. Eventually the whirlpool of people pushed out from the courtyard onto the main street, and I caught sight of the center of attention: a shivering band of men and boys awash in a brand of terror so unique even I could identify them as refugees. They looked more desperate than those from the first round, wild-eyed and concave in all the wrong places. They clutched scraps of paper marked with the addresses of in-laws, cousins, family friends, anyone who might be willing to take them in, and thrust them in the faces of my parents and neighbors, exchanging bits of information about the front lines for directions to their relatives' houses.

One man from the group reached out and grabbed my father's forearm, holding his address close to my father's nose with a shaky hand. His face was shadowed, empty troughs beneath his cheekbones.

"They're killing them," the man said.

"Who?" said my father, studying the paper for clues.

"Everyone."

"Would you like some soup?" said my mother.

Inside, on television, I saw what it meant for a city to fall. The footage was foreign. Any Croats in Vukovar were either fighting or being captured, so the Croatian news network had intercepted a German broadcast, their correspondent narrating in a mix of unfamiliar consonants. The feed was live and the voice-over untranslated, but the refugee, my parents, and I stared at the screen, as if looking at it hard enough would somehow advance our German skills. The cement façades of homes were disfigured, scarred by bullets and mortars. JNA tanks barreled down the city's main street, followed by convoys of white UN Peacekeeping trucks. Alongside the road, in a place that had probably once been grass but was now trampled and muddy, lines of people were lying facedown, their noses pressed into the dirt and their hands behind their heads. A bearded soldier with an AK-47 walked between the rows. He fired. Somewhere, someone was screaming. The camera jerked up and away, capturing instead a collapsing church steeple. The dull roar of a distant explosion rumbled through the TV speakers. In the background more bearded men with black skull flags marched down the empty street, singing, *"Bit će mesa! Bit će mesa! Klaćemo Hrvate!"* There will be meat; there will be meat. We'll slaughter all Croatians.

"Please turn that off," the man said.

"One minute," mumbled my father.

Just then Luka burst into our flat, the doorknob coming to rest in the same dent I'd made.

"Ana! *Vukovar je pao!*"

"I know," I said. I gestured to the television and the hunched man at the table with his back to the screen, who was devouring the soup that was supposed to have been my father's lunch in quick, greedy swallows. Luka reddened and greeted my parents. He thrust his hands in the pockets of his jeans and the four of us stood around the TV, surveying each other's reactions to the on-screen carnage.

"Does your mother know you're out?" my mother said.

"Yes," Luka said, a little too fast. He grabbed my arm and pulled me toward the door.

"Maybe you should both stay here. I'll make you a snack."

"Mama." I slumped my shoulders in protest. I knew Luka had come because he'd deemed the desecration of Vukovar a good reason to skip class, but our chances of leaving were better if we acted as if nothing had changed. "We have to go to school," I said. "We're gonna be late." But my mother, who refused to negotiate with whining, ignored me and began mixing Rahela's formula. Luka and I skulked into the living room.

Having downed the soup and eager to escape the television, the refugee followed us and sat on the far end of the couch. His face was coated in stubble and mud, dirt smeared across his shirt and lodged beneath his overgrown fingernails. He made me nervous, and I wished my parents would be more attentive to their guest, but they were busy trying to get Rahela to eat something—an effort that had essentially become force-feeding—and neither of them noticed.

"He took my wife," the refugee said. "I heard her screaming through the wall."

Luka and I just stared, afraid to move.

"He had a necklace strung with ears. Ears off people's

heads." The man cupped his head in his hands, pressing his fingers to his ears as if to check whether they were still attached. I yearned to go to school. After what seemed like much too long, my father poked his head around the corner.

"You'll be back straight after class is through?" He raised his eyebrows.

"Yes," I said, unaccustomed to curfews but willing to compromise.

"Go on then."

We sprang from the couch under cover of clattering pans and collapsing building footage, and my father winked at us as we slipped out the door.

When I got home from school the refugee was gone. My parents didn't say anything about where he went, and I didn't ask. At sunset my father and I walked to Zrinjevac to look at the weather column at the edge of the park. He was wearing his mechanic's jacket and I'd donned a coat and scarf, but it was balmy for November and soon we unzipped. My father pointed to the thermometer, explained the barometer, and lifted me up so I could run my fingers on the glass case that housed statistics for seasonal temperature averages and wind measurements.

"Maybe you'll grow up to be a weatherwoman," my father said. "You'd have to study hard, though."

"Yes, *Tata*," I said, but my mind was elsewhere. I climbed

onto the rim of a nearby fountain, grabbing my father's hand for balance as I strutted the perimeter of the now stagnant pool. "What's going to happen to Rahela?"

"If she doesn't get better she might have to see a doctor far away. But she's going to be fine."

"What's going to happen for Christmas?" It was still more than a month away, but winter had always been my favorite season, the Trg ablaze with fairy lights and filled with vendors selling roasted chestnuts in paper cones, snow layering up on our balcony and in the streets below, the days off school. I was getting too old to believe in Sveti Nikola, but I still looked forward to leaving my boot on the windowsill and waking up to find presents stashed inside. This year, though, I wasn't so sure; nothing seemed totally out of reach of the air raids and our dwindling food supply.

"What do you mean?"

"Are we still going to have it?"

"Full of worries tonight!" my father said. He grabbed the fringe of my scarf and brushed it against my face, tickling my cheek. "Have you got your scarf tied too tight? Of course we're going to have it!"

There was something about talking with him that made me feel better, no matter the conversation. My mother used to say my father and I thought in the same circles. I never understood it until I watched us later, in memories—when we were gazing at the sky (and we often were) we could unconsciously turn in the same direction and extract the same face from the clouds. At the park, I laughed and my father lifted me up off the fountain rim and I was skinny from biking and rations and he carried me on his shoulders the whole way home.

The electricity faded in and out in fits that sometimes coincided with air raids but often seemed related to nothing at all, the whim of a damaged wire. When it happened during the day we didn't notice at first. Then, when the shadows edged inward, one of us would reach for a lamp in the fading afternoon sun and be met with disappointment. Eventually we got used to its intermittent presence, and after a while didn't even bother to light the candles we'd stockpiled, instead resigning ourselves to those activities to be carried out in darkness.

Then the water went. We'd had periods of outage before, but now it was gone often, and for longer stints. A twist of the faucet released a coppery sludge, then the angry hiss of air pressure. One morning before school, my mother woke me early and sent me to the courtyard with a pair of gas cans to bring back water from the pump for soup and bathing. City officials and other grown-ups called it the "municipal pump," as if it had been designed for this purpose, but it was really a fire hydrant rigged with a wrench and some piping by one of the men in the building.

Down in the concrete clearing I swung the cans by their handles. The air was crisp, but in the sun it still wasn't too cold. The landscape had transformed into something desolate: the cigarette and newspaper kiosks were all boarded up, the old man and his chocolates packed away, his folding table leaning against an alley wall, abandoned. The pump at least livened the place up again, if only for a few minutes at a time. When I came to the corner, I saw that most of the building's residents were already outside clutching an odd collection of containers and broke into a run; the water often ran out and I'd been late the day before and only got half a canister. Two girls I knew from school were at the pump and they waved me to the front.

"Don't cut the line, Jurić!" an old lady yelled at me, but I called back an excuse about Rahela being ill and went ahead to meet the girls. When I got there a stream of water hit me in the chest, the wetness spreading down my torso; Vjera— the perpetually pigtailed girl—had pressed her hand over the spigot, and the water shot out through her fingers like pent-up rays of sunlight.

"It's *cold*!" I yelled, but already I was laughing. She aimed the water at my face now, and I caught it in my mouth, spraying it upward like the angel fountain in Zrinjevac. I grabbed at the pipe and twisted it in her direction, pegging her in the backs of the legs. We were hysterical now, laughing so hard it didn't even make a sound. The old lady's tolerance ran out and she came at us full-hobble, swinging her empty gas cans until one hit me upside the head.

"Get out of here before I call your mother," the woman said. "All your mothers!" Ashamed, I quickly filled one of my canisters and darted home.

Inside my mother pressed a hand to her hip and pulled at the strands of wet hair plastered to my face.

"Ana, were you wasting the water?"

"It wasn't my fault. Some girls from school sprayed me," I said. Silence hung between us and I mumbled a sorry to break it.

"Let's hope everybody has enough to drink now," she said. Then after a while, she smiled a little and swiped again at my hair. "At least I don't have to boil any for you. You've already had quite a shower."

I smiled then, too, and watched as she heated the water on the stove and bathed with a washcloth in the middle of the kitchen. My mother's hair was the color of burnt chestnuts, and when she moved, it shone.

That night I arrived home from school to find my mother and father standing face-to-face, staring hard at one another. Something was wrong. My father was home too early; his fists were clenched. When the door swung in and hit the wall, they jumped. My mother turned to wipe her eyes. My father began plunking dishes and spoons down on the table with too much force. My mother busied herself, too, was throwing tiny clothes that had once been mine and were now Rahela's into a suitcase on the floor.

"Rahela," I said. My parents seemed to slow slightly at the mention of her name. "Where is she?"

"She's sleeping," my mother said. They'd moved the cradle into the threshold between the kitchen and their bedroom, and I peered in. Too much blood on the blankets, down the front of her shirt. Her breathing shallow.

"What's going on?"

"The medicine's not working. She has to go."

"To the hospital?"

"There's nothing they can do for her here. There's a program transporting out of Sarajevo. We're going to take her tomorrow."

"Transporting where?" I said.

"To America."

I looked around. There were no other cases, no adult clothes in the bag. "By *herself*?"

"It's a medical program. They'll take good care of her," said my father. "Once they fix her up she'll come right back home."

"I want to go to Sarajevo with you," I said.

"No," said my mother.

"We'll see," said my father.

The power was on for an hour or two, and my father made a series of calls, his hand cupped over the receiver to guide his voice through the shoddy connection. At first I assumed he was trying to reach MediMission, but I noticed him later scribbling out what looked like a map, which he folded and put in his back pocket.

After dinner, when an especially violent air raid rattled the windows of our flat, my mother sprang up and held me and I knew I could win her over.

"Did you finish your homework?" she asked when we returned from the basement.

"I don't have to since I'm not going to school tomorrow," I tried.

My mother sighed.

"I want to say goodbye to her, too."

"Better go to bed then. We're getting up early."

On the couch I lay listening to my parents shuffle around the flat.

"She shouldn't be going with us," my mother said. "The road isn't safe."

"It's not safe here either, Dijana. What if something were to happen while we were gone? It's better we stay together." I heard the paper crumpling and remembered my father's drawing. "Besides. Look. I called Miro and he gave me the latest intel. We'll have to take the long way, but it'll be clear. We'll be fine."

I stared at the ceiling, imagining the ride through the mountains with Luka's father's map, then some Medi-Mission stranger carrying Rahela in the airport, on a plane, in America. I knew little of America besides what I'd seen on television, mostly cowboy movies they played on state TV Saturday nights. The United States seemed to me a wonderland full of actors who subsisted on McDonald's, and I wondered if Rahela would go to live with someone rich and famous. On the news men in suits were always calling on the States to help protect us, but no one had shown up yet. Maybe they were just too far away. I slept fitfully, the kind of sleep in which you never quite lose contact with the waking world, and after just a few hours I heard the clack of my mother's shoes alongside my couch.

"Time to go," she said. My arms and legs felt leaden and I struggled to dress, rummaging through my clothes in the morning dark.

7

"Ivan, *molim te,* don't drive so fast. We don't need to give them a reason to pull us over." My mother pressed her free hand against my father's knee. With the other arm she cradled Rahela, who was too weak even to cry. On the horizon, day had not yet broken. It was cold; the back window was stuck half-open, and my father gave me his jacket to use as a blanket. Whenever he turned too sharply, Rahela's suitcase banged me in the shin and my mother implored him to slow down. At some point I fell asleep.

When I woke the sun was noon-strong through the streaky windshield and we had already crossed the border into Bosnia; the signposts were written in both Cyrillic and Latin alphabets and the road circled the bases of the Dinaric

Alps in a serpentine coil. We called the road a highway, though it wasn't really—not the kind with streetlamps—and in the spaces between more important destinations it was only two lanes.

Like the areas in Croatia far from Zagreb, Bosnia was mainly full of nothing: vast expanses of rocky soil, so that even the grass looked like it'd prefer to be rooted somewhere else. Clusters of cement-block houses appeared every so often but seemed to dissolve against the bleach-bright sky as we sped past. Finally, signs presented us with digestible distances to Sarajevo: 75, 50, 25 kilometers.

"Allaaaaaahu akbar," the adhan began as we passed a peripheral mosque at the limits of the capital. We didn't have mosques in Zagreb, at least not ones with public presences, and I cranked the window down the rest of the way to soak in the mysterious strains of the muezzin's call. Rahela slept through it, and I craned my neck around the headrest to survey the rise and fall of her chest.

Sarajevo was on edge, the expectation and anxiety almost palpable. The war hadn't yet come to Bosnia, and the haze of a city left to wait was familiar, though more like a remembered dream than an actual place I'd lived. We passed through the city center, the curvature of mosque domes and sharp angles of Yugoslav skyscrapers forming a rugged skyline. Still, Sarajevo and its inhabitants seemed similar to, if a bit cheerier than people in Zagreb. Markale market was not yet infamous; the parliament building stood boxy and firm, though it was the bloodshed here, not ours, that would catch the attention of the international community in the end. Gazing through the back window at children my age playing stickball in the street, I thought of our war games and generator bike fights and wondered if the things I'd come to consider ordinary were not so normal after all.

My mother traced her finger along a sheet of directions, and my father maneuvered through the alleys in accordance with her commands.

"That's it!" she said suddenly, and my father pulled the car up on the curb to make room for passersby on the narrow street. I recognized the MediMission logo, red and gray and loud, affixed to a corner concrete building. Clutching Rahela, my mother ran across the street without even checking for traffic.

"Lock the car," my father said, tossing me the keys and ducking through the undersize doorframe.

The waiting room gave off the impression of having once been a different kind of room hastily decorated to look like a doctor's office. The carpet was stained; the plastic upholstery of the chairs was hard and cracked. It smelled of antiseptic and rotting fruit. Still, it was more official-looking than the living room–turned-clinic we'd been to in Slovenia, and there was comfort in this formality. But Rahela was shaking with fever now, and a nurse took her from my

mother and into an exam room. Dr. Carson, with her insuf-
ferably white teeth and a matching lab coat, appeared from
the back soon after and ushered us inside.

"Good to see you again," she said. No one replied.

By the time we reached her room, Rahela was already
strapped down to the infant-size examination table, one flex
of plastic tubing in her nose and another in her foot. Her
chest and mouth moved as if she were crying, but produced
only the faintest trace of what appeared to be a full-blown
wail. I tore a corner off the exam table paper and scrunched
it into a ball.

"Okay let's flip her," the nurse said.

"What's going on?" said my mother.

The nurse rolled Rahela onto her stomach, then refas-
tened the straps restraining her arms and legs.

"We have to do a lumbar puncture to check for bacterial
infection," Dr. Carson said in sterile but much improved
Croatian. She snapped on her latex gloves; a long needle
gleamed on the tray beside her.

"Lumbar?" said my mother. "You're going to put that in
her spine?" She lunged toward Rahela, but my father caught
her by the elbow and pressed her firmly against the wall,
whispering things I couldn't hear.

My mother began to scream. Somehow it was easier to
watch the needle. I uncrumpled the paper and shredded it,
the scraps falling to the floor.

My father forced my mother down into the room's single chair. The doctors turned Rahela back over, shot her with pain medication, gave her a pacifier. She looked comfortable for the first time in months.

"All right then," said Dr. Carson, placing a hand on my mother's shoulder. For a moment I saw what looked like sadness flicker across the doctor's face, but it was gone quickly. "Here are the forms for Rahela's transport to the Children's Hospital of Philadelphia. They have some of the best pediatric specialists for renal failure in the world. We'll have her on the plane as soon as she's stable." Dr. Carson gestured to the second of two piles of paperwork on the counter. "And here are the foster family consent forms." My father looked up and my mother lowered her eyes.

"Foster family?" my father said. "Dijana, what is she talking about?"

Dr. Carson jiggled some change in the pocket of her lab coat. "Your wife informed me that your visas were denied?" she said, pausing for my father to affirm this statement. He didn't. "Rahela will be admitted to the hospital upon her arrival, where she'll be housed in the intensive care unit." Dr. Carson was gaining speed now, employing the most professional of the range of tones in which we'd heard her speak. "However, after emergent care is completed, there is an outpatient treatment portion, for weekly dialysis and examinations."

"Outpatient?"

"Rahela will stay with a volunteer emergency foster family until her program at the hospital is complete. Rest assured that all foster families are screened for safety by MediMission—"

"I thought you people were just going to fix her! Fix her and send her home!" The vein in my father's neck, the one that usually signaled that I'd done something wrong and was going to get a whack with a belt, had bulged out precariously far, banging along with the rhythm of his heart. I shied away instinctively, but all the anger and frustration instead compacted into a single tear that passed over his cheek. It was the only time I'd ever seen him cry. "I can't even take care of my own children," he said.

Dr. Carson tried for a reassuring smile, but it came off lopsided. "You are taking care of her. This is the only way Rahela will get better."

"Fuck off," said my father.

"I'll wait outside so you can say goodbye."

I stared at my sister. For once she was quiet. Her eyes were glassy and she looked deep in thought or far away, as if she had already crossed the ocean. I wished I knew more about her and less about the patterns of her sickness. She was so small, so busy surviving that we hadn't gotten the chance to be like other sisters, but her hands still fit well in mine. I hoped her foster family in America would be kind, would tell her stories and take her to the park and sing to her.

"We'll see you soon, baby," my mother was saying over and over. My father put his hand on Rahela's head, ran his fingers through the black hair that was beginning to curl, and said nothing.

"When you get back I'll teach you everything," I whispered to her. "How to walk and talk and color and ride a bike. And everything will be good."

Outside, my mother sobbed so ferociously that she got dizzy and had to sit down on the curb. My father sat next to her and rubbed her back.

"I'm sorry I didn't tell you sooner," my mother said. "I didn't want you to get upset. This is the best we can do." When her breathing steadied, we got in the car and drove out of the city.

At border control a meaty guard checked our documents dispassionately, becoming suspicious only when he came to Rahela's picture. Babies had no passports of their own, only pages within their mothers'.

"And your daughter?" he asked.

"She's with her grandmother," my father said. Both my grandmothers had been dead for a decade, and though I knew it was a lie designed to simplify, I didn't like its implications. The guard handed our passports back through the window, and my father snapped the rubber band tight around them and stretched across my mother's lap to stow them in the glove compartment. The guard waved us through the crossing.

We drove in unbearable silence. I ached for the distraction of staticky music, talk radio even. When I thought of Rahela on her way to America an unexpected emotion welled up in me: relief. Then, when I recognized the feeling, shame. What was wrong with me? I was supposed to be sad. I forced my eyes shut in hopes of squeezing out a tear, and got one or two before my forehead lit up with a jagged ache from all the clenching.

"Mama, I need some water," I said, half because of the headache and half from the desire for my parents' full attention, something unattainable since Rahela had been born. My mother sighed and turned to look at me, her face contorted with such anguish that immediately I wanted to say never mind, that I was okay. But my father, as if he'd been waiting for an excuse to stop, had already veered toward a derelict gas station. A huge piece of arrow-shaped particleboard had been nailed to the abandoned pumps. TRUCK STOP, it read in unpracticed permanent marker scrawl.

We passed a mechanic's garage, graffitied and doorless, and pulled into the car park of a building labeled, a bit more carefully than the first sign, RESTAURANT. It was a bucolic structure; the wood was stained black but maintained its treelike properties—the imperfect curvature of trunks, the knots and whorls of unfinished planks. The gravel lot was completely empty.

Inside was a single room with high-beamed ceilings and picnic tables. We approached the cafeteria-style counter and collected orange trays and rolls of tin silverware. There was no menu, just a few steaming pots on the line. A woman in a dirty apron appeared from the back and eyed us cagily.

"How'd you get down this way?" she asked.

"What do you mean?" my father said. "Aren't you open?"

"This place is always full at supper. The roads must be closed."

"We came down from Zagreb to Sarajevo, now back. They were clear."

"They must be closed," she said, beckoning at our trays. We handed them to her and she slopped down bowls of dense bean soup and hunks of bread. Next to the cash register, thick glass mugs of soured milk perspired, leaving wet patches on an adjacent napkin pile.

"And three of those," my father said, gesturing to the drinks.

"I don't want any. It's bitter," I said.

"It's good for you," he said, taking my mug onto his tray.

At home my mother always cooked, and it was the first time I could remember going to a restaurant. I ate greedily, sopping up the beans with my bread, even downing the tangy milk in the end. My mother ate nothing.

"Do you think the roads are really closed?" my mother asked as we returned to the car.

"We were just there a few hours ago," my father said, though I noticed him glance at his watch. "It'll be okay."

———

We drove for an hour, then two, passed signs for Knin and Ervenik. A pickup truck in the opposite lane flashed his headlights at us.

"Slow down. There must be cops," my mother said. My father braked and another car appeared, this one driving much faster, laying on his horn as he went by. "Maybe we should turn around."

"There's no space for a U-turn," my father said, looking around. But as we rounded the corner the roadblock came into view. "Shit. *Shit.*" I pulled myself up and rested my head atop the driver's seat to get a better look. A cluster of bearded men stood talking and laughing in the road. They wore mismatched fatigues, shoulder-slung ammo belts, and black sword-and-skull arm patches. They had cut down a large tree, which prevented passage on our side of the road. The other side was blockaded with sandbags.

"Can't we get around?" my mother said. "Tell them we just want to get home."

Two men stood apart from the group, motioning disjointedly at us.

"Shit."

"Okay, just pull over!"

"What's happening, Mama?" I said.

"Nothing, honey, we just have to stop for a minute."

"Mama—"

"Just sit down, Ana." My father cranked open the window as one of the soldiers staggered toward the car. The glimmer in his eye matched the reflection of the sunlight off the vodka bottle he held. In his other hand was an AK-47. A Soviet stamp covered the butt of the weapon, and the paths where the ink had dripped and dried looked like tear tracks.

"Is there a problem?" my father asked.

"Need your ID," the soldier slurred. My parents' faces grayed as my mother searched the glove compartment for our passports. Giving up our IDs would provide the soldier with the greatest weapon against us: the knowledge of our names. Our last name specifically, the one that carried the weight of ancestry, ethnicity.

"We have a child," my father said. "We're just going home."

"Jurić?" the soldier read aloud. My parents were silent. The soldier readjusted his gun, looked away. *"Imamo Hrvate!"* he called over his shoulder. *Hrvati*. Croatians. Despite his drunkenness, he still managed a clear inflection of disgust. Another soldier approached and pressed his gun against the soft skin of my father's neck. "Everybody out," he said, then, turning to the rest of the men, "Get the others."

"Mama, where are we—"

"I don't know, Ana. Just be very quiet. Maybe they want to search us." The car bobbed on its corroded shocks as we climbed from our seats. A line of cars had formed along the side of the road. Farther off, a group of civilian prisoners stood on a patch of browning grass, shifting their collective weight uneasily. I stared at them, tried to get someone to look back at me, but no one would. I was jolted from my gaze when a soldier jammed his gun into my back, sending a shock of pain up my spine.

"*Tata!*" I called out to my father as the soldier wrapped a thick coil of barbed wire around my wrists. The soldier let out a laugh and a mouthful of air that stunk of alcohol. Tides of the soured milk pitched against the walls of my stomach.

"Fuck you! Fuck all of you!" my father was yelling, struggling against his own wire cuffs. The soldier behind him struck the back of my father's knee with the barrel of his AK. My father's leg twisted in a way it shouldn't have, and blood ran down the back of his pant leg. He was quiet.

I made my way over to him, leaned my head on his hip, and instinctively reached for his hand, but the wire around my wrists sunk into my flesh. "We're going to be fine," he said, softly now. "Just don't get separated." Beside him, my mother was shaking a little, even though she was wearing her coat. I'd left my jacket in the car, but somehow I didn't feel cold.

The realization that my parents, too, felt pain and fear frightened me more than any strangers could. Panicked thoughts came like a rush of river water—they were going to take our car; we were going to be beaten; they were going to send us to the camps. They herded us into the group of other prisoners: a series of men wearing painters' jumpsuits and stolid expressions, a teenage couple trying to touch one another and recoiling when the wires caught their skin, a woman with a run of blood down her thigh, an old man with white stubble and scuffed black orthopedic shoes. Others.

"*Hajde!* Let's go!" barked the leader of the soldiers. He staggered toward the forest that lined the road.

I focused on not moving my wrists beneath the wire, watching my feet as they sunk into the underbrush with each step. The child of a concrete city, I had never been in a forest before. It was cold and dank-smelling, like the basement of our skyscraper. The viny brushwood seemed to grab at the tops of my sneakers. I thought of Stribor and his kingdom and wished for a glimpse of magic inside a hollowed oak, a miraculous escape route. As we walked farther into the forest, the afternoon sunlight was swallowed by shadows.

"*Tata,*" I whispered. "Why's it so dark in here?" But the group had stopped and he didn't answer. We'd reached a clearing, the forest floor packed so thoroughly under the heels of combat boots that there was no more plant life, only dirt and rotting acorns. In front of us were the remnants of an extinguished fire and a large hole in the ground.

Behind me someone was shouting. One of the painters had tried to run back toward the road, but his gait was off-balance with his arms tied behind him. A soldier caught him quickly, and, after a smack of the rifle across the legs, the man was on his knees. The soldier pulled the man up by his hair, moving his head side to side at an unnatural tilt before letting him drop again to the ground. The man lay in the dirt, and the soldier wiped a clump of hair from his hand before angling the butt of his gun and dispensing a swift blow to the back of the head. Blood—runny—and a dent where bone used to be.

"Anyone else?" the soldier said. His teeth were brown.

The soldiers organized us into a single-file line. They shoved and jabbed. If someone didn't move fast enough, they bludgeoned. They arched the line perfectly around the mouth of the pit.

The first time, the noise that came out of the AK didn't sound like a gunshot. It sounded like a laugh. There was a unified gasp as the first victim crumpled and fell into the void below. For a few seconds, a minute even, nothing happened. Then another shot, and the man next to him— another one of the painters—went.

Witnessing these men's deaths taught the rest of us two things: they were going to do this slowly, and they were going left to right. This was not the most efficient way to kill people. But it was not the least efficient either. It was good target practice for the new recruits. It was slow enough to make the prisoners squirm. It wasn't messy. Bloody, maybe. But once they fell, they were already half-buried.

My father looked down at me, then back to my mother on his left side. His mouth twisted as he pulled his eyes away from hers, then spoke to me in a sharp whisper.

"Ana—Ana, listen to me." A shot. "We're going to play a game, okay? We're going to trick the guards." A shot. "They're drunk—it'll be easy if you pay attention. All you have to do is stay close to me, very close—"A shot. "Then when I fall down into the hole, you fall at the same time. Just close your eyes and keep your body straight." A shot. "But it won't work unless we both fall at the very same time, okay?" A shot. "Do you understand? Don't! Don't look at me."

I didn't understand what was happening, really, how we could trick the guards out of shooting us. But my father seemed sure that if we both fell at the same time we would be okay, and he was always right.

"Is Mama going to fall with us, too?" A shot.

"No, she—" My father's voice cracked. "She's going to go first." I looked at my mother, watched my father watching her, the way something in his irises extinguished.

"Ana!" My father's whisper was much harsher now, frantic. "Listen. Once we fall we have to stay absolutely still and wait until it's quiet above us. Then we'll get out together. Okay? Just remember—" A shot. My mother swayed on the rim of the muddy cavity. A dot of crimson appeared at the curve of her lip, streamed down her chin. She seemed to hover there, as if she'd jumped on purpose, landing quietly, not with the thud of the others before her.

I felt myself yell as I realized what had happened. Another shot, one that echoed. I waited, watched my father, then held my breath and fell.

It was dark and sticky and it smelled like sweat and piss. I turned my face to the side so I could breathe. Something heavy came down on my legs, but I felt far away from my body and couldn't move. I concentrated only on the corner of my once white T-shirt as it soaked up other people's blood. I used to think all languages were ciphers, that once you learned another's alphabet you could convert foreign words back into your own, something recognizable. But the blood formed a pattern like a map to comprehension and I understood the differences all at once. I understood how one family could end up in the ground and another could be allowed to continue on its way, that the distinction between Serbs and Croats was much vaster than ways of writing letters. I understood the bombings, the afternoons sitting on the floor of my flat with black fabric covering the windows, the nights spent in concrete rooms. I understood that my father was not getting up. So I waited, my head light and spinning and my eyelids heavy, and came around to the stench of stale fear and the beginnings of decay.

"Don't worry about it. We'll get the bulldozer in from Obrovac," the leader of the soldiers said. Already the bodies around me were cooling, beginning to take on the puttylike feel of dead flesh. My heartbeat thundered in my ears, panic coursing up my neck. But the soldiers obeyed orders, and I listened as the footsteps disappeared and the echoes of the footsteps disappeared, stayed motionless until I convinced myself I had heard them starting up their jeeps.

"*Tata*," I said. I knew already, but inched closer against him anyway, nudged his shoulder with mine. "Wake up." His eyes were clamped shut tight, as if he were counting for a round of hide-and-seek, but there was blood—at his neck, on his lips, in his ears. "Wake up!" It was impossible to take a deep breath. I tried to move, but my legs were pinned down beneath the leg of the person who'd fallen next to me, a teenage boy missing the back of his head. The weight of his body made it worse. I was sure I was suffocating and kicked wildly, trying to shake him off. My hands were still bound and I struggled to sit. Then, using the dead as step-stools, I climbed out of the ground.

I pulled my wrists out of the wire—squeezed one hand through violent and quick, then unwound the steel and freed the other. Strings of my skin clung to the barbs. Blood dripped in staircases down toward my fingertips. We hadn't been very deep in the forest, and I followed the boot prints out to the road. The soldiers had left the felled tree but had taken the sandbags with them. They had set our cars on fire. I saw the charred skeleton of what I thought had been our car pointing like a giant arrow, and decided to continue in the direction we'd been driving, homeward.

It seemed important to keep walking, but my legs were stiff with shock and the path ahead blurred in and out of focus. I moved with excruciating slowness. Night turned to dawn though I didn't notice the change until it had already passed, as if I'd been a sleepwalker awakened by the sunlight. The shadows were shrinking as I arrived on the outskirts of a village in the glow of a new morning.

II

Somnambulist

1

I woke in the cobalt part of dawn. It was too early to leave but there was no chance I'd fall back to sleep now. Not wanting to wake Brian, I compelled myself to stillness for a minute or two, tried to match the rise and fall of my chest with his, but already consciousness had quickened my heartbeat and I found it difficult to keep from fidgeting. I slipped from his bed and he breathed a deep, surfacing kind of breath but did not wake up.

I returned to my dorm to change, tried to smooth the cowlick on the right that emerged with exceptional stubbornness whenever something important was scheduled. Outside the cold burned my throat but I continued on foot anyway, to kill the time. The roads were slushy, leftovers from a late-night snowplowing, slippery beneath my sneakers as I crossed the avenues and headed uptown. A few business owners were pushing up their grilles to start the day, but overall the city was stark and quiet, as empty as Manhattan gets. For long stretches of my walk I didn't cross paths with anyone.

The lobby of the UN headquarters was not what I expected. Though I'd been attending college in New York for nearly three years, I'd managed to avoid the complex on the East River. Now, inside and waiting in a metal detector line, I felt an odd mix of anticipation and disappointment. Over the years I'd lost faith in the UN—their interventions, in my country and across the globe, were tepid at best—but I'd still assumed the compound would be impressive, decorated with vainglory. In parts it was: the four-story ceilings made me feel small; the balconies of glass and concrete curved around the entrance hall in a slick modernist wave, suggesting progressivism. In other ways, though, the interior was unremarkable. The checkered marble floor was covered in strips of stained industrial carpet. The surveillance cameras were so conspicuous I was sure they were fake, and that streamlined equipment was positioned at more clandestine angles.

The woman who'd asked me here had called over Christmas break. I was easy enough to track down; I hadn't strayed from the people or places to which I was headed when we'd first met. She told me that after her stint in Yugo Peacekeeping she'd returned to New York and muscled her way through the bureaucracy to a liaison position. Now she was working on a new project, forming a committee to focus specifically on human rights. She told me she needed me. I told her I was at college in the city, and she said, "Remarkable," which offended me though I knew she had a point. Then I said something cheerful like "Fridays are perfect. I won't even have to miss class!"—something she was pleased with and I regretted before I hung up the phone.

I was early, and took a seat on a bench to wait. I gazed at the men in suits, wondering if any of them had been in the decision room or on the ground during my war. The woman—Ms. Stanfeld—had never been anything but kind, and I felt guilty about the derision running through me as I scanned the lobby for her face. Finally I caught her in my peripheral vision: dressed in a suit and high heels, her hair straightened and pulled into a bun. The last time I saw her she was in combat boots and a blue flak jacket, a tangle of wavy hair beneath her helmet. Her face was the same. It occurred to me that my appearance had likely undergone a more radical transformation—I'd grown about a foot and a half since then—so I stood and started in her direction. Before I even tried to get her attention, she called out to me.

"Ana Jurić?" It was a last name I hadn't heard in a long time.

"Ms. Stanfeld." I thrust my hand out prematurely and it dangled.

"Please, call me Sharon."

"How did you recognize me?"

"The eyes." For a moment she looked unsure whether she should say more. "And we don't see those shoes much around here." I snuck a peek down at the Converse high-tops I'd pulled on in a last-minute fit of groggy defiance.

I followed Sharon out of the main lobby and down a corridor. She excused herself to go to the bathroom and I wandered the hall. I poked my head into open conference rooms trussed in heavy curtains and adorned with religious-looking paintings that, upon closer inspection, were devoid of any actual religion, eagles and haloed planet earths in place of crucifixes.

Farther down the hallway I noticed a set of ornate wooden doors and a plaque declaring CHAMBERS OF THE SECURITY COUNCIL. I imagined the delegates of a decade ago convening on the other side of that wall, discussing the body count of my parents and friends and determining that yes, something would have to be done to keep up appearances, but that it would be best to stay out of such a messy conflict. I slipped my fingers around the handle and tugged gently, but the door was lighter than it looked and opened wide. A rush of air wind-tunneled into the room and a few delegates in the back row turned to look at me.

I felt a hand on my shoulder. It was enough to startle me into loosening my grip, and the door swung closed. Sharon was offering me a cup of coffee and a frosted croissant in wax paper.

"They'll be done in a few minutes. Then a quick coffee break and we're on." She tried to snap her fingers, but the wax paper got in the way. I followed her to a smaller room with fossilized adhesive on the wall where a plaque had been removed.

She tracked my gaze. "It's our room now," she said with pride. "But I haven't had half a second to put in the application for new signage. Why don't we go get settled at one of the front tables?" She handed me the cup and the pastry. "Any of the 'reserved' spots is fine."

The room was windowless and paneled in dark wood, the tables and chairs arced in a semicircle. I chose a seat and took a swig of the coffee that turned out to be hot chocolate. I choked it down; I usually took my coffee black. The sweetness stuck in my mouth, and it dawned on me that, for Sharon, I would always be ten years old.

In America I'd learned quickly what it was okay to talk about and what I should keep to myself. "It's terrible what happened there," people would say when I let slip my home country and explained that it was the one next to Bosnia. They'd heard about Bosnia; the Olympics had been there in '84.

In the beginning, adults operating somewhere between concern and nosiness had asked questions about the war, and I spoke truthfully about the things I'd seen. But my de-

scriptions were often met with an uncomfortable shifting of
eyes, as if they were waiting for me to take things back, to
say that war or genocide was actually no big deal. They'd
offer their condolences, as they'd been taught, then wade
through a polite amount of time before presenting an excuse
to end the conversation.

Their musings about how and why people stayed in a
country under such terrible conditions were what I hated
most. I knew it was ignorance, not insight that prompted
these questions. They asked because they hadn't smelled the
air raid smoke or the scent of singed flesh on their own balconies; they couldn't fathom that such a dangerous place
could still harbor all the feelings of home. Soon I changed
my approach, handpicking anecdotes like the Great Ding-
Dong Ditch affront on the Serbian man's flat, or the games
we invented in the shelters, until I'd painted Zagreb with the
lighthearted strokes of some carnival fun house. The version
of things they ended up with was nonthreatening, even
funny. But to create a palatable war was tiring and painful,
so one day, I stopped completely. I grew and my accent
faded. For years I didn't reveal anything at all. I passed as an
American. It was easier that way—for them—I told myself.

But the UN delegates, now making their way to their
seats, knew who I'd been a decade ago. They would be thirsty
for gore. I wasn't sure what to tell them. I'd stayed up late
thinking of what to say, had tried to organize things into an
outline, but all these years later I still had no narrative to

make sense of what had happened. Across the room two teenage black boys shuffled into the front row and slumped low in their chairs. Africa, I thought. Lost Boys, or RUF child soldiers. I wondered whether Sharon had recruited them, too, or if they were someone else's project.

Sharon stood and gave an introduction while the projector blinked a big red NO SIGNAL on the screen. I watched an intern jiggle the connection wires. After a second reset the slide show appeared—"Children in Combat" in 3-D Word Art autofocusing overhead.

"Presenting first is Ana Jurić," Sharon said. "Ana is a survivor from the Yugoslavian Civil War." The slide exhibited before-and-after maps of Yugoslavia and its subsequent color-coded divisions. "At age ten, she was also involved in rebel combat missions against Serb paramilitary forces." A quiet murmur floated across the tables at this. "I'll let her introduce herself more fully though," Sharon said, which I took as my cue to stand.

Unsure applause rippled through the room, and I walked to the spot where Sharon had been standing. The auditorium felt much bigger from the front. I pulled the folded index cards from my pocket, but the bullet points now seemed useless. I coughed, and it echoed across the chamber. A memory of my father resurfaced. I had been nervous about performing a solo part in my third-grade Christmas concert. *Just sing loud,* he had said. *If you're loud, everyone will believe you got it exactly right.*

"I'm Ana," I said. "I'm twenty and in my third year at NYU, studying literature." There was a time when I would have been afraid of this room, of the dignitaries and their stiff, suited language, but now I felt more weary than scared. I'd grown out of fear like my childhood clothes, and after the initial adrenaline subsided my voice settled.

"There's no such thing as a child soldier in Croatia," I declared as the next slide flashed—two teenage girls sporting camouflage and scuff-marked assault rifles. "There is only a child with a gun." It was a semantic argument, and bullshit at that, and just like in the lecture halls at university they were eating it up.

The girls in the picture were strangers, but they could have just as easily been me. Caught in that void between childhood and puberty, skin still smooth but limbs gawky from growth spurts. Each held a Kalashnikov across her chest. The taller girl had her other arm over the shorter one's shoulder; they might have been sisters. Both gave half smiles to the camera, as if they remembered from another time that one was supposed to smile in photographs.

Who had taken these pictures, I wondered as I continued on with the speech, recounting our journey home, my parents' murder, the village I'd gone to after. Certainly not the locals, who wouldn't find the image notable enough to warrant a photograph. Too early in the war for trauma tourists, who appeared only after the danger was gone. Must have been journalists, a breed of people I still couldn't understand. Outsiders who claimed the moral high ground, then stood back and snapped photos during encounters with bloodied children.

"Combat was not an option," I said. "It was just a thing we did to live. A part of home."

The slides made the girls look foreign—animals captured on safari—but we were far less exotic than that. When I thought of my own weapon I remembered not its existential power but its weight, heavy against my slight frame. The way its strap rubbed a raw spot on my shoulder. The almost ticklish sensation of my stomach absorbing the pulsating mechanical rhythm as I shot from the hip.

We were not like the children of Sierra Leone who, a continent away, were fighting their own battles that same year; we weren't kidnapped and spoon-fed narcotics until we were numbed enough to kill, though now that it was over I sometimes wished for the excuse. We took no orders, sniped at the JNA from blown-out windows of our own accord, then in the next moment played cards and had footraces. And though I had learned to expel weapons from my everyday thoughts, speaking of them now I felt something I wasn't expecting—longing. As jarring as the guns were to the pale crowd before me, for many of us they were synonymous with youth, coated in the same lacquer of nostalgia that glosses anyone's childhood. But I knew no matter how

I twisted my words I could never explain that I felt more at ease among those rifles than I did in their New York City skyscraper.

Instead I tried for pragmatism, to say something that might at least help someone else. "You should know that your food aid does not reach the people it's supposed to," I said. "In the place where I stayed, there were no Peacekeepers, and the Četniks stole the aid meant for civilians. If you drop the food and leave, you're just feeding your enemy. We had guns, but they had more. Firepower is the only thing that determines who eats."

Eventually I felt the telltale warmth of a person beside me and realized Sharon had returned and was waiting for me to finish. "Thank you for your time," I said. The audience clapped more assuredly now; they were either intrigued by what I'd said or glad it was over. Sharon squeezed my shoulder, then transitioned into her segment on Serbian concentration camps. I looked over at the African boys, whose eyes were permanently reddened from too much rubbing or crying or coke, concealing some unidentified tragedy. I returned to my seat, relieved I had gone first. But when they got to the photos of the mass graves, I slipped out a side door and vomited in a potted plant. I didn't come back for the rest of the presentation, not wanting to see someone I recognized.

2

I crossed the front grounds of the UN complex—a tundra of concrete and winterized fountains—and passed through the exit gate. Sharon and I were supposed to have lunch after the event, but I figured there was still about an hour left if the other boys were to speak, and I could no longer stomach the sight of the place or the memories it churned within me. I negotiated my way across First Avenue traffic and climbed the steps back toward Tudor Village. I'd have to stay nearby to make a quick return to meet Sharon. More than my debt to her, I was realizing now, the chance to talk to someone who'd known me even briefly in Croatia had been the real reason I'd come. Maybe she could tell me something about what happened to the people I'd left behind.

The late-winter air was still chilly, but at least it eased my nausea. I'd always found solace in Manhattan, felt secure among its buildings and streets crowded with strangers whose lives might be just as jumbled as mine. As far as university went, I'd chosen the city more than the school. Neither of the Americans I'd come to call my parents had gone to college, and I had only vague notions of what I might want to study. So with no other criteria I recalled Zagreb—its alleyways and trams, the autonomy and mobility that came with the compactness of a city—and set my sights on New York. But now, as I walked down Forty-fourth Street, examining this unfamiliar piece of Manhattan, I felt out of place. The street could have belonged to another city entirely, so different in aesthetic and purpose from the West Village, where I spent most of my time: clean sidewalks sparsely populated by people in ties and buffed leather shoes, black cars with drivers and diplomatic license plates idling curbside. I passed a string of UN Program offices and the UNICEF building, names that had meant so much hope to me as a child across the ocean and so little to me now.

I stopped in a bodega to buy a roll of breath mints. While digging around in my jacket for change I saw my phone flashing with a text message from Brian.

Mornin babe. Where'd u go?

I didn't want to lie, so I wrote nothing and stuffed the phone back in my pocket. Brian and I had been dating for a year, but he didn't know anything about who I really was. I'd

told him, as I had everyone else at college, that I was born in
New Jersey.

At first I was confident in the choice to keep my past life
a secret. I could experience college and the city without the
old sadness in wait at every turn. For a while, it worked. I
made a few friends, met Brian, stayed out too late smoking
and drinking and dancing, walking home wide-eyed and
enchanted by the city lights. Slowly, in a place uncontami-
nated by the specter of childhood, I was learning to live a
normal life. Then, at the start of my third year, the towers
had fallen.

I was in an 8:00 A.M. chemistry class making periodic
table jokes with my lab partners when a professor from a
neighboring classroom appeared in the doorway. She let
herself in.

"Hank," she said, "you've gotta see this." She searched
through Dr. Reid's desk drawers while he looked on, annoyed. She found the remote and aimed it upward with a
shaky hand. The television, having been left in video input
mode, produced a static growl. She turned to a news chan-
nel.

The fire was lurid even through the grain of the old set,
startling in both intensity and size, but it was when the
cameraman zoomed out that the entire class gasped in recognition. Professor Reid flipped the emergency switch to
cut power to the gas line, deactivating our experiments, and
we circled around the television.

"You are looking at obviously a very disturbing live shot there," said the news voice-over. "That is the World Trade Center, and we have unconfirmed reports this morning that a plane has crashed into one of the towers."

"Oh god, which tower is that?" said a girl in the back of the lab.

"What kind of pilot was flying that low over New York City?" a boy beside me said. "Fucking idiot."

"My brother works in South Tower," the girl said.

"What if it wasn't an accident?" I said.

"What do you mean not an accident?" said the boy. "What the fuck was it then?"

Our professor punched the keypad of his cellphone, but whomever he called didn't pick up, and he snapped the phone shut.

"I want you to go back to the dorms," he said. "If you live off campus find someone you can sit with for a while." We collected our books, except for the ashen girl, who stayed below the television.

"It was the North Tower," I said, pointing to the ticker text. "I'm sure your brother's fine."

"Guys," Dr. Reid called as we reached the door. He didn't look up; he was pressing keys on his phone again. "Take the stairs."

Outside I tried to get a look downtown, but I couldn't see anything. I wondered where Brian was, and felt around in my backpack for my cellphone. My American parents had given it to me for my birthday the month before, but I still wasn't used to carrying it around and was constantly misplacing it. When I found it the screen revealed several missed calls. I tried to call Brian, then home, but was met each time with a busy signal I'd never heard before, the sound of millions of people simultaneously on the phone.

Not knowing what else to do, I ran back to my dorm and found Brian pacing the front hall. I was relieved and a little shocked to find him whole and fine and right in front of me. Instinctively, I realized, I'd been expecting the worst.

"You're okay," I said, trying not to sound too surprised.

Brian kissed me on the forehead and we went upstairs, where my floor mates were already crowded in the common room. We sat staring at the television, watched the strike on the second tower and its collapse a few hours later. The ticker had changed from "disaster" to "attack." Eventually I got through to my family, an inexplicably whispered call, as if we were afraid speaking too loudly might send something else toppling. I was fine, I said over and over, trying to placate the woman I'd come to call my mother. And I *was* fine, I assured myself when I hung up. After all, nothing had happened to me.

Brian wanted to stay, but I feigned a research paper and a string of apologies, and reluctantly he returned to his own dorm. I wanted to be alone. Even after everyone had gone to bed I stayed up watching the towers that were no longer towers, what everyone was now calling Ground Zero. A desire to be close to the wreckage overwhelmed me. I went out and walked south until I got to the fire engine roadblocks, stood there for a while, awash in emergency light. The air was still thick with the smell of burning plastic and molten steel, dry, itchy breaths filled with plaster particulate.

When I returned to the common room the news was replaying the day's footage—jerky shots of asphalt concealed by a layer of ashes and dead people's paperwork, documents that had been considered important, maybe even classified, just that morning. The coverage returned to real time, a live helicopter shot of the skyline. A cloud of smoke lingered over the spot, tinged orange from the reflection of the city's lights. I tried again to quell the solipsistic thought I'd been evading all day—that trouble would follow me wherever I went.

It was now six months since the attacks, and the everyday things were returning to normal, first through an attitude of compulsory courage—*fear means letting them win*—then in a slow reinstating of routines, until we were again wrapped up in the mundane inconveniences of city life: knocking radiator pipes, subway construction reroutes, and the usual array of vermin. The country was at war, but for most people the war was more an idea than an experience, and I felt something between anger and shame that Americans—

that I—could sometimes ignore its impact for days at a time. In Croatia, life in wartime had meant a loss of control, war holding sway over every thought and movement, even while you slept. It did not allow for forgetting. But America's war did not constrain me; it did not cut my water or shrink my food supply. There was no threat of takeover with tanks or foot soldiers or cluster bombs, not here. What war meant in America was so incongruous with what had happened in Croatia—what must have been happening in Afghanistan— that it almost seemed a misuse of the word.

My phone rang and startled me, and I answered in a shaky voice. It was Sharon.

"Ana? Where'd you go?"

"I just needed some air. Should I meet you in the lobby?" I realized I had wandered farther west than I should have. I jogged back across the avenues and up to the gates of the UN, where a tour group was clogging the entrance portals. I hit Redial on Sharon's number, but she appeared through the exit moments later with an armful of file folders and my index cards.

"I figured you wouldn't be able to get back through that mess," she said. "Do you want these?" She handed me the index cards. "You hungry?"

I wasn't, but I was eager to get away from the UN and have Sharon to myself.

"I've got a reservation. We can walk."

I trailed behind her back up the stairs, in awe of the ease with which she carried herself in high heels. I still clomped whenever I tried to wear them, and the older I got the more unlikely it seemed I would ever learn the grace other women had. Each time we passed an expensive-looking restaurant, I held out hope we'd be going someplace more casual, where I wouldn't make an ass of myself. Sharon pecked at her BlackBerry and gestured absently to UN-affiliated properties—the Malaysian consulate, the hotel where all the bigwigs stayed. I looked at them inattentively, but could think only of how I might begin the conversation I'd been suppressing for a decade.

The sun broke through a patch of gray, warming my cheeks and sending India's mission building shimmering. At the top, the inset porch was now awash in a spring gold, sun spilling through the latticed skylight and glancing off the mirrored cut-ins along the walls.

"It is a beautiful one," Sharon said, leaning back on her heels. "Something futuristic about it, almost."

I'd been thinking the opposite—that the russet granite suggested desert, an ancient-temple kind of beauty, but I said nothing and followed her across the street.

The restaurant looked a little dingy, its awning faded and curtains caked in dust. When we entered, though, I was dismayed to find the place was indeed upscale, if not exactly clean. The tables were sheathed in stodgy white linen even for the lunch hour. I looked down at my sneakers.

"I'll have the house red," Sharon said to a waiter in a metallic vest.

"Can I have a Coke, please?"

The waiter smiled and took my wineglass away with him. The room was lit with patchy spotlights, and I squinted at the menu. There were no prices on anything.

"I think that went very well, don't you?" said Sharon. I told her I thought so, too, but in reality I wasn't so sure. I fiddled with my napkin, folding and unfolding the little cloth rectangle, and asked about her project. She responded with stock lines about busyness and moved her file folders beneath her chair.

"But enough about that. How's college? And your sister—Rahela?"

The use of my sister's name, the one no one had called her in years, caught me off guard. "They—we—call her Rachel here."

"And she's well?"

"She's good, yeah. I'm surprised you remembered her."

"Petar often spoke fondly of your family when we were on duty together. Particularly during the period in which you were ... missing."

Speaking of Petar. For all the times the question had lingered in my mind, it was difficult to shape in my mouth. The finality of knowing. "Do you—" I faltered. The waiter returned with our drinks, and I hoped Sharon, who had not picked up the menu, would tell him to go away. But she

ordered a steak salad with mustard dressing, and, unpre-
pared, I ordered the same. When the waiter left, Sharon
sipped her wine and looked at me expectantly. "What were
you saying?"

"Nothing."

She paused but decided to take me at my word. "Then
tell me more about you. I want to hear all about your new
family, your new life."

I clenched my teeth at her use of the word. *New*, like I
had traded one family for another in a used-car deal. I swallowed the resentment and told her that my family was kind
and had taken good care of me. Rahela was healthy now, as
if nothing had ever been wrong with her at all. We'd spent
most of the last ten years in a suburb of Philadelphia, where
everything was clean and calm. That I had come to New
York to get away from that quiet. Sharon nodded along like
a woman at church. She meant to be encouraging, I knew, or
else she was pleased with herself, but either way it bothered
me that my life was something for her to evaluate and take
some kind of credit for. "Anyway," I said. I looked down at
my plate. "I wanted to ask you about Petar."

Sharon stopped nodding.

"Do you know what happened to him? The day we left?"

"No," she said. "The men I sent—they couldn't find him.
Then I was in Germany for a month, and after that Bosnia,
out of communication. I was sort of hoping you had—"

"I haven't," I said.

"I tried. I wrote letters. Even asked the people who set up the new embassy. But there was nothing."

"What about all the other guys in the unit?"

"I think of all of them, of course, but none of them were as close—Petar and I were friends. And, after you, I just wanted to know that everything was okay."

"Petar told me he saved your life."

"That, too—I owe him. Really it was probably more than once. His unit actually used their guns and we were carrying ours around like handbags."

My face must have betrayed my anxiety because Sharon said, "I'm sorry. Sometimes I just feel like if I don't laugh about it, something really ugly could take root in me. I'm sure you understand."

I said I did.

"You know, in the end, you're my biggest success story."

I thought of Sharon's speech, the photos of the grave excavations. All the others, like my parents, who hadn't yet been found.

"I don't know if *success* is the word."

She smiled faintly. "Maybe not. Truth is I don't think I'll ever get over the things I saw there." She paused. "But I shouldn't be putting that on you."

I told her it was okay.

"Petar would be so proud of you."

I mumbled a thanks and concentrated on my salad until the waiter mercifully appeared with the check. I reached for my wallet. Twenty and studenthood was an interim existence in which I frequently found interacting with "real adults" awkward, them waving off my offers to split bills as something ridiculous, and making me feel even more like a child.

"Don't even think about it."

"Are you sure?" I said, though in this case I was thankful; my work-study check was sure to take a hit from the priceless menu. Sharon gave an exaggerated nod as she tipped back the last of her wine.

Outside, the burst of spring had given way to a thin, cold drizzle. Sharon pulled the belt of her trench coat tight as we stood together on the curb. "Do you ever think about going back?" she said.

"I tried not to think about it at all until you called." I moved to pull my coat closed, too, but the zipper was jammed. "Do you?"

"I don't think it's good idea. For me." She stuck her arm out to hail a cab. "Looks like the skies are about to open up. You need a ride somewhere?"

I shook my head. Anyway, we were going in opposite directions. A taxi pulled to the curb on the other side of the street. "Guess I'll take that," she said. We shared a mannered hug and she ran across the street, still poised in her heels on the slick asphalt. I watched her into the cab, but she was typing something on her BlackBerry and didn't look up again.

As I walked to the subway my mood blackened, something like anger but about what I couldn't pinpoint. Frustration, maybe, that I still understood so little. Instead of clarity and insight, adulthood had only brought more confusion. At the next corner I dumped the index cards in the trash.

3

The city was crowded and wet and grim, with that air of gray desperation it sometimes took on in March. Lunch had gone long and I was going to be late for my appointment with Professor Ariel.

I tried to gauge whether I had enough time to return to my room to retrieve the book he'd loaned me, but decided against it and headed straight for his office.

Reading was one of the only ways in which I allowed myself to think about the continent and country I'd left behind. Though I hadn't told the professor anything about myself, he seemed to know I was not at home in the world, and so he lent me books—Kundera and Conrad and Levi and a host of other displaced persons. I'd read one and return to his office, where he'd wax eloquent about the authors with such intimate detail I was convinced they were all his close friends. I'd just finished *The Emigrants,* and though most of the week's anxieties had been UN-focused, the book hadn't been much easier on my mind. I'd followed the wandering protagonist—at once forlorn and whimsical—all the while with an uneasy feeling that the professor somehow knew more about me than I cared to reveal.

I ran up the stairs to his office and knocked though the door was half-open. The room was small and warmly lit, with shelves covering nearly every surface. Stacks of overflow books lined the floor. Professor Ariel sat at a desk in the center, looking little and frail amid his collection.

"Come in. Sit down," he said in his trembly way. "What did you think of the Sebald?" I moved some papers from the chair and put them on his desk. Behind him on the wall a giant poster of Wisława Szymborska, whom he'd also made me read, watched over our meetings like a chain-smoking guardian angel.

"It got to me," I said.

"Remarkable prose, isn't it?"

"Yes." It was true, but that wasn't the reason. "Not just that, though. The characters. To come face-to-face with people who never recover from their traumas. It was . . ."

"Disconcerting?"

I nodded.

"And yet Sebald continually points to the imperfections of memory. Not what we usually think of as the 'searing' of a certain trauma into one's mind. That haunting lucidity. What do you make of it?"

That had been what scared me most. What if my memory of my parents' final moments was all wrong? I felt certain I had kept them fresh and protected inside me. The idea that the whim of the subconscious might corrupt what little I had left of them was too much to accept. "But, maybe it's not that way for everyone. Maybe some people do remember," I said.

"Certainly. But that comes with its own problems, no? Consider the character of Ambros Adelwarth."

"His uncle?"

"Tormented by such clear images of his past—"

"He opts for electroshock therapy. To wipe out the thoughts."

"Precisely."

"So what am I supposed—I mean, what are we supposed to take from it?"

"Damned if you do—" He smiled a little, then turned to look out the window. He began talking about Sebald's recent death, a car crash of questionable explanation, but I was feeling too rattled to respond. "Ana, you all right? You're looking a bit peaked." He said my name the Croatian way, not with the long, flat *a*'s most Americans used.

"I'm fine. Sorry," I said. "Just a little under the weather."

"Sebald has that effect on people. I call it the 'spell of despair.'"

I tried to protest, not wanting him to think I couldn't manage his assignments, but he turned and stared right at me and I fell silent.

"Where did you say you were from again?"

"I—well. Originally?" I had not said. I didn't want to say. But it came out anyway. "From Croatia. Zagreb." A strange, weightless feeling came with having spoken the truth. I gripped the side of the chair as if I really was at risk of floating away.

Professor Ariel did not seem surprised. "Mmm," he hummed. "I thought so."

"What?"

"I had an inkling. Not Croatia, exactly. Just from somewhere else. Though the Balkans makes sense."

"But how could you tell?"

"You have an old soul. I should know—I've got one, too. Also, you read too much." He winked, and I allowed myself a little smile back. "The good news is your friends will catch up." He swiveled back toward the corner bookshelf. "Now, for next week. Can you handle another Sebald? I've got his latest around somewhere . . ." Slowly he stood and jimmied the book off the shelf with a skeletal finger. "Here it is. *Austerlitz*."

"Sorry I didn't bring the other one back. I came straight from—a meeting."

"Never mind. You keep it anyway. I'm sure I have another copy."

He shuffled around his desk and put the book in my lap. "Go on then."

"Thank you," I said. But something else had caught his attention and he was far away now, running his fingers along the spine of a book as if it were braille, or the hand of someone he'd long loved, so I closed his heavy office door behind me.

I returned to my dorm, glad to find the hallways quiet and my roommate gone. I should call Brian, I thought, but could not bring myself to do it. Now that I'd told Professor Ariel even just a little about me I felt dangerously open. If I saw Brian I might tell him, too, and I was not ready to deal with the consequences of my deception. Instead I filled my oversize skateboarder's backpack—remnant of my high school antiestablishment phase—with homework and Sebald and dirty laundry, and left. At Penn Station I bought a dollar bag of oversalted popcorn and climbed aboard the first in a series of commuter trains to Pennsylvania.

By the time I boarded the commercial jet in Frankfurt I hadn't slept in two days and was afraid of nearly everything. I was frightened by the pressure in my ears at takeoff, of catching the sickness of the man who was throwing up into a paper bag across the aisle, of whatever was waiting for me on the other side of the ocean.

When we landed flight attendants took turns reading the

airline tag around my neck like I was lost luggage. One grabbed my wrist and dragged me toward customs, where I moved through a series of roped-off queues and signed my name to a form I couldn't read. An announcement over the intercom caught her attention, and she stared at the wall clock and tapped her foot. A man with too many badges rifled through my passport, eyeing my makeshift visa with its crooked staple. Behind him I watched suitcases wind around a black track. The officer asked me a question that, from what I could understand, was about whether I'd recently been on a farm. I looked at his badges and shook my head.

The officer stamped my passport and sent me onward, and the flight attendant said goodbye. At the baggage carousel I found my suitcase and followed everyone else toward a set of glass doors. The doors looked sealed, with no knobs or handles, but no one else seemed to notice. I thought about yelling out that everyone should be careful, but couldn't think of how to say it in English. As the first people pushed ahead I narrowed my eyes, anticipating a spray of broken glass. But the doors slid open at the last minute, like magic.

On the other side, groups of excited loved ones clustered around the opening. A little boy attached himself to his mother's leg; two friends hugged and jumped and screamed in one another's ears. Beyond them, men in suits bearing signs with people's names ringed the lobby. I continued through the crowd, head tilted to compensate for the swirling feeling inside me, until I ran right into a man holding a toddler who looked like my sister.

The man looked down, and for a moment it was unclear which one of us was more terrified. The woman beside him—who was holding a handwritten sign bearing my name with diacriticals in odd places—shuffled through a handful of paperwork. She was short and tan, and her face was set in a smile.

"Rahela?" I peered up at the healthy, curly-haired little girl perched in the crook of the man's arm. She'd grown so much she was almost unrecognizable, except around the eyes, where we had always looked alike.

"I thought the airline was supposed to bring you—well—" The woman found the paper she was looking for. *"Dobrodošli u Ameriku, Ana,"* she read haltingly from her sheet.

"Hvala." I searched again through my school lessons for any English words that would fit together and make sense. The woman bent down and hugged me.

"It's so nice to meet you," she said.

Their names were Jack and Laura, and they said it was okay for me to call them that. But Rahela called them Mommy and Daddy in her high-pitched toddler voice, and for the first few months, I called them nothing at all.

———

I changed trains in Trenton and fell asleep in a saggy leather SEPTA seat. I dreamt of bodies. They were nightmares I'd had years ago, when I first arrived in America. Dreams in which I'd be cliff-diving from the rock ledges in Petar and Marina's fishing village and, in a midair exchange, was no longer headed for the warm Adriatic but was instead careening toward a pile of bloated corpses. Then, as I was landing, a powerful tingle radiated from my neck to the backs of my knees and jolted me awake. The train pulled into the station and the conductor yelled, "Last stop!" and I gathered my things.

On the platform I watched the train ready itself for reversal, part of me already wishing I could go back with it. I trudged down the town's main thoroughfare, lined with interconnected strip malls: a two-story pet supply, the Kmart where I worked summers, all the major fast-food chains, and Vacuum Mania.

Sometimes I felt guilty that Jack and Laura had moved here for Rahela and me. I wondered if they ever missed their life before us. For years they, too, had been city dwellers, their apartment just enough for newlyweds and the baby they couldn't have. Then Rahela arrived, and soon she was rosy-cheeked and growing, toys and clothes brimming from her allocated chest of drawers, annexing the arms of furniture. Of course they knew they'd have to give her back. But with her presence they began to want the things they'd always dismissed as the desires of people older than they were.

They bought a cheap piece of land on a hill that was going to become a neighborhood, and began to build.

When construction started I was nothing to my American parents but the older sister mentioned in Rahela's MediMission fact sheet. Then, before the building was finished, I was there.

"Which bedroom do you want?" Laura asked me on move-in day. The thought of my own bedroom was an alien concept and I defaulted to silence, thinking I'd misunderstood. In the end I picked the room with the bigger window because it reminded me of the balcony in Zagreb. The hill overlooked acres of farmland and, beyond that, forest. When family and friends came to visit the new house, all of them remarked on the beautiful view. But in those first months I spent each day searching the skyline for a building, craving something dirty or metal to break through the dark green. I never got used to the forest, not after months or years, not even in daytime, when the sunlight passed through the leaves. I made up excuses to withdraw from neighborhood games of Manhunt that ventured too close to its edge. At night the trees seemed to lean inward, casting shadows on my wall. They were chestnut oaks, Jack said, when I asked him after some sleepless night of tracking their silhouettes out my window. Like in Stribor's forest, I tried to tell myself, but I could think of nothing but the white oaks and rotting acorns in the place my parents had fallen.

America was not what it looked like in the movies. I had

been right about the McDonald's at least; they were every-where. But the bravado and gallantry, that spirit of adven-ture touted in the Westerns so loved across Yugoslavia, was absent in the life I found in Gardenville. In Zagreb I had always been excited about a trip in the car. In Gardenville you needed the car to do anything, even to buy groceries. There were no bakeries anywhere. Everything in the super-market was presliced and prepackaged. In stores bigger than any I'd ever seen in Europe, stores that had everything, I followed Laura around incredulous that I could not find a fresh loaf of bread.

The culture was noticeably conservative, even in juxtapo-sition with the dual traditions of communism and Catholi-cism back home. In Croatia, topless women graced the covers of most newspapers and were common on the beaches, but in America nudity of any kind was something shameful. In Zagreb I ran the streets without curfew and bought cigarettes and alcohol for the grown-ups. In Gar-denville, adults nursed a perpetual fear of kidnappers, and I stayed close to home.

Conversations, particularly with respect to me, were crafted carefully. After those initial bursts of curiosity, no one spoke to me about my past, even within the family. Laura developed euphemisms for my "troubles," the war and its massacres reduced to "unrest" and "unfortunate events."

Throughout that first summer I passed the days clinging to Rahela, which was harder now that she could walk. I sat

in a tiny chair and pretended to eat the plastic food she pre-
pared in her plastic kitchen, or followed her up and down
the driveway in her Flintstoneesque foot-powered toy car,
unwilling to let her out of my sight. Sometimes I whispered
to her in Croatian, to see if she remembered. She'd parrot
back a word or two, but the things she babbled of her own
accord sounded like English.

When it was time for her nap I'd hide in the crawl space
beneath the porch and look at her picture books, practicing
English, matching the illustrations to words. Sometimes I
scoured the newspaper for any headlines with "Croatia" or
"Serbia" in them, which I pasted in a notebook I hid beneath
my bed. When Laura could will me out into the open, she'd
speak to me loudly, as if volume was the reason I couldn't
understand. Having studied English all my school days, I
could comprehend most of what she said, but struggled to
summon the right words in the right order fast enough to
respond. She bought me summer school workbooks, and I
powered through the math problems and guessed on all the
reading fill-in-the-blanks until I had completed enough
pages for her to declare me finished. Then I'd return to my
spot beneath the porch and fight the urge to sleep. I stayed
awake most nights and was always exhausted, but sleep
meant dreaming, and so I avoided it.

One afternoon we had a barbecue in the new backyard.
When it got dark, I heard rumbles in the distance.

"It will rain?" I said.

"I don't think so, kiddo," Jack said. He was right. The sky was cloudless.

Then the explosions started. Bursts of red and orange clustered along the horizon, followed by a series of violent crackles. I yelped and took off toward the house, brushing past Jack.

"Hey, Ana! Wait!" he said. "It's just the Fourth of July!" I could not understand what the date had to do with an air raid and was not about to stop and find out. I dove beneath the porch, tucking my head between my knees and covering my neck with my arms like we'd learned to do at school if we didn't have time to get to the shelter.

"Ana. It's okay." He was lying in the grass on his stomach now, his head poked into the crawl space. "It's the Fourth of July. It's a celebration of—of the end of our war. They're just fireworks. For fun."

"You have a war?"

"No. Well, yeah, but a long time ago. Hundreds of years." He'd grass-stained the shoulder of his shirt and his glasses were crooked on his face.

"Fireworks?"

"Yeah you know, like, the BOOM"—he mimed a big flash with his hands—"and the pretty colors?"

"We had it. In the New Year's Eve. Before the war."

"Yes, right. For celebrating."

I reached out and straightened his glasses on the bridge of his nose.

"Thanks," he said. After a while he put his hand on my knee. "So it's okay. All right?"

I nodded.

"Do you want to go watch?"

I shook my head. "You. Please."

"Well I'll just be over there if you change your mind." I hugged my knees to my chest and watched him return to the party. He ran his hands through his hair and whispered something to Laura, who shot sideways glances back at the porch, and I didn't come out for the rest of the night.

At home I shed my muddy sneakers and stood alone in the kitchen. Little magnetic frames featuring pictures of Rahela and me clung to the refrigerator—her as a baby, crawling, walking, graduating kindergarten; me as a sixth, seventh, eighth grader, teeth in transitional positions.

"Hello?" I said, but no one was there.

I pulled a chair from the table toward the kitchen's highest cabinet. The file box inside contained the family's essential documents—marriage certificate, property deed, social security cards, insurance records—the ones it would be the most unpleasant to replace. I pulled a manila envelope from the back of the box, a large, slanted "Ana" scrawled across it in felt tip.

Inside was my expired Yugoslavian passport and my unused American one, the documents asserting that I'd actually been born in New Jersey, and a pair of photographs creased down the middle from when I'd folded them and shoved them in my pocket ten years ago.

The first was a picture of my family in Zagreb the Christmas before the war—me on the table; Rahela, a newborn, asleep in my lap. My mother and father, who'd been engaged in a tussle with the camera's automatic timer, had run into the frame late and were captured mid-movement, my mother flipping her hair behind her shoulder, my father trying to slip his arm around her waist. I had taken the photo to a camera shop once to see if it could be fixed. No, the man behind the counter had said, there was nothing he could do to unblur them.

The second photo was me on the beach in Tiska, two or three years old, wearing an oversize sweater and squatting down to touch the blue-green water. I stared into the lens with a wide grin. My father had no doubt been behind the camera, and I wondered what he had been saying that made me smile like that.

I looked again at the photo of my parents and tried to picture them more precisely. Maybe Sebald was right, and time and trauma had darkened my memory. Sometimes I could see fragments of them—my mother's severe cheekbones, my father's fair, bushy eyebrows—but I could neither zoom in nor cling to these moments of clarity. Long ago I forgot what they smelled like. I could no longer conjure my father's soap or my mother's perfume. Slowly, I was forgetting them.

I heard the door slam in a way Laura would not approve of and knew my sister was home. Her backpack still slung over one shoulder, she didn't notice me; instead she immediately submerged her head in the deepest sector of the freezer and began sorting through generic-brand popsicles. Clutching the photos and the envelope, I shoved the box back on the shelf, closed the cabinet, and jumped down from the chair.

"Hey, Rahela," I said. She didn't respond. "Rachel!" She pulled her face up from the icy drawer. "Hi. How was school?" Rahela was in fifth grade now, like I had been when she'd gotten sick.

"I only like the grape ones," she said, peeling off the iridescent wrapper. "Or Fudgesicles. Miss Tompkins was a real jerk today. She made us do multiplication time tests at recess because Danny Walker wouldn't stop making armpit fart noises during morning announcements. Hey, what are you doing here? Mom didn't say you were coming."

"She doesn't know," I said. "I mean, it's a surprise."

"Want to come to my soccer game tomorrow? Who's that?" She pointed her popsicle toward the photo in my hand. Excess syrup dripped from the wrapper.

"No one," I said. "You're getting popsicle on your shirt."

"Crap." She wet the corner of a dish towel and dabbed at

the stain on her chest while I went upstairs to my room. "Don't tell Mom I said 'crap'!" Rahela yelled up from the kitchen.

I had attended the same elementary school as Rahela, though it hadn't been easy to get me enrolled. As summer waned I overheard anxious conversations between Jack and Laura about the upcoming school year. Registering me for school was going to be a problem, I gathered, because I had entered the country on a forged visitor's visa, and it was hard to sign someone up for school who technically didn't exist. I watched Laura sit on hold with the INS helpline and pore over photocopies of a policy book from the library, but she wasn't getting anywhere. One night, frustrated, Jack dumped the entirety of her research directly from the kitchen table into the trash. He didn't say anything afterward, even when Laura yelled at him, and instead retreated to the basement with the phone, where he stayed until long after I'd been sent to bed.

Jack had uncles. He had uncles who worked construction. He had uncles who owned racetracks. He had garbageman uncles, a fire chief uncle, and even a mayor-of-a-small-town uncle. He had uncles in prison.

They came at night. They wore odd clothes. Uncle Sal dressed all in black—a colossal medallion of Jesus's face strung from a gold chain and submerged in a tuft of chest hair. Junior wore a red suit with flame-licked shoes one night, a pink one with white snakeskin boots the next. They smoked in the house. Laura gritted her teeth each time they flicked back their lighter caps. They brought Rahela and me presents: gold wristwatches and pocketknives that Laura put on high shelves to "keep until you are old enough."

The Uncles convened standing up, forming a horseshoe around the kitchen table, half-joking about how no one could stand with his back to the door. They spoke a miry blend of English and Jersey-accented Italian and laughed too loud. Every night, the conversation ended the same way: one of the Uncles would say, "I'll take care of it for ya," and clap Jack on the back. They'd go out the front door, which no one else used, slip into their Cadillacs, and drive down the hill with their headlights off, leaving silvery oil stains on our new driveway.

When they were gone Laura would fling open a window to let out the smoke and Jack would sit on the edge of the couch, remove his glasses, and run his hands over his reddened face. Then he'd reach for his guitar and play until he returned to his normal color. Laura, who usually managed to put Rahela to bed sometime during the visit, would shoo me upstairs. I'd climb the stairs halfway, then sit and watch through the slats in the banister, trying to decipher the meaning of the visits, but all I could ever discern was an ongoing debate between Jack and Laura about whether or not asking the Uncles for help was a good idea.

I didn't say a word for the first month of school, sat staring through class and spent recess trolling the perimeter of the blacktop until a piercing whistle demanded our return. Sometime in October, after weeks of patience, my teacher called on me to read out a paragraph from the chapter book we'd been studying. I produced a halting string of unrecognizable words and my classmates snickered. When I got home I ripped all the pages from the book and tried to flush them down the toilet.

Laura and Jack asked me if I wanted to join a soccer team. I didn't know what soccer was but was pleasantly surprised to find out it was football when I arrived at my first practice. The excitement was short-lived, though—Americans had somehow managed to ruin the game with all sorts of rules: the coach put me on defense and told me I wasn't supposed to cross the halfway line or try to score a goal. The neatly manicured lawn and fixed nets made my favorite game unfamiliar.

"I think I don't like the soccer," I told Laura.

"That's okay," she said. She leaned in, secretively. "I hate sports, too." I thought about telling her that I actually liked sports but didn't want to hazard a return to the soccer team, so I gave her a thumbs-up and we never went back.

I spent my free time writing to Luka. I told him about the strangeness of English and the desecration of football. I jotted notes on the backs of homework assignments during recess and sat in bed with sheets of loose-leaf paper, leaning on outdated volumes of *World Book Encyclopedia*. I couldn't remember Petar and Marina's address, so I wrote letters to

them and sent them to Luka, too. I never heard back. Still I
wrote and licked airmail stamps and pretended that Luka's
prolonged silence didn't mean anything was wrong.

My teacher began sending home reports of my every
move at school—how I spent my recesses scribbling, that I
refused to socialize with other children and didn't raise my
hand in class. She sent me to the guidance counselor. Jack
and Laura worried, and I felt awful, too, the sleepless nights
getting me nothing but bluish circles under my eyes. Laura
offered to take me to a doctor who she said could "look into
my head" and help me feel better, but my grip on English
figures of speech was tenuous and the thought of a doctor
opening my brain was terrifying.

I knew my time for grieving was running short. People
were getting impatient. It wasn't their fault. It was near impossible, even for me, to contain Gardenville and Croatia in
the same thought. So a few weeks later, when we were assigned a project about hometowns, I made a poster of New
Jersey, transplanting the least offensive of my childhood
memories into the apartment where I'd first lived with Jack
and Laura, before the new house was finished. My teacher,
who knew better, rewarded the lie with a good grade.

The more I lied, the closer I came to fitting in. Sometimes I even believed myself. People assumed I was just
bookish or shy, and I was, or had become so. Nobody in the
new neighborhood had ever seen Jack and Laura without
Rahela and me, and had no reason to think we were any-

thing other than a biological family. I threw out the book of
news clippings. I stopped writing to Luka.

For the first two years I was away at college, my family had
left my room alone. Now, slowly, others' unwanted belongings were finding their way in—photo albums, Laura's broken sewing machine, and clothes to be donated to the
Goodwill formed piles in the corner behind my door. It was
unfair of me to expect them not to use a perfectly good
space, I knew, but I still felt a sense of loss for the place that
had once been only mine. I surveyed the rest of the room,
which looked the same—single bed pressed against the
windows, shelves filled with my first books and a series
of glass fishbowls containing the seashell collections I'd
amassed from summers at the Jersey shore. On the wall
hung a sequence of photos of Rahela, Laura, Jack, and me
on Rahela's fifth birthday at Disney World, and posters of
terrible punk-noise bands I'd gone to see at the Electric Fac-
tory on Friday nights when I was in high school.

The remnants of a flower stencil peeked out from behind
my desk, and I smiled with the thought that Laura and my
mother might have bonded over their mutual distaste for
my tomboyishness; Laura had put the blossoms on the wall
and I'd promptly pushed my desk against the spot. When I'd
chosen a denim comforter for my bed she'd sewn pink rose-
buds in rows up the seams, and whenever she left the room

I turned the comforter over to hide the flowers. Now, the roses were faceup again.

"Ana's home, Ana's home!" I heard Rahela shouting downstairs amid the heel-click of Laura's cowboy boots. I slipped the envelope of my past life under my mattress and went downstairs.

"Hey, baby!" said Laura.

"Hi, Ma."

The first time I called Laura "Mom" was an accident. I'd been playing with Rahela in the driveway when she fell and skinned her knee. The wound was filled with gravel and bled a lot and I scooped her up and ran inside, calling "Mama! Mom!" I found Laura upstairs folding laundry, the cordless phone tucked between her shoulder and chin. When I entered the room saying, "Mom, Rahel—Rachel got hurt," she raised her head and let the phone drop.

"Sue, I have to call you back," she said loudly at the phone now on the floor. I handed her Rahela and we went in the bathroom and bandaged her up, and Laura didn't mention it, though she smiled at me for the rest of the day, as if she was wondering whether or not I had realized what I said. I had, and figured there was nothing I could do to take it back now. But for years onward, each time I said "Mom" or "Dad" a silent prefix of "American" existed in my mind. They were my American parents, and the distinction made me feel less like I was forgetting the other set I'd abandoned in the forest.

"I didn't know you were coming home. I was just in town. I would've gotten you from the train."

"I needed the walk."

"Oh gosh, that's right. How was your speech?"

"What speech?" Rahela said.

"Ana was giving a very important presentation at the United Nations," said Laura. "Tell me everything! Did you take a picture?"

"Take a picture of myself giving a speech? No. It was no big deal."

"Maybe if you had longer arms," said Rahela.

"Huh?"

"Then you could take a picture of yourself."

"But she wouldn't have because she never humors her mother," said Laura, feigning exasperation.

"You can have my name tag." I dug the crumpled guest pass out of my pocket.

"Take what I can get," Laura said, and stuck it to the fridge.

At dinnertime we met Jack for pizza and bumper bowling.

"What are you doing home, girlie?"

"Just visiting."

"Remember, Ana was giving that *speech* today," Laura said.

"I didn't forget," said Jack. He pulled me into a bear hug,

and I liked that I would probably always feel little inside his embrace. "How was it?"

"Odd," I said.

"Did they put sanctions on you? They're putting sanctions on everyone and their mother these days."

"I'm gonna give you all sanctions if you don't come play," said Rahela, squeezing between us on the bench.

"Surprisingly accurate use of the word," I said. In the scorekeeping computer, Jack named us after *Taxi Driver* characters, and we all bowled terribly and laughed hard and for a few hours that was enough.

Going to bed was a different story. During my first months in America I'd tried to fend off the nightmares by avoiding sleep altogether. I sat up keeping watch, worried that someone would break in and slaughter Jack and Laura. Then when I tried to give in, I couldn't get comfortable. A mattress and box spring was a stark contrast to the cushions of my Zagreb couch; my back hurt and I twisted beneath the sheets.

Most nights, I'd give up and tiptoe down the stairs, through the kitchen, and into the family room, where Jack would be playing the guitar. When I appeared at the edge of the room he would sigh, then motion with his head for me to come and sit. A striped blanket hung on the back of the nearby armchair, and I'd pull it off and trail it behind me on my way to the couch. Jack would continue to play, swaying slightly as if to console himself.

Spring nights he'd lean his guitar against the sofa and flip on the television to watch baseball. The Mets were his team, a vestigial preoccupation from a childhood played out in the Italian ward of Newark. Muting the volume, we'd watch the silent game and he'd tell me the names of the players and their batting averages, explain foul balls and strikes and ground rule doubles. He repeated himself when I didn't understand, and when he sensed me getting overwhelmed he stopped, content to sit quietly in the television flicker. Baseball lingo permeated my vocabulary, and though I knew I didn't need to talk to make him happy, I learned more English by discussing the specifics of the game. Baseball calmed me down; every play and mistake had corresponding consequences, each scenario governed by a set of regulations I could memorize. It was a game I imagined my real father would love as well, the steady cadence of throwing and swinging as rhythmic as a whispered song, the innings' narrative arc like a bedtime story.

When the Mets invariably lost, Jack would switch off the TV and return to his strumming and swaying. I'd lie down with my ear pressed to the leather of the couch and match my breathing with the vibrations of my father's music.

Now, though, it was both too early in the season and too late at night for baseball; even Jack was probably asleep, so I lay awake through the uneasy hours for as long as I could before the dreams set in.

"You sleep okay last night?" Laura said the next morning.

"Bad dream."

"I thought I heard you yelling."

"Sleep-talking." When I was little, I'd wake her several times a week that way.

"Does it happen at school?"

"God no."

"You sure you don't want to talk? You never really told me how the UN thing was."

"I don't want to talk about it," I said, though I loathed the disdain in my own voice. "I'm going out."

I retreated to my room, pulled on jeans and a sweater, and made to leave, then caught a glimpse of myself in the hall mirror, disheveled, and doubled back for my brush. My hair hung down past my shoulder blades and had darkened with age, was the sandy brown color of my father's. The freckles across the bridge of my nose were faded from winter, but they would multiply at the first hint of sun. My eyes, so dark they were almost black, had bothered me in my teenage years—incongruous, it seemed, with both my paleness and the blond, blue-eyed model in every American ad and magazine. But now I saw they were unmistakably my mother's, perhaps the single feature we shared. I pulled my hair into a ponytail and went downstairs.

I spent the morning and into the afternoon in a coffee shop—built two years ago to look old—working on a paper about *Wide Sargasso Sea* and wondering how it was possible that whenever I was in one place I could feel so sure I belonged in the other. Brian had left a voice mail asking if I wanted to have dinner. I called him back but was relieved when he didn't pick up. I pecked out a text message instead, saying that I had gone to visit my family but I would see him on Sunday, and I was sorry for not having called sooner. I left the phone atop my notebook for a few minutes, waiting for him to write back, but he didn't.

Behind the bar a boy I'd had a crush on in high school appeared from the back room and began scraping coffee grounds from the cappuccino machine. I tapped him on the shoulder and we attempted an awkward, over-the-counter hug.

"You on spring break, too?" Zak said.

"Yeah," I lied.

"But you're not working?" He nodded in the direction of the Kmart across the lot, where I worked summers.

I told him I needed the extra study time, but that it was good to see him, and made a halfhearted return to my stack of homework.

"Well, I was about to take lunch," he said, coming out from behind the counter. "Wanna go over anyway? Old times' sake?"

Zak and I had belonged to intersecting circles of friends throughout high school, and had over the years flirted in sarcasm and baseball jargon. He loved the Phillies; I'd assumed the Mets as my own cause, and whenever we found ourselves at a party together we bickered about which team was worse. We became friends in our own right in the final year of high school, and took to sitting in the back of Zak's car, listening to sports radio and kissing.

In the summer before we'd gone off to college, Zak had often trekked across the parking lot to visit me, and we'd played Wiffle ball in the back of the store. Now we slipped through the automatic doors and passed by Sporting Goods to collect a bat.

"You still dating that guy at school?"

"Yeah."

"That's too bad."

We found some space in the patio furniture aisle, and Zak put on a show of pitcher's stretches. "I'm glad you're around. This town gets smaller and weirder every time I come back."

"It was always weird," I said.

"My parents are going gray."

"That's your revelation? Your parents' hair?"

"You're the worst." He threw the ball with more force than he should have, and I connected bat and ball with a satisfying thwack. The ball careened out of Outdoor Living and into Health and Beauty, taking out the deodorant display in a domino-style cataclysm. From behind the rubble an arthritic, red-vested woman threw us a look of contempt.

"SECURITYYYYY!" she roared, a sound incongruous with her tiny frame. A fat man with armpit stains emerged from the stockroom; I recognized him, but he didn't know me, or didn't care. He stared at the deodorant, then at us, and adjusted his flashlight belt holster.

After we'd been searched for evidence of shoplifting and ejected from the store, I walked Zak back to work.

"I know what you mean, about feeling strange being here."

"I know you do," he said, and kissed me on each cheek.

"How European of you," I said. In truth he had startled me. I tried to think of some tipsy exchange in which I might have revealed something about my past, but was sure I hadn't. Back behind the counter, Zak mixed me something caramel-flavored, and I sat for an hour paging through notes and glowering at my blank notebook, producing a single sentence before I gave up and went home.

That night Rahela appeared in my doorway in her pajamas. "Whatcha doing?"

"Homework. What are you doing?"

"I had to pee. Can't you sleep?"

"People don't sleep in college," I said, which was not exactly a lie. "Go back to bed."

Instead Rahela pulled back my comforter and wriggled her way in. "I heard you yelling last night."

"It was just a bad dream. Sorry if I woke you up."

"Tell me about the night I was born."

"Where did that come from?"

"I'm just curious," she said. "I mean, you're the only one who knows."

Rahela knew, in theory, that we'd been adopted, had been told enough to account for her earlier memories of my accent, for the fact that our sable eyes didn't match Jack's and Laura's dark green and watery blue ones. She knew, empirically, but she didn't feel it. For her, there was no one before our American parents, and the loss of these other people, the parents of technicality, was objectively sad but nothing more.

I thought of my father's stories, the way he'd made my own birth sound so exciting. My parents had been in Tiska and had to drive two towns down, where there was a hospital: *You were almost born cliffside—you just couldn't wait to get out and go swimming!*

"Once upon a time," I said. "We lived in a little flat in the middle of a great big city."

"What's a flat?"

"Like an apartment."

"A flat apartment?"

"Okay just listen."

Rahela quieted.

"Our mom was going to have you very soon, but it was a cold winter and a blizzard hit the city. The snow was this high"—I swung my hand in the air to mark a meter's height—"like up to your chin!"

"Up to your chin?"

"Yeah, I was nine years old. Our dad joked that if I walked on an unplowed road all that would be left of me would be the pom-pom on my hat.

"You waited until the middle of the night. Our godparents came running over from their apartment through the snow and dug out the car so Mom and Dad could get to the hospital. I had to stay in the house, and I was so mad about missing out that I cried like a baby. But then, just a few minutes after Mom and Dad had left, Dad came running back up into the apartment. It was so cold that he'd grown tiny icicles in his eyebrows!"

"What happened?"

"Everyone was screaming at each other. The car was stuck in the road!"

"Did you call an ambulance?"

"Dad didn't think an ambulance would get there in time."

"You just left Mom out in the snow?"

"They had to—there were no cellphones back then. So Petar and Dad ran and got Mom out of the car and carried her toward the center of town, where the roads had been cleared. Then they found a taxi driver who took them the rest of the way, though he charged them triple the price.

"You were stubborn and Mom was in labor with you for twenty-seven hours, so it turned out they should've just waited for the ambulance. But everyone called Mom

Cleopatra and the Queen of Sheba for months afterward because of the way they hauled her downtown, and Mom wouldn't let Dad live down how nervous he was."

"Can I see the picture?" Rahela asked after a while.

"What picture?"

"From yesterday. The picture of you that you said wasn't you." I felt foolish for thinking I had outwitted her and reached across her to tug the envelope out from under the mattress. I felt for the gloss of the photo among the other papers, but when I pulled my hand from the envelope I was instead holding the Christmas picture of our entire family. Rahela grabbed it before I could return it to the packet.

"This isn't the one—" I watched the image pass through her eyes and register. "Is that . . . me?" she said. "And that's, those are—"

"Our parents."

"Does Mom . . . I mean—" She looked at the photo, then back at me. "Do Mom and Dad know you have this?"

"Of course." Laura had been the one to talk me out of carrying the photos around in my jeans pocket, relegating them to their place in the file box, for "safekeeping." "All right, let's put it away for now," I said. "You've gotta get to sleep."

"I just wanna see it a little more."

She held the photo so close to her face it looked like she was staring right through the paper. I thought of our parents and felt sorry that she could only see them blurred.

"Do I look like them?"

I examined her, the wavy hair and warm complexion. "You look a lot like Mom."

She looked embarrassed. "Can I still see the pictures? While you're away at school?"

"Sure. I keep them in the file box. Just don't take them out of the house or anything. Don't lose them."

Eventually she nodded off, and I tucked the photo back into the envelope and carried her to her room. I stayed up most of the night reading *Austerlitz*. I had read many books by writers long gone but found myself lingering on the fact of Sebald's death only three months before, and was fixated on the notion of holding someone's final thoughts in my hand. I called Brian but hung up after two rings. I'd talk to him tomorrow, once I got back to the city and sorted out what I was going to say to him that night.

4

Brian was a year older, the kind of person I'd imagined meeting at college—sensitive, worldly, independent—and I had first developed a crush on his intellect. He had studied abroad in Tibet; he had been to the Louvre and the Uffizi; he read Chomsky and Saussure for fun. If anyone was going to understand my story, it would be him. Several times I'd come close to telling him everything, but each time I tried I'd gotten nervous and backpedaled the conversation another way.

"I missed you," I said when we kissed in the street. "I thought maybe I'd finally take you over to my uncle's place, if you want." I could feel myself talking too quickly. Brian pulled away a little. "What's wrong?"

"Nothing," he said. "Just—"

"What?"

"You kind of blew me off this weekend."

"I was home. I sent you a message."

"You didn't say goodbye."

"I wanted to get an early start. I'm sorry."

"It's okay." He conceded that I hadn't missed much over the weekend, that he'd spent most of the time in the library working on his thesis, a study of universal grammar theory via Nicaraguan Sign Language. Previously isolated across the country, deaf students had been brought to a special education school with the intent of training them in spoken Spanish, but on the playground and in the dorms they'd rapidly developed a signed system of their own. Linguists flocked to the site, eager to witness the birth of a new language.

"It's really amazing," Brian said. "After only a few years they had developed subject-verb agreement and classifier systems." I liked listening to him talk about the project, how he got so excited about the finer points of grammar, but I knew nothing of the topic beyond what he'd told me, so the conversation soon petered out. He saw *Austerlitz* protruding from my purse and pulled it out. "Oh, not Sebald again."

Brian and I did not have the same taste in books, which led to a kind of intellectual jousting I usually enjoyed. But I did not feel like debating, not about this.

"Where are you getting this old-man stuff?"

"From an old man," I said. "But I like him."

"Ariel or Sebald?"

"Both."

"What is it about him? Is it the loopy sentences? The man does know his way around a comma."

"Maybe." Really it was because of the feeling of grief that ran through his books like a subterranean river. But I didn't want to say that aloud. Not yet.

"He's a bit of a German apologist, though, no?" Brian said.

"I think it's more complicated than that."

"Of course it is. But if there's ever a time you get to draw the moral line in the sand, it's the Holocaust. I mean, his father was in the Wehrmacht."

"That's not his fault, what his father did."

"It's not. But it still makes things . . . thorny."

"Which makes the book good."

"Or ethically objectionable."

I kissed him to make him stop talking. "You're just grumpy because I've read a book you haven't. Don't worry—you can borrow it when I'm done." I tried to smile and held my hand out to him.

"Fine, I'm stopping," he said, and we locked pinkie fingers in what had become our signal for a truce. "But only because I'm starving."

People's use of the word *starving* when they obviously were not had always bothered me, but it was especially irritating at college, where every night was a buffet of excess. I thought of the piles of roast chicken and potato salad and fluorescent yellow corn bread the school was likely serving for Sunday dinner, then throwing away.

In Croatia I had been a normal-size fifth grader. In America I was skinny. When I went for my first physical, I didn't hit the minimum on the growth charts for weight and height. The doctor instructed Laura to give me nutritional milk shakes twice a day along with my regular meals, so that night after dinner she poured a cup of gritty chocolate liquid and sat me down on a stool at the counter. I told her I wasn't hungry, but she put on her sternest expression and told me to drink. I saw a flash of my own mother's impatience in Laura's irises and drained the whole cup. But when I stood to place the glass in the sink I was alarmed by an unfamiliar bubbling in my stomach. My limbs were heavy and my throat contracted. I was suffocating. I ran out to the back porch and threw up over the railing.

"The doctor said that might happen," Laura said when I'd calmed down. "You were just full."

I told her feeling full was awful and I never wanted to do it again. I panicked and threw up every night for the rest of the week.

"Well, if you're on the brink of death we can just go to the dining hall," I said to Brian.

"Don't you be grumpy now." He squeezed my pinkie finger, a reminder of our pact.

We boarded the train, and he slouched picturesquely beneath the DO NOT LEAN ON DOORS decal, hands in the pockets of his army surplus jacket.

"Hey, I got you something," he said.

"What for?"

"No reason. Saw it and thought of you. Some vintage store."

He unfurled his hand to reveal a sun-bleached shell fragment strung on a bronze chain. He dropped the necklace into my palm. "It's a piece of the moon." He smiled the mischievous, crooked smile I'd come to love.

"It's perfect. Thank you." Fumbling with the clasp, I put the necklace on and tried to draw myself from the depths of my foul mood. We came up from the subway where the remnants of Little Italy converged with Chinatown, and headed to my uncle's restaurant.

Uncle Junior had been called Junior for so long that Jack could not remember what the name of the "original" had been. Even *uncle* was an approximation of things; he was probably more like a great-uncle or second cousin. With his parents gone, no one wanted to admit to him that we couldn't remember his name, so we never asked.

The restaurant was called Misty's after his dead dog, a name everyone in the family did remember because of the time Misty took a shit under the table during Thanksgiving dinner. Inside Misty's was dim and warm, and the hostess recognized me and let me have my pick from the row of green leather booths along the wall. Junior appeared shortly thereafter in pinstripes, a red carnation pinned at his breast pocket.

"Hello, beautiful," he said, kissing my forehead. "And who is your gentleman caller here?" I introduced them and Junior planted a wet kiss on his cheek while Brian tried not to look surprised. "Welcome to my place," Junior said, and poured us red wine from a carafe. "The *seppia*'s fresh tonight. You want that?"

"Sounds great," I said. Brian ordered pasta and Junior yelled something in bastardized Italian back through the kitchen doors, then pulled a Yankees cap from behind the bar and went outside for a smoke.

"So that's the infamous uncle," Brian said. "How have you never brought me here?"

I hadn't wanted Brian to meet Junior; I had been keeping him away from all my family, afraid of what they might let slip about my past. But now I was half-hoping Junior would say something that would force me to tell the truth.

"I didn't want to scare you off."

"I didn't realize you were *that* Italian."

"I'm not," I said. Then, when he looked confused, "I mean, he's kind of exceptional."

Brian made some Godfatheresque gestures and laughed, then kissed my hand.

"Watch where you put those lips," someone whooped from the corner booth, where a group of men were hunched

over their tumblers playing cards. Brian gave them a sheep-
ish smile and dropped my hand.

"I don't know them," I whispered.

The group laughed. Junior poked his head back in the
door. "That sounded too happy. You up to no good?"

"No, Jun," was the collective response, morose, like a pack
of schoolboys in trouble.

"They bothering you, Ana?"

"We're fine," I said.

"Yeah, well, just knock it off in there or I'll make you pay
for the drinks this time." The men returned their focus to
the card game.

"You know," said Brian. "Maybe next time you take off to
go home you could invite me."

"Why? I've told you how awful Gardenville is."

"I don't care about Gardenville. I'd just like to go with
you. Maybe meet your family or something? You met mine
last fall."

"I know, but—"

"Why don't you want me to meet them, Ana?" His use of
my name made me feel like a child.

"Why do you want to meet them so badly?"

"Why wouldn't I?" He was rubbing his temple the way he
did when he was frustrated. He sighed, then grabbed at my
hand again across the table. "Just—I don't want to fight. I'm
graduating in two months. I need to start applying for jobs.

Decide if I'm going to stay in the city. I was thinking, maybe, you might want to move in with me."

Something was happening to my face, a tingling at my cheeks, and I couldn't tell if I was blushing or going pale.

"We could find a place, a studio or maybe a loft, probably in Brooklyn, but we could look for something close to the train so it'd be easy for you to get to class—"

We had talked about living together obliquely before, but not like this. Not with a real plan.

"Brian—"

"You don't have to make a decision right away. But I wanted to bring it up before your housing deposit is due—"

"Brian," I said. He looked startled. "I just—"

"You don't want to live with me?"

"It's not that. I have to tell you something."

My throat was dry. I slipped my hand out from under his, took a gulp of water, and tried to think rationally. Once, another time when I'd almost told him, I'd brought up the war, just to see if he'd heard of it. He had, of course, had even read a book about it, some journalist interviewing Bosnians in concentration camps. He knew what a bloody and complicated thing it had been. Surely he would understand why I'd kept it from him. Plus, he was my best friend; more than that, we were in love.

"Look, on Friday when I left your room I didn't go straight to Pennsylvania."

Now it was his turn to pale. It occurred to me that he probably thought I was cheating on him.

"I was giving a speech at the UN."

"The UN? What for?"

"The thing is, I'm not actually—" I searched for a word. "Italian."

"What do you mean?"

"I was born in Croatia. Zagreb. Well, it was Yugoslavia then. When I was ten, the civil war started. My parents got killed."

"But what about your parents in Pennsylvania? And your sister?"

"We were adopted. Rahela—Rachel's my real sister."

I told him about Rahela's illness and MediMission and Sarajevo. About the roadblock and the forest and how I'd escaped. About how the UN presentation had brought on the old nightmares. Our food arrived and got cold. When I finished, Brian was still holding my hand, but he didn't say anything.

"Are you freaked out?"

"No," he said. "I mean I am. Not for me, for you. But that's not that point. Shit, Ana. I'm sorry. Are you okay?"

"I'm sorry, too. I should have told you sooner."

"It's okay. I'm still trying to process all this. But it's okay."

Junior appeared with the wine again and slipped into the booth next to me. "Heya, princess. It's good to see you. You should come around more often."

"Yeah," I managed. "School gets busy. How are you?"

"Same shit, different day. I got some tax man so far up my ass it's like my colonoscopy all over again. But fuck it. How's the family?"

"They're good. Rachel's getting big."

"I bet. I've gotta get down there for a visit. Your father always throws good barbecues. I'll make more of that 'lemonade.'"

"Definitely. This summer."

"Well, sir," Junior said to Brian. "Don't want to steal this pretty lady away from you any longer."

"What are you thinking?" I said when Junior had gone.

"A lot of things," Brian said. "I feel so sad for you."

"And?"

"And. And I know this is gonna sound bad, but I can't help wondering if it changes things for us."

"It doesn't," I said. "I'm still me."

"You can't tell me this stuff doesn't affect you at all."

"No, you know me." I pulled my hands under the table, rubbed at the thin white rings of scar tissue at my wrists. Wounds I'd explained away with an invented bicycle crash. "We're supposed to be happy right now. You just asked me to move in with you," I said, though that moment felt far away.

"I know. I just mean it's a lot to work through. But, Ana?"

"Yeah?"

"I'm willing to do it, okay?"

"Okay," I said.

"Want to get out of here?"

"Don't think you're leaving without dessert!" said Junior, rounding the corner with two bowls of panna cotta.

"Thanks, but we're really full," I said.

"Dessert is a separate compartment," said Junior and set the bowls down on the table. Brian, who intuited that it would be quicker to eat the dessert than argue with Junior, took a few big spoonfuls, and I followed.

"Uncle J, can we have the check?" I said between bites.

"Unfortunately I can't help you. No such check exists."

"Come on. We want to pay you."

"You're students. Forget it."

"All right," I said, willing to give in if it meant we got to leave. "Thank you."

"No problemo. And tell your father to call me for chrissakes."

Out on the street it was much windier than it had been when we'd gone in, strong gusts cutting through my jacket. Brian always sped up in the cold, and I struggled to match his pace.

"Have you ever thought about going back?" he said.

"Sometimes. But I don't know what for."

"It might give you some closure."

"Oh, here we go." Annoyed, I stopped trying to keep up.

Brian slowed, too. "Hey, don't do that. I didn't mean anything by it."

"You don't know the first thing about dealing with this stuff."

"I know. You're right." We were blocking the sidewalk, and he broached the gap between us. He tried to pull my hand from my pocket, but I jerked away.

"It's cold."

"Ana, I'm sorry. Just come home with me. Elliot's still off at some design conference. We'll have the place to ourselves. We can ... decompress." He was holding on to my wrist inside my jacket pocket, and I interlaced my fingers with his. I could feel myself relenting. I didn't want to fight with him, and I didn't want to be alone.

Brian and I had quiet sex that felt like an apology. Normally we were relaxed with one another, having learned the patterns of each other's bodies. But now we were overly careful, each of us fumbling to show the other we were willing to repair the trust I had broken. When it was over I felt a longing for the blitheness I had ruined.

"What is it?" Brian said.

"Nothing."

"I can see you thinking."

"Really, nothing."

"How do you hold all this stuff inside such a little person?" he said, pressing his palm to my chest. "Don't you feel like you're going to explode?"

"I'm more worried about you."

"What about me?"

"What you're thinking, about all this."

"I'm thinking that's why you like Sebald."

"Oh, don't start."

He smiled his crooked smile and ran a finger across my cheek. "Seriously though."

"Isn't there anything you want to know?"

"Everything," he said. "But not tonight. We have time. Tonight let's just do this." He slipped his arm beneath me, and I laid my head on his chest.

I listened to his heartbeat slow. "Brian?" I said after a while. He didn't respond. I slid from his bed and searched his desk for a piece of scrap paper. *Sorry to leave. Been having trouble sleeping.*

I took a detour to the library. I was nearly finished with *Austerlitz* and needed a new book. The circulation desk was about to close for the night, and the work-study girl scowled when I walked in and showed my guest pass. I found myself typing "Croatia" into the catalog database, and followed the resulting call number to the Eastern European section at the back of the stacks. I pulled the biggest nonreference book—*Black Lamb and Grey Falcon*—from its place on the shelf and thumbed through the first few pages in the volume of over a thousand. It had been published in Britain in the forties, and I was wary of what kind of light a dead English-woman might shed on modern-day anything, never mind a country so drastically changed as mine. But when I turned to the dedication page my breath seized at the stark precision of its single sentence: *To my friends in Yugoslavia, who are now all dead or enslaved.* I snapped the heavy cover shut.

The book hadn't been checked out since 1991, and the work-study girl made a point of looking me over before stamping the due date card with the twenty-first century. I thought of the person who'd borrowed it more than a decade ago, when I was still across the ocean. A journalism student, I decided. An overeager one, looking for some deep background to inject sense into an article about ethnic cleansing.

I went home but didn't open the book again. I could not shake the thought of friends gone missing. I turned on the computer and trolled the Internet in search of Luka. I'd done it only once before, but finding no trace of him had sent me into a weeklong depression and I'd forbidden myself from making it a habit. Now, I reasoned, I couldn't feel much worse. But Luka's life, if he was still alive, had produced no techno-footprint. At two in the morning my roommate, Natalie, came home drunk and fell asleep with her shoes on. I walked to the bodega and bought a Coke and a frozen burrito. Going to bed now would surely bring on another set of nightmares, so, sufficiently caffeinated, I went to the common room, turned the TV on loud, and read Rebecca West's book until the sun came up.

Over the next few weeks I told Brian pieces of my story—the sandbags and air raids and snipers in Zagreb, the Četniks in the forest, and the little village afterward. He was patient and didn't push me if I stopped mid-thought, but it didn't matter; I could feel myself slipping, and had no way to contend with the fact that all his kindness and understanding could not fix me. Each night I'd wait for him to fall asleep, then return to my dorm to pace the halls. Once I stumbled over my shoe and woke him.

"You can stay, you know. Elliot's probably at Sasha's for the night."

"I don't want to keep you up."

"You have work to do? You can turn the desk lamp on."

"It's not that. The dreams I told you about. I wake up yelling."

"I don't mind."

"I do."

"But if we're going to live together—"

"Brian, don't."

"A few bad dreams are no big deal in the grand scheme of things."

"Look, I'm sorry. I just can't have that conversation right now," I said. I fumbled with my shoelaces in the dark and left.

———

"There you are," said Professor Ariel when I appeared in his doorway one afternoon. "That big research paper in Brighton's class keeping you busy?"

"Yeah, sorry. And I've been reading . . . something else."

"Come, sit."

I put *Austerlitz* down on his desk.

"Lovely, no?"

I nodded.

He leafed through the volume. "I find the symbolic use of train stations throughout to be his most successful integration of photos. What have you dog-eared here?"

"Gosh, I'm sorry. I don't even remember doing that."

"The wily ways of memory." He chuckled. "Not a problem. Here." He handed me the open book, and I skimmed the page I'd bent. It was easy to find what I'd been trying to save.

"This," I said. "'I had never heard of an Austerlitz before, and from the first I was convinced that no one else bore that name, no one in Wales, or in the Isles, or anywhere else in the world.'"

"What do you like about it?"

"The isolation, I guess. That he can describe an emotion so perfectly, without any adjectives."

"A rare talent."

I passed the book back over the desk and nodded again.

"What do you make of his critics?"

It hadn't occurred to me that there could be critics of such a writer. Brian was one thing, but he hadn't even read the book. "What do you mean?"

"He's got no new material. That it's just more of the same."

"Of course it's more of the same. What else is there to write about when you have this?"

"That is the counterargument," Professor Ariel said.

By mid-April the gray skies were receding, and I tried to let the sunny weather permeate the vacant feeling inside me. Brian attempted to coax me into talking about what was bothering me, and in response I picked petty fights with him until we had spiraled into a cycle of bickering and making up. I studied more than I needed to just to fill time. There were only three weeks left in the semester, and then I could get out of this city.

One night Brian and I ate Chinese takeout in his bed. He was reading an anthropology textbook, and I held *Black Lamb and Grey Falcon* open on my lap but could not concentrate. I was running out of time to decide whether we should live together. The dreams showed no sign of letting up, and I continued to pull away from Brian in every moment I most needed him.

"Do you think two people are meant to stay together forever?" I said.

Brian looked up with a tentative smile. "Did you read *Us Weekly* in the supermarket line again?"

I glared at him and he mumbled an apology.

"Some people do it," he said. "My parents are still married. Yours, too. I mean, your parents in Gardenville—"

"I know what you mean."

"So what's got you worked up then? Trouble in Rebecca West paradise?"

"I'm not worked up," I said with a sharpness that suggested otherwise. "It's just, housing deposits come due next week. I don't know what to do."

Brian closed his book and moved closer to me on the bed. "I've got an idea."

"It's not that easy."

"So you have bad dreams. We'll deal with them. Maybe they'll even go away. Is that really what you're worried about?"

"Worrying isn't rational. No one makes a conscious decision to freak out about something."

"Look, you've got a lot on your mind. And you're not sleeping, and finals are coming up. I get that. But these nightmares—all this stuff—it's no reason for us to put our lives on hold."

"Yeah, that's it. I'm overreacting." I was being unfair, I knew, but could not stop myself. I was so tired of his being even-keeled in the face of all that was upsetting and ugly and illogical. I wanted a reaction out of him. "Maybe I'm even hysterical. A hysterical woman," I said.

"Whoa, Ana, I didn't—"

"I know you didn't. You didn't have to—I can tell you're thinking it."

Brian dropped his chopsticks into his carton of noodles and stood. "You know what? Fine. I have been trying and trying with you, but you just refuse—I'm not sure I can take this anymore."

"I think we need some time apart." When I saw the words reflected on his face I wished I hadn't said them. "Maybe we could just take a break, and talk again in a couple weeks."

Brian didn't say anything.

"Brian, I'm sorry. Really."

"Okay. Can you just—" He nodded toward the door.

I left Brian's room and walked Fourteenth Street all the way to the Hudson. In the gutter someone had dropped a pen and I eyed it uneasily. For years I had forgotten about the mines disguised as litter, but now I was staring at someone's trash half-expecting it to explode. I cursed Sharon and the UN for stirring up trouble. Telling my story was supposed to be a good thing but it had just made everything worse. And now I'd been terrible to Brian and lost him, too.

"What's wrong with you?" I said. I yanked at the necklace Brian had given me, but it held fast and my neck stung where the metal dug into my skin. I unclasped the chain and balled it up in my fist. The river glowed auburn with the lights of Manhattan and Jersey City. I considered throwing the necklace in the water. Had I died in the forest, at least I would be with my family and ignorant of such profound loneliness. But then there was Rahela. I dumped the chain in my coat pocket. Not knowing what else to do, I called my mother.

Laura answered in a groggy voice. "What's the matter?"

"Shit, I'm sorry. I didn't realize how late it was. Did I wake you?"

"No, no, it's okay. What's wrong?"

"I don't know." I could feel my voice cracking.

I let Laura whisper placations into the phone but knew she could not console me.

"I think—I want to go home."

"Do you want me to come get you?"

"No. I mean I want to go back to Croatia."

"What?"

"Just for the summer."

"Honey, I'm not sure that's a good idea. It's dangerous."

"The war's been over for ages."

"Only two years since Kosovo."

"So what am I supposed to do, hide out in Gardenville forever?"

"But a trip like that—do you think it makes sense to open old wounds?"

"Open them?" I almost laughed.

"I just don't want to see you hurting again."

"I'm already hurting. I am at a standstill with this shit. I'm never going to get better. Not like this."

"Look. You're upset. Take a day to cool off and we'll talk more—"

"I'm not asking your permission," I said. "I just need you to send me my passports."

I hung up and kicked the curb until it hurt through my boot. "I'm sorry," I said to the river. The wind off the water was frigid, and I turned up my collar against the cold.

In the dorm Natalie was asleep, and I got into bed, too, staring through the dark at the speckled drop-ceiling tiles. I hadn't slept more than a couple hours a night for over a month, and the dream bodies were encroaching on my consciousness. Even before I'd dropped fully into sleep I felt their cool, rubbery skin against mine as surely as I did the cotton weave of my sheets. I threw back the blankets and stood too quickly, setting the darkened room spinning.

Lurching to my desk, I shook the mouse; the screen hummed to life and Natalie rolled over. In the glow of computer light I tore a piece of paper from my notebook and wrote a letter to Luka. I filled the beginning lines with perfunctory hellos and inquiries about his family. I wrote that I was living in New York City, which I knew would impress him, and that my visit to the UN had set into motion a twist of events that had made going back unavoidable. *Basically, no one here knows who I am, not even me, and I think coming home might set me straight.* The word *home* looked strange on the page, but I left it. I was trying to sound positive, or at least not on the verge of a mental breakdown. *I think of you often. Not knowing whether you're alive drives me crazy some days. So email me, or write me back, or something. And I'll see you soon.* I listed my contact details at the bottom of the letter, folded the paper into thirds, addressed the envelope to his parents' house, and stuffed it in my schoolbag. Then I entered the Web address of a discount airfare site I'd seen on a commercial replayed over and over during one of my all-nighters, emptied my bank account of a summer's worth of Kmart labor, and booked a ticket to Zagreb for the day after school let out.

5

It wasn't until three weeks later, as the plane was cutting through the clouds over the Balkan Peninsula, that the trip seemed like a very bad idea. Luka hadn't written back, hadn't called or emailed. I had to find out what had happened to him, but the closer I got the more I worried about what I would discover. *Black Lamb and Grey Falcon*, which I'd effectively stolen from the library, felt leaden in my lap. I'd packed stupidly, I thought, with the type of retrospective clarity I'd been experiencing in bursts throughout the night of fitful plane sleep. In the end Laura had mailed me my American passport, but not my Yugoslavian one, which I'd need if I wanted to get a new one. When the flight attendant handed out customs cards with checkboxes labeled

"Citizen" or "Tourist," it struck me that Croatia was a country to which, technically, I'd never been.

I shouldered my backpack, descended the stairs, and crossed the tarmac toward the graying building of Zagreb International. The mass of concrete tapered out into two skinny terminal arms. Three other propeller planes were parked opposite the one I'd just disembarked, and from the looks of it the airfield was at full capacity.

Despite a concerted effort to keep myself calm—the war had been over for years now; we were practically a member of NATO goddammit—I spent my first minutes on the ground waiting for something to blow up. Inside the terminal, the yellow Information signs cast a sallow light through the hall. My sneakers clung to the dirty tiles, sticky with humidity and spilled soft drinks. All these years later and the place had yet to shake its Eastern Bloc aura—the posturing with size and cement, a woman with a brash smear of cherry lipstick she can't quite pull off. I made my way past a cluster of confused tourists to the front of the immigration line. I liked the power that came with pushing through a crowd, the kind of shoving that would be unacceptable in America. I didn't say excuse me.

"HelloDobarDan," said the customs agent when I reached the window. He put a hand out in request for my documents. Upon receipt of my American passport he mumbled something in broken English and reached for a stack of immigration forms.

"Dobar dan," I tried. The words were rough in my throat. *"Kako ste vi danas?"* I'd conjugated the phrase formally but correctly, and stroking his mustache, he looked me over as if I'd presented him with false papers. I met his gaze. He returned the blank forms to the top of the pile.

"Welcome back," he said in Croatian and waved me through.

Outside families were coming together. A set of toddler twins in matching sunglasses flung themselves at an elderly man. A young man in a Dinamo jersey flagged down his weary fiancée and lifted her off the floor in their embrace; the color crawled back into her cheeks when they kissed. A man in a dark suit met another in like clothing. At first they looked like corporate associates, but when they hugged and clenched their jaws, I recognized their reunion immediately as the business of burial. I looked away.

The baggage carousel squeaked along at a lethargic pace. Many bags had been strangled with industrial-grade plastic wrap. I spotted my suitcase, relatively unharmed, heaved it off the belt, and walked out into the open lot.

The airport was far outside the city, so I handed my bag to a man in an official-looking reflective vest and boarded a bus marked ZAGREB CENTAR. I realized it was a mistake as soon as the driver requested twenty kunas, too much for a regular bus ride. It was probably a private company designed to scam tourists, but I hadn't seen any other public transport in the lot, and my suitcase was already in the belly of the bus.

"I haven't changed any money yet," I said to the driver in English, suspecting he'd take the news better that way.

"Two-zero kuna to Autobus Station Zagreb," he said, palm out. I handed him a five-dollar bill, which he pocketed without issuing me a ticket.

After a stint on the new highway between the airport and city, I exited Autobusni Kolodvor and walked into the city center. Zagreb seemed both smaller and more beautiful than the simulacrum I'd constructed in my head. Red and yellow tulips bloomed in beds across the city, and the cobblestone walkways, soaked in summer sun, looked cleaner than I remembered. While people on the street were clothed in fashions long passed in America, they looked well fed, with no outward signs of distress. Only the occasional shelling damage in the building façades gave any confirmation that a war had taken place.

I continued down Branimirova, a street that had become unrecognizably commercial. Boutiques peddling jewelry, jeans, and cellphones had cropped up to create an unbroken, mall-like storefront. I thought of the gifts I'd brought for Luka and Petar and Marina—things I'd found new and exciting in America when I'd first arrived—and felt embarrassed. From the looks of it, they'd imported everything already.

Hotels, big international ones, stood behind the market. I knew the city must have had hotels when I was young, but I could neither remember them nor imagine who would have wanted to stay in them. On the left Glavni Kolodvor came into view—Zagreb's Grand Central, everyone joked, though in reality it was older than the New York terminal.

Until this point I'd been walking straight, avoiding the question of an exact destination, but soon I'd have to turn off if I wanted to go to Luka's parents' house. Property usually only changed hands via inheritance, so it was unlikely that they had moved. Luka would be there, too; students lived at home with their families while attending university. Was it better to go and get it over with, or stop at the hostel first and try to wash up? Should I try to find a pay phone with a phone book to see if his family was even still listed? I decided it was best to go look for him right away—chances were slim that a hostel shower would put me in a clearer state of mind. But the weight of whatever I might find there was slowing my steps. The prospects of having lost or coming face-to-face with the person who'd known me best were equally terrifying.

By the time I reached Luka's front stoop I was so nervous it was all I could do not to run away. What if he'd been killed by some back-alley sniper, or burned beyond all recognition by a mine in the park? What if he was angry with me for getting out? What if we didn't like each other anymore? I rang the doorbell and listened for footsteps. There weren't any that I could hear, but then the lock clicked and the door opened to reveal the foyer through which I'd tracked mud countless times, and a tiny woman in fuzzy slippers and a housecoat. It was Luka's grandmother. Luka and I had visited her flat down the street occasionally after school. Even in the darkest months of rationing she'd managed to slip us something sweet. But now she looked much older, more hunched. Beneath the open robe she wore a black blouse and a woolen skirt hiked up to her flaccid breasts. Her hair was tied in a dark scarf. She was in mourning.

"*Baka,*" I breathed, not meaning to say it aloud. She looked me over, her eyebrows raised at my use of a familial term.

"Who are you?"

"I'm, uh—"

"No soliciting." She closed the door in my face and I retreated to the bottom of the stoop, where I sat sweating and trying not to panic. In Bosnian villages, where Luka's grandparents were from, once you went into mourning for a close family member, it could go on for years; for a particularly troubling death one might never wear color again. I allowed myself to fall into an antifantasy of what had happened to Luka—death by land mine, malnutrition. I envisioned his funeral, a small stone marking his remains up on Mirogoj.

The morbid string of daydreams made Luka's appearance on the sidewalk before me even more startling. I shot up when I caught sight of him farther down Ilica, and felt him look me over, first with the general curiosity that one directs at a person lingering in front of his home, then with the more exacting gaze of trying to place someone.

Luka was tall and broad-shouldered, a departure from the scrawniness we'd once shared, but he was recognizable in other ways—his hair still thick and stiff, the same serious, close-lipped smile. I caught in his eyes the exact moment he recognized me.

"My god," he said. We hugged, and his arms exuded an unfamiliar strength. I pulled away in a rush of self-consciousness that I smelled of sweat and plane food. Luka kissed me on both cheeks and took my suitcase into the house.

His family was in the kitchen—Baka crocheting at the table, Luka's mother aproned and dishing out potatoes, his father in police uniform, home for lunch, wiping the droplets of soup stuck in his mustache on the back of his arm.

"Use your napkin," Luka's mother said.

"Mama," Luka said, and all three of them looked up. Baka stared at me, confused by my presence in the house. Luka started to say something, but his mother had already bypassed him and taken me by both hands.

"Ana?" she said. "Is it you?"

"Ja sam," I said. She pulled me into a smothering hug, and Luka's father stood and placed a beefy hand on my shoulder.

"My god."

"Ana," Baka muttered, contemplating who I might be.

"Welcome back," said his father.

"I'm going to make some calls," said Luka's mother.

"Ajla, wait." I'd never called Luka's mother by her first name before, and it surprised us both.

"What is it, honey?" She put down the phone and gave me an encouraging smile. I wanted to ask her about Petar and Marina. But she was happy. Everyone was.

"Nothing," I said. "Never mind."

Luka dragged my suitcase up the stairs but bypassed the spare bedroom, which was filled with luggage and a peculiar collection of dated housewares: chipped china, rusted cast-iron pans, and a cardboard carton of slotted spoons.

"Baka's staying in there now."

I remembered Baka's black clothes. "Your grandfather?"

"He's—she's in mourning."

"I'm sorry."

"It's okay. He was old. I mean, we were expecting it."

I'd never come across death when I was expecting it, but I doubted that would make it any easier.

"Still," I said. "Is she okay?"

"She's tough." Luka had always been stoic, but the detachment with which he spoke about his grandfather was unnerving. It occurred to me that he may have gotten used to saying goodbye. He picked up my bag again and we headed to his room. Except for a bigger bed and a desktop computer, it looked the same. "You can sleep here. I'll go downstairs."

"I'd rather take the couch," I said.

"Suit yourself."

"Did you get my letter?"

He went to the bottom drawer of his desk and pulled out a rubber-banded stack of envelopes addressed in my unsteady ten-year-old scrawl.

"Didn't you get mine?"

I shook my head. "But those are old. I wrote you last month, to say I was coming."

"Well, I didn't get— Oh. The postal codes all changed after the war. A lot of the street names, too. It might get here eventually; it takes them a while to sort through the stuff rejected by the computer system. And if you don't write *First Class,* god knows what they do with it. Hey. Why did you stop writing? In 'ninety-two?"

"I don't know. I guess I just got scared."

"That something happened to me?"

"That you wouldn't write back," I said, though I'd been equally afraid of what he'd say if he did.

Outside around the backyard table everyone spoke much faster than I remembered. Luka's mother, from a Herzegovinian family, had thirty-one cousins and invited them to everything. About half of them had actually shown up, and they crowded around the patio in mismatched chairs hailing from various decades. From what I could make out, the cousins were engaged in an argument that swung with a bizarre effortlessness between the profligate behavior of parliament's ruling party and two different brands of spreadable cheese.

Luka sat across from me, a mischievous grin surfacing whenever a member of his family called for another round of *rakija*, brandy cooked in bathtubs by old ladies in the mountains and sold on the side of the road in Coca-Cola bottles. The alcohol just made me sweatier; the temperature hung steady at thirty-seven degrees even though it was dusk, and I had grown accustomed to air-conditioning. Each shot of brandy lit a fire in my mouth and carried a torch down into my chest. Had I really drunk this when I was young? And as medicine? As if in answer to my thought Luka's eight-year-old cousin slammed his glass on the table and let out a drunken belch.

I should have gone to the hostel, I thought, as the group filled the yard with spirited laughter. The language that in my mind had existed for so long only in past tense was alive again in conversation and pulsing from the radio. Every time I spoke I was met with a correction of my childlike grammar. English words welled up in my mouth and I swallowed them with difficulty.

Now the cousins, already into their second bottle of *rakija*, had nicknamed me American Girl. I mulled over the vinegary phrase with distaste, struggling to construct a grammatically sound sentence I could wage against them. In the end, self-consciousness blocked all productive channels of thought, and I resigned myself to eating in silence.

Afterward I climbed up to the roof and tried not to cry.

"What was I thinking?" I said to Luka, who had followed

me. "I can't stay here." Luka, who'd always gotten nervous when I was sad, turned away. I knew it was only because he liked to be alone when he was upset and wanted to afford me the same privacy. After a while, though, when I hadn't calmed down, he sat beside me, pulling his knees to his chest to get traction with his bare feet against the clay roof tiles.

"You're just tired," he said. He put his arm around my shoulder, tentatively at first, then letting his full weight come down on me.

"I want to go home," I said, all too aware I had no idea where that might be.

6

In the morning I felt better. I'd spent the night in a jet-lag coma, dreamless, on Luka's living room couch, its worn upholstery retaining just enough texture to leave a checked pattern on my cheek. The couch was the same one they'd always had, recognizable in an innocuous way—just an old couch in the home of an old friend.

Still, when I saw Luka standing in the kitchen I felt unsettled. He offered me a plate as he took one down from the cabinet, but we were clumsy with one another; he pulled away too quickly and I felt the china slipping between our hands. I set it safely on the counter and sorted through my archive of go-to conversation topics, searching first for something witty, then just anything to say.

I smeared Nutella over the remains of yesterday's bread,

and Luka mixed a pitcher of fluorescent yellow Cedevita. As a public health initiative we'd been organized into lines in the school yard and handed little cups of the stuff, chalky powder injected with vitamins and stirred into water, to make sure we got something of nutritional value in the weeks when food was hard to come by. They hadn't expected an entire generation to become addicted to the concoction—lemonade on steroids—but we had, eventually making its producers the most successful pharmaceutical company in the country.

I put the glass to my lips and felt the juice fizz in my mouth.

"*This* is what my life has been missing," I said.

"They don't have Cedevita in America?" Luka asked. "I thought they had everything there."

"They don't need it in America. It's war food. Speaking of." I remembered the gifts I'd brought for Luka and his family, mostly food I'd found exciting when I first arrived in America. "I forgot. I brought you some stuff from over there," I said. "It's probably stupid."

"You brought me a present?" Luka's voice was almost syrupy, and for a moment I thought he might be mocking me. "Can I have it?"

In the living room I unzipped my bag and pulled out the plastic sacks that accounted for a third of the space in my suitcase. Inside was an "I ♥ NY" T-shirt, M&M's, Reese's peanut butter cups and a jar of Jif, and three boxes of instant macaroni and cheese. Now I felt silly offering him a bag of gifts for a little boy.

"I kind of underestimated the state of things here. I'm sure you have all this stuff by now—"

"Cool! What is this?" Luka said. He pulled out the Jif and tried to smell it through the lid.

"You really haven't had it before? But you've got a mobile phone. I just got a mobile phone in America."

"We only have them because the government didn't feel like repairing the bombed-out landlines. Though you can imagine how obsessed everyone is." Luka was struggling to talk through a mouthful of peanut butter. "So superficial. Everyone in this fucking country gets their shit paycheck, wastes it all on clothes from Western Europe, then complains about how they don't have any money. Idiots."

"That's what happens when you ban Levi's, I guess," I said. During the height of communism jeans had been a symbol of rebellion, Americanness. For some reason the aura hadn't worn off.

"Too bad I didn't know you were coming. I would've made you bring me a pair."

"Ana." Ajla's voice trailed in from an upstairs room. "Come here."

"I thought everyone was stupid for caring about that stuff," I said.

"This is really good," Luka said, scooping out another spoonful of peanut butter. I downed the rest of my Cedevita and went upstairs.

I found Ajla in her bedroom among an array of unmatched socks. "Do you have any washing?" she said. "It might rain tomorrow and I want to get everything out on the line. Come, sit."

I sat cross-legged opposite her and plucked a matching set of socks from the pile.

"Sorry if the cousins were a bit much for you yesterday. I didn't think of it."

But I knew holding a big meal in my honor was the utmost compliment she could give. "It was great," I told her. "The food and everything."

"So how is it," she said. "In America? The family?"

In truth, things were strained between us. I'd only spoken to Laura once more after I'd snapped at her. She'd called a few times, but I hadn't answered. She'd sent my passport. Finally I'd forced myself to call her back the day before I left. I'd given her my flight details and she'd told me resignedly to be careful. But I did not want to tell this to Luka's mother. "They took good care of me," I said.

"Are they happy for you? That you're coming back home?"

"They worry a little. But they understand," I said, and hoped it was true.

"They sound like good parents." She pulled me into an

awkward embrace. She smelled of rosemary and bleach and something else I remembered but could not name.

"Ana!" Luka was yelling from what sounded like the opposite end of the house. "Come on! I'm going to be late."

But I couldn't put it off anymore. Halfway down the stairs I reversed and stuck my head back through his mother's doorway. "Do you know if Petar and Marina are—" I paused. "Okay?"

Ajla's smile waned; she looked ashamed. "I don't know," she said. "I haven't tried to contact them in a long time."

"You're sure you're okay?" Luka looked wary as we walked to the Trg, like the sight of the city might set me off crying. We spoke Cringlish, a system we'd devised without discussion—Croatian sentence structure injected with English stand-ins for the vocabulary I was lacking, then conjugated with Croatian verb endings.

"I'm fine," I said. "I'm just having culture shock."

"You can't get culture shock from your own culture."

"You can."

In the Trg the morning sun bounced from tram to tram in spectral refractions. I felt myself beginning to move with the rhythm of the city again. The buildings were still tinted yellow, a remnant of the Hapsburgs; billboards hawking Coca-Cola and Ožujsko beer were propped up on rooftops with the familiar red and white lettering. Teenagers in cut-offs and Converse high-tops formed sweaty clusters beneath the wrought-iron lampposts. And Jelačić was at the center of the square, sword drawn, right where I'd left him.

"Wait. Where is it?"

"Where's what?"

"Zid Boli." The Wall of Pain had been constructed over the course of the war, each brick representing a person killed, until the memorial of brick and flowers and candles spanned the whole square. I'd made my parents bricks there, when I'd gotten back to Zagreb, and it was the closest thing they had to a gravesite.

"They moved it."

"Moved it? Where?"

"Up to the cemetery. A few years ago. The mayor decided it was too depressing to have it in the Trg. Bad for tourism."

"It's *supposed* to be depressing. Genocide is depressing!"

"There was a big fight about it," Luka said. "Shit, that was our train." We arrived at the tram stop just as a full car pulled away and were alone on the platform.

"I've got to drop off some forms at my college," Luka said, fanning the papers in my face. "We can go up to the cemetery tomorrow if you want."

But I could not visit my parents there, not really, and I felt a creeping sadness at the thought. I pushed it from my mind.

"It's funny, you at college," I said instead.

"I've got good marks."

"I just mean you're all grown up."

"Same as you," he said. "What are you studying?"

"English."

"English? You still haven't gotten the hang of it?"

"Not the language. Literature and stuff. What about you?"

"Finance." I was underwhelmed by his choice. I'd imagined him as a philosopher or a scientist, holed up in some library or laboratory in a profession that would allow him to scrutinize the minutest of details like he'd always done. "In third year at high school, all the adults were asking me what I wanted to study at university. I hated talking about it so I just made up the most practical answer I could to shut them up. Then, when it came time to apply, it actually sounded like a good idea."

"Sounds stable."

"It's not as boring as you think."

A man with a shaved head and unshaven face was staggering down the platform in our direction. His cheeks were sunken, his eyes shifting rapidly inside deep-set sockets. He clawed at his face as he walked, bumping shoulders with Luka as he passed. An odor of sweat and urine followed him.

I tried to refocus on our conversation, but the man spun around and now came toward us with a purposeful look. He clamped his hand down on Luka's shoulder.

"Did you touch me?" the man asked.

Luka said he hadn't. The man pushed Luka, asked again.

"No," Luka said, more forcefully. "Keep walking."

"You wanna fight?" The man swayed. "I'll show you a real fight." He reached into his sock and stood up quickly, wielding a serrated knife.

Luka stood in front of me protectively, straightened his shoulders. "Just calm down," he was repeating. The man grinned and tightened his grip around the handle of his weapon.

I scanned the empty platform, wondering where all the witnesses had gone. Had I really come this far to be stabbed in the middle of the Trg in broad daylight? I was sure something terrible was about to happen, but panic eluded me. I found myself thinking of the next logical move. The violent Zagreb was, after all, the place I knew best. I considered a way to jump the man from the side and knock the knife from his hand, planned my route to the nearest shop where I could run for help if Luka was hurt, rehearsed a dialogue with the shopkeeper in my head. The man pressed the blunt side of the knife against Luka's cheek.

But nothing happened. A crowded tram slowed to a stop, and Luka and I ran to the farthest car and ducked in, melting into the commuters as the doors shut behind us. The man stared up from the platform, then stuffed his knife back into his sock.

Luka, who had been calm throughout the encounter, was

now cracking. Streaks of perspiration had formed at his hairline, and he pulled the back of his unsteady hand across his forehead.

"I take it that doesn't happen often, then?" I asked.

"You often get knifed by hoboes in New York?"

"Well, no."

"I'm going to buy a gun," he said. He was breathing like we had run farther than just a few meters. The spot on his face where the man had pressed the knife was scratched, but he hadn't broken the skin.

"It wouldn't help anything," I said.

The tram was going the wrong direction, and we rode it three stops before we noticed.

The economics college was the modern, windowless cube I had imagined, an exemplar of everything that was dismal about Communist architecture. I stood in the lobby while Luka circled between offices in a bureaucratic shuffle. I spotted a computer kiosk and waited for the dial-up, then checked my email. One from Laura, who, unaccustomed to email, had written the entirety of her message in the subject line: *Are you there yet? Are you safe? Love, Mom.*

Hi, Mom, I wrote. *I'm here in Zagreb. Staying with some family friends.* I thought of the man on the subway platform. *Safe and sound, don't worry. Will write again soon.*

Nothing from Brian. We had been in contact only a few

times after our fight, via perfunctory text message: *U doing okay?; Can I come get my copy of* Bleak House*?; Good luck w/ finals.* The night of my flight I'd written him an email to say that I was going to Croatia, that I was sorry for hurting him and hoped we could talk soon.

I opened a new message. *Hi. How was graduation? Just wanted to let you know I got here safely and am thinking of you.* I closed the window without sending it. Maybe he hadn't written because he didn't want to talk to me anymore.

I went to the bathroom and was met with the kind of public toilet I had conveniently forgotten, a ceramic basin recessed into the floor. I adjusted my stance, engaged in the awkward reallocation of clothing, but it was a skill set of balance and willpower I seemed to have lost, so I resigned myself to waiting until we returned home.

"Would've been easier if you had a skirt on," Luka said when I mentioned it. His words were steeped in a masculine dismissal I found startling.

"When have you ever seen me in a skirt?"

"I'm sure you got new clothes at some point."

"Why are you being like this?"

"Like what?"

"I don't know. Different."

He slowed his steps as we left the college. "Sorry," he said. He veered close to the edge of the curb, and I took hold of his elbow and pulled him back onto the walkway. "I guess I'm a little overwhelmed."

"By what?"

"You're back. It's a lot of shit."

"It's my shit."

"It's not just your shit," he said. "You don't get to claim the war as your own personal tragedy. Not here." I watched his eyes flicker like he was deciding which cards to play in a hand of poker. "What's the family like?"

"They're nice," I said. "They're Italian. I mean, they're American, but—"

"I get it."

"Rahela's eleven. She thinks she's American. Everyone does. They call her Rachel."

"Rachel," he said, testing it out with his accent, a heavy rolled *r*. "She doesn't really think that, though, does she?"

"She knows," I said. "But she doesn't feel it."

"Hey! Luuu-kaaa!" A thin voice punctured the quiet between us. "Wait up!" I heard the click of heels, and we stopped as the girl approached. Her black hair, smoothed and straightened, swayed in just the right rhythm as she walked. The pointed patent-leather toes of her shoes protruded from the cuffs of her jeans. She seemed to belong to a decade I could not pinpoint.

"How have you been?" she was saying to him but looking at me. I looked down at my flip-flops.

"Danijela, this is Ana. An old friend, from primary school."

"Drago mi je," I said, and felt a fake smile stretch across

my face as she planted a kiss on each of my cheeks with unnecessary force.

"Ne, zadovoljstvo moje," Danijela said, and I recognized the same smile reflected back at me. She and Luka talked about registration for fall classes while I studied her olive skin, the kind my mother and Rahela had. I thought of the school yard girls who had made fun of my hand-me-downs and teased me for inheriting my father's fair, freckled complexion, calling me Czech or Polish. I wondered if this girl had been one of them. I was relieved when she flipped back her phone to check the time and said she had to go. She and Luka made vague plans to meet for coffee, and she winked at him as she left.

"What was that all about?"

"What?"

"That," I said, fluttering my lashes.

"Girl I used to date," he said, suppressing a smile at my impression. "She's not that bad. She's actually kind of smart."

"Used to?"

"Yeah. As in don't anymore."

"She looks smart." I pushed out my chest.

"What's it to you?"

What is it to me? I thought. She was annoying, yes. But maybe I was just jealous that he was not as lonely as I had become.

"What about you? You got a boyfriend?"

"There was a guy. But I'm taking a break from dating."

As we neared the tram stop, I said, "You all right to get on the tram without your AK?"

"Let's get some ice cream first."

I submitted to more questioning over a shared bowl of chestnut gelato. I told him about the Uncles and how I'd learned to pass as American.

"But I don't get it. Why didn't you just tell people the truth?"

"A lot of reasons. Mostly because they didn't want to hear it. But also because I couldn't figure out how to get over it without getting rid of it."

"That's crazy," Luka said. "I'd never be able to hold it all in for ten years."

"I got used to it."

"Then why'd you come back?"

"All right, Freud," I said. I dropped my spoon into the bowl for emphasis and hated him, briefly, for being right.

Back at Luka's house we sat in front of the TV—there were two new channels, bringing television networks to a total of four—soaked in a Mexican soap opera that Luka's mother forbade us to change, and waited for the sun to go down. But it had only gotten muggier as the day wore on, and I began to remember why the residents of Zagreb always fled the city in the summer.

"Just wait," said Luka's mother as she ladled servings of vegetable soup over shallow bowls of mashed potatoes. "I heard there's going to be a heat wave."

"This isn't the heat wave?" I said. Luka's mother looked at me and smiled, a smile that seemed to say *You've been gone quite a long time.*

"What about a portable air conditioner?" I said. "In New York people get little window units." But the suggestion was met unanimously with looks of horror.

"Air-conditioning will give you kidney stones," Luka said. I was gradually recalling those mundane moments—the ones that had until now given way to more traumatic memories—of a childhood governed by collective superstition: *Never open two windows across from each other—the* propuh *draft will give you pneumonia. Don't sit at the corner of the table; you'll never get married. Lighting a cigarette straight off a candle kills a sailor. Don't cut your nails on a Sunday. If it hurts, put some* rakija *on it.*

I tried to think of a singularly American superstition. I'd learned a few from the Uncles—something about not letting one's shoes touch the kitchen table—but those were all imported from the Old World. Perhaps a country of immigrants had never gotten around to commingling the less desirable pieces of their cultures. Either that, or life there wasn't difficult enough to warrant an adult's belief in magic.

Finally, after nightfall, it was cooler outside than in the house. At around nine Luka's father came home, finished off the leftover soup, and promptly fell asleep in front of the television.

"Do you want to go out?" Luka said.

I was eager to feel the night's breeze and started toward the closet where I'd traded my shoes in for house sandals, a requisite of Bosnian households.

"Don't you want to change?"

"Oh, you mean, *out* out?"

"There's a new disco that just opened up by Jarun," he said. "I haven't even been yet. I mean, if you want—"

"Let me just change my shirt or something."

Luka went out to the garage and pumped his mother's old bike tires fat with air while I dragged my suitcase into the bathroom and tried on all my shirts, assessing which would look best under black-light strobes. I looked in the mirror, and another rush of self-consciousness ran through me. Maybe it was because of Luka's ex, her mascara and pointed shoes. Or maybe I was just tired of looking sweaty. I piled my hair on top of my head, securing it with my entire supply of bobby pins in an attempt at a humidity-proof hairdo.

"You drown in there?" Luka called through the door. I swung it open too fast, nearly clipping him in the side of the face.

"Fancy," he said when I emerged into the kitchen. "Let's go."

I hadn't been on a bike in years, and whenever I changed gears the handlebars jerked crooked in my grip. At first

Luka laughed when I nearly crashed, but by the time we got to the club I was frustrated and he looked at me with something approaching shame. What was the matter with me? I thought as Luka locked our bikes to a tree. I had spent half my life on a bike, on these streets, and now I could barely steer the thing.

"Let's get a drink." Luka grabbed my wrist and pulled me toward the door, bypassing the line.

"What are you doing?"

"Show them your passport."

I handed my passport to the bouncer, who studied it like it was an archaeological artifact, running his fingers along the indented national seal on the cover and examining the pages to see what other stamps I had procured. Then he gave it back and waved us into the club.

"Tourists have money," Luka explained.

Inside, the club was tinted purple and filled with cigarette smoke and the pounding rhythm of some remixed hip-hop song that had been popular last year in America. Overhead, industrial fans tilled the sweaty air through the room and out the back patio doors.

We pressed through the crowd onto the terrace, where it was calmer and we could actually hear one another. Behind the outside bar, the bartender stood shirtless with his back to the counter, hunched over a blender. He glistened as if he'd been oiled.

"Hey! Tomislav!" Luka called.

"Hey." Tomislav turned and grabbed Luka in a backslapping man-hug over the bar. He was sporting a giant gold hoop in one ear. "How you been? What can I get ya?" Luka ordered a beer, and Tomislav cracked the cap off against the side of the counter and handed it to him. "And who's the pretty lady?"

Even in the dim light I could see Luka redden. "It's actually, um, Ana," he said, taking a swig of the beer. "Jurić."

Tomislav stared, then a flash of recognition passed across his face. "Ana? Like from primary school? Are you shitting me?"

We exchanged perfunctory how-are-yous, each of us assuring the other that we were, despite the odds, totally fine.

"What are you drinking?"

"I'll have the same."

"I'll get some more from the back," he said, disappearing behind a black curtain.

"I heard he was working here," Luka said. He wagged his head slightly. "It's fucked, what happened to him."

"You mean his brother? Getting killed like that?"

"That's not the worst of it." After his brother's death Tomislav's parents were inconsolable, even forgetting to feed him at times, Luka said. Then, a few years later, after the war was over and things seemed to be returning to normal, Tomislav came home from school to find his father lying faceup in the bathtub. He had stabbed himself three times in the chest and his eyes were still open. The note was wet and illegible, and the only thing investigators could agree upon was that a man must be filled with an exceptional amount of rage to opt for that method of suicide. But more than the mystery, it was the eyes that changed him; in that instant of discovery Tomislav had seen his future in the gaze of the dead.

By his first year of high school, Tomislav's mother had moved across town to stay with her boyfriend, and he and his sister were left to live alone with the decidedly angry ghost of their father, their rent paid by his pension. It was fine, he'd insist, whenever Luka or any of the other guys at school asked, good even, because he could have girls over whenever he wanted, and he had become quite the chef if he did say so himself.

"But he's not okay?" I said.

"Of course he's not. He was one of the smartest in our class and now he's a shirtless pirate bartender."

Tomislav reappeared with a case of beer and was loading the bottles into a fridge beneath the bar top.

"Sorry it's a little warm," he said, thrusting a beer into my hand. "On the house. Welcome back." He winked, and I chalked another line on my invisible tally of "orphaned by war."

Tomislav poured three shots of vodka, and we clinked glasses. Then, called into service by a pair of giggly bleach-blondes, he left Luka and me alone to nurse our beers. I could feel the vodka bubbling at the bottom of my stomach and reddening my cheeks.

"Hey, do you—" Luka paused, looking uncertain. "Want to go dance?"

I followed him back inside to the dance floor, and for a moment I missed Brian. I hadn't danced with anyone but him for a long time. Now Luka and I were taking care not to touch one another, but the room was packed and we were pressed together by the swell of the throng. The first time I jerked away. Despite the crowd and the dark I felt exposed, too aware of my body, unsure what to do with my arms. I had never been a very good dancer and usually tried to make a joke of it. Now I was finding comfort in the fact that Luka was even worse than I was—he was biting his lower lip in concentration, always half a second behind the downbeat. Still, the next time we touched we lingered for a moment. There was something pleasant about the feeling, but, when I looked up at Luka, I could not read his face. I wondered what he was thinking, then remembered Brian again and felt guilty.

Luka leaned in, his face close to mine. "Want another beer?"

"Definitely." He pressed his way back toward the bar, and I stood alone swaying to the music. When he returned he slapped me on the back like one of the guys, and I took a slug from the bottle and felt the old Luka again.

———

In the dead of night I woke on the couch short of breath. Luka and I had come home late; judging from the color of the sky I'd only been asleep for an hour or so. I crept into the kitchen and searched the desk until I found the address book. I located Petar and Marina, their details in Ajla's slanted script. Next to the entry she'd drawn an asterisk, with no other markings beside any other entries on the page. I'd never paid close attention to their address when I was young, but the street name was familiar. I started to dial their number, but hung up halfway through. I pulled on jeans and sneakers, slipped sideways through the front door, and set out on Luka's mother's bicycle.

I'd never been out in Zagreb alone at this hour. The sky was navy blue and the roads were empty, the desertedness both tranquil and eerie. Occasionally I passed a bakery—the only storefronts with their lights on—and caught the scent of tomorrow's bread.

The cool air swept my hair back, and I felt more at ease on the bike. Petar and Marina's building was a few miles away, but the road was flat and I pedaled quickly, stopping only to check the address I'd written on the inside of my wrist. They lived on the second floor, so I left the bike in the lobby, hopeful that no one would be awake to steal it, and took the stairs.

When I reached number 23 I began to get nervous. Why

had I thought this was a good idea? I tapped on the door, lightly at first, then more forcefully. Finally I knocked so loudly a man wearing only slippers and underpants appeared in the adjacent doorway.

"Cut the racket."

"Excuse me, sir," I said, employing the most formal language I could muster. "Sorry to wake you, but do you know if the Tomićs are home?"

"Who the hell are you?"

"I'm Ana. I'm an old friend."

"Well, they haven't lived here in ages! Kovačs live there. Three kids. Noisy fuckers."

"How long have the Tomićs been gone?"

"About ten years now."

"Do you know where they went?"

"Moved back down to someone's grandfather's place. Mimice or Tiska or something. Well, I don't know about Petar. He was in the war. Who did you say you were again?"

"Well—"

"Fucking hell, forget it," he said, and went back inside.

Downstairs I pushed the bike out into the street and sped down Ilica, where the early risers were just waking up.

The next afternoon it was so humid we barely moved.

"I don't understand how you've managed to import *Walker, Texas Ranger* but not air-conditioning," I said, gesturing at the television. Luka looked for an instant as if he wanted to throttle me, but he didn't reply. It was too hot to fight.

Luka and his father wandered the house in their underwear. Luka was lean and lithe, understated muscles rippling as he paced the living room. I looked him up and down; he was about Brian's height. Thinner legs, but broader shoulders. Darker skin. It was a good body, desirable even, and I liked looking at it, could feel my eyes lingering on his abs as he passed. But there were the other parts of Luka—the small smile, the wiry black hair standing on end—that had stayed the same. In those parts he was ten to me.

Miro's stomach hung low over the band of his briefs, a tub of pasty flesh in stark contrast with the deep tan of his forearms, which his summer police uniform exposed. He was sweating from places I didn't know one could sweat, and it was gathering in creases of parts that shouldn't have been creased. The house was filled with the tang of bodies.

"I've been thinking," I said, trying to sound nonchalant. "You wanna go somewhere?"

"Like for a pizza?"

"Tiska."

"Tiska. You sure you want to go down that way, on the southern road?" There was only one main road that spanned the country north to south. A day's drive from Zagreb to Split, then a few smaller offshoots to take us the rest of the way down to Tiska.

"I'll be fine."

"I heard you leave last night."

"I couldn't sleep. I just went for a bike ride." He knew I was lying, I could tell, but he had seen history blaze across my pupils, and left it alone.

"I'll see if I can get the car."

In the morning Luka began a campaign of pleading with his mother to let us borrow the family Renault 4. As children we'd been much freer than American ten-year-olds, but now there'd been a strange reversal: Luka and all the other university students were living at home, beholden to their parents.

In the end it was unclear whether or not we'd actually gotten permission to take the car, but we acted as if we had, Luka palming the keys from their nail on the wall. The car, which had once been white, was now mostly rust. We packed the trunk with clothes, water jugs, two orange blankets, and a machete from the shed and left without saying goodbye, in case we weren't supposed to be going.

We stopped at the grocery store for provisions. We filled a cart with cases of milk—the kind in cardboard boxes that doesn't need to be refrigerated—bags of granola, farmer cheese, and a fresh loaf of black bread. In the first winter of the war, after my parents had been killed and we were hungry, Luka and I had swept through this same store, gathering packets of powdered soup and carrying them to the pet food aisle, which no workers monitored. We tore at the packaging with our teeth and passed a packet between us, salty and stinking of onions. In Croatia, at the start of 1992, this did not feel like stealing. I glanced at Luka for any sign of this memory, but he had probably been in the store hundreds of times since then, and he pushed the cart toward the checkout. We paid.

A few minutes later, before we'd reached the highway entrance, Luka pulled off the road into the parking lot of the technical high school.

"You drive?" he said.

"Yeah. Not stick though."

Luka got out of the car, and I slid over the center console into the driver's seat. Driving stick was like a seesaw, Luka explained. About keeping a balance of pressure. "Press that pedal on the left all the way to the floor."

I pressed the wrong one, and the engine revved wildly.

"Your other left." The car was so old it had a manual choke, and he reached across me to slide the vented lever up until the motor sounded less like it was being strangled. I looped around the lot for a while without stalling, shifted into first, second, third.

"All right," he said, gesturing for me to turn out onto the main road. "You're ready."

"WHAT DO I DO?" I yelled. I had caught a traffic light on a steep incline, and when the light changed and I took my foot from the brake the car began an unfamiliar backward slide. I slammed the pedal back against the floor.

"Just give it a little gas." Behind me the drivers honked. I pulled my clutch foot up too fast, and the car sputtered, then went quiet. Someone passed us on the shoulder. Luka reached over and turned the car off, then told me to restart it, but I just glowered at him until the light had gone red again.

"Calm down," he said in an unfazed manner I found infuriating.

"Fuck this." I wrenched the key in the ignition; the engine howled as I gunned it across the intersection. More honking. I pulled over.

"You were doing fine. You have to learn. I can't drive the whole trip."

"That was not fine."

Luka sighed. "You're impatient," he said, which, because it was true, hurt more than a harsher insult. We switched places. "You're driving once we get out of Zagreb," he said, and flipped on the radio.

On the highway I was calmer. I was driving again, but without stop signs and traffic lights it was easier. We took off our shoes, threw them in the backseat, cranked down the windows, and let the breeze flow through the car. The air was hot, but at least it was moving. The dashboard vibrated with the folk-techno mash-ups that pervaded the country's airwaves. A mix of traditional Muslim and Mediterranean melodies overlaid with thumping house beats, they'd become the new postwar pop. A far cry from the nationalistic anthems of our childhood, they were what Luka termed a "cultural cease-fire," an effort to bring the segregated nationalities back into communion with one another.

"I like the new songs," he said, fiddling with the dial to clear out the static as we passed the last of Zagreb's suburbs. "It's genius, really. People in the discotheque, all drunk, rubbing up against each other to music that everyone thinks came from their own heritage."

Outside of Zagreb things quickly became rural—sheep and chickens and rows of corn along the roadside—and it was hard to tell one farm or cluster from the next. Luka spoke about the end of the war and which friends from elementary school were doing what, and I told him stories about Rahela and American high school and New York City.

I looked at the clock; we'd been driving for a few hours. Bullet-dented road signs showed we were approaching the place where the road split toward Sarajevo. I got nervous and swerved to follow a sign toward Plitvice Lakes National Park. Luka noticed but didn't say anything. Plitvice was famously beautiful, even outside Croatia, and I'd never been there, so it was an easy enough stop to justify.

At the park I pulled my camera from the trunk and slung its oversize strap across my chest. We talked our way through the front gate without paying. The woman manning the booth said she was just relieved to hear someone speaking Croatian. She could go a whole day without coming across another Croat, she said, spent hours conversing in pantomime and broken English with tourists from Italy and France. The German tourists were better, she said, because she knew a little German.

"Everyone learns German in school now because they were quick to recognize us as a country," Luka said to me.

His sidebar didn't slow the park attendant down at all—the problem with the Germans was that they were a little rude and all dressed like Boy Scouts, and anyway we should go in if we liked, because it was silly that Croats should have to pay to see their own park.

"Once, when the war was just over, my mother and I went to Germany to visit her sister," Luka said as we passed through the gate and onto the main trail. "I was fifteen and wearing a Croatian flag T-shirt, police academy issue, and in the Frankfurt airport a man came up to me and asked me if I was Croatian."

"Never a good sign."

"I said yes, and he said he'd lived in Germany for a long time but was a Croat, too, and was sorry for all I'd had to go through. He gave us a box of expensive chocolate and walked off.

"That was the only good thing I ever got just for being a Croat. Until now."

"I guess this was a first for me," I said. Once on the subway I'd stared too long at a couple speaking Serbian, lingering in a manner that must have betrayed comprehension.

"*Govorite srpski?*" the boyfriend had said.

"*Hrvatski.*"

"Oh!" they'd said simultaneously. The boyfriend had stuck out his hand, and we'd shaken. We'd spent a few minutes in desperate friendliness, and I'd gotten off at the next stop, which wasn't mine. Nothing good had come from that; they'd looked embarrassed and I was late for class.

Luka and I passed a gilded plaque laid in the ground that read, IN MEMORY OF JOSIP JOVIĆ. Plitvice had been at the center of the war before the war even began—the region was one of the first to be seized because the Serbs wanted cross-country access to the sea. During the takeover, which came to be called Bloody Easter, Croat and Serb police forces had clashed, and the resultant dead officers, one on each side, were eulogized as martyrs. It was months before the air raids started, but technically, the war's first blood spilled here.

The edge of the park didn't look like much—we were still at a high elevation and we'd have to hike down to get to the water. We examined the map the woman in the window had given us and decided on a route that would take us past the biggest waterfall.

The lakes, the pamphlet suggested, were named entirely after legendary people who had drowned in them.

"I wonder what they called them before all these people drowned," Luka said, stuffing the paper in his back pocket.

"Probably nothing. No need to differentiate."

"Why were they all drowning anyway? It's a lake. It's not like you get caught in a riptide."

"Did your dad know the guys who fought here?"

"Huh?"

"On Krvavi Uskrs. The cops who got killed."

"God, I forgot about that. Is this too close for comfort?"

"The whole country is too close for comfort," I said. I'd meant it to sound like a joke, but it came out wobbly and Luka didn't laugh. "Let's just go look at the water. Surely there's a reason all these Germans are wandering around a sad little battlefield."

"He didn't know the guy," Luka said. "I think he was from Zagora."

We arrived at the edge of a bluff and peered down at the lakes, the water a shocking turquoise. The shallows were bridged by wooden-slat walking paths, and the sound of the falls overwhelmed the garble of foreign languages. The place was so obviously beautiful it was almost disturbing—perhaps people had drowned here because they'd wanted to, or at least allowed themselves to succumb to that unfathomable blue. Its beauty was completely unmarred by the bloodshed, and it was easy to see how tourists could push all that history from their minds.

We found a secluded place at the bottom of the canyon to put our feet in the water. Touching the water wasn't allowed, a sign in several languages warned, but Luka didn't seem worried about the rules, and I was emboldened by the ticket woman at the gate, who'd called the place mine. The water was clear and warm, and I watched a fish brush against Luka's ankle. He flinched, then faked a cough to pretend he hadn't noticed. I laughed and switched on my camera.

The camera was a Polaroid, the pop-up kind, which I'd bought at a garage sale before I'd gone to college. I'd purchased it out of a desire to be interesting—Gardenville could bring out that kind of desperation in a person. The camera gears whirred, and Luka looked startled by the mechanical grinding amid the white noise of rushing water.

"What is that?" he said, right as I snapped a picture. The camera churned the photo square from its front slot. A specter of Luka materialized, mouth agape and eyes wide and black against the brilliant blue background. I held the photo up, and he scoffed. "That's so . . . American." It wasn't the response I'd been expecting, and I knew he didn't mean it in a good way.

"It's not!" I said, defensive. "It's old. People had Polaroids here, too."

"Seriously, what's more 'instant gratification' than this?" He flicked the photo. "You can be nostalgic within three minutes."

"It's not like that. This photo's one-of-a-kind. Impossible to copy. It's like art."

"Art, eh?" Luka said, taking the photo and shaking it.

"That actually doesn't work. Shaking it. It's a myth."

He stopped and handed me the photo. We drew our feet from the water and let them dry on the cracked wood. Then I stood and slipped the Polaroid into my pocket. I thought of Sebald and his photos—maybe they were his way of bypassing the slipperiness of memory. "Anyway, they're for Ra-

hela," I said. We trekked up out of the valley and back toward
the car and the road and the coast.

Luka's mind was a cavernous place I couldn't navigate,
though the ambling course of our conversations was familiar. I was both fascinated and annoyed by his willingness to
pull apart things I would have left in one piece, just like he
had when we were small.

"Communism is fascism, in all practical applications," he
was saying now. "Can you think of a Communist country
sans dictator?" But I was thinking of Rebecca West, of how
the people she'd met in Yugoslavia were all killed or enslaved, tangled up in this same debate at the start of the
Second World War. Croatia had been on the wrong side of
history then—a puppet state of the Germans and Italians—
and had killed its share of innocents. I hated this most of all,
that my anger could not be righteous against such a murky
backdrop.

"True," Luka said, when I mentioned the fascist faction
in the forties. "But before that they were starving us out; we
couldn't even own land. We've been fighting for thousands
of years. And most of those guys got executed when Tito
came into power. That's just how it is."

He spoke with some finality, and I was relieved when the
conversation swelled past the ghosts of ex-governments and
into a broader sweep of ethics. We began with Voltaire

(Luka loved the witty attack on religious dogma, it being the driving force behind our ethnic tensions as far as he was concerned) and pushed up through Foucault (whose amoral take on power infuriated him), I all the while feeling that my American education had left me remarkably ill-equipped for a discussion of philosophy. Luka seemed to have read at least chunks of the seminal texts in high school, while I kept up by regurgitating lines from the single critical theory course I'd taken my freshman year, until I saw a sign that marked the impending road split. I pulled over and reached for the map in the glove compartment.

"What are you looking for?" said Luka. "You just need to follow the signs for Dubrovnik."

I ignored him and traced my finger along the road, squinting to read the names of the smallest villages.

Luka put his arm across my lap, blocking the map. "Ana. Look at me."

"What?"

"I'm here. I'll go with you wherever you want. But you can't shut me out."

"I'm not—"

"Whatever it is. Maybe I can help."

"I don't exactly have a master plan here."

"I could've asked my dad for old intel or something. You should just be honest with me."

"I know. I know."

"You promise?"

"I promise," I said. It was a lie even as it was coming out of my mouth. There was still one thing I hadn't told him, had never told anyone.

"Okay," he said. "Where do you want to go?"

I pointed to a part of the road with a bend like a boomerang and restarted the car.

Back on the road I felt almost dizzy with anticipation. I'd pictured a return to this place hundreds of times—had dreaded it and yearned for it—but in all my imaginings it never involved feeling so faint. I studied the landscape for clues, but nothing was familiar, or everything looked the same. We passed strips of black pine and ash, some vibrant green, some blackened and bare from wildfires. I whiteknuckled the steering wheel and pushed my foot down hard against the gas pedal. I could see Luka watching me from the corner of his eye.

"What are you doing?"

"Nothing."

"Do you want me to drive?"

"I'm fine." The tree line was becoming less patchy, more mature, until thick bands of white oak lined both sides of the highway.

"Seriously, Ana, you're going too fast. The cops will double the bribe if they see your American license."

I glanced at the quivering needle of the speedometer but didn't slow down.

"If you just pull over I can—"

"I don't want to stop here."

A small side road, almost completely obscured by overgrowth, caught my eye. I craned my neck to watch it take a steep drop down into a valley. Luka protested again, but I shushed him. My stomach lurched, but I tried to ignore it; there were probably a lot of villages in the valley, with a lot of sinuous little offshoots that followed the same arc.

Then, after a few minutes the main road made a harsh curve, and I knew.

"Oh my god."

"What is it?"

I slammed on the brakes and swerved to the shoulder. We slid to a stop on the roadside grass, the smell of burning brake pads drifting through the open windows.

"What the hell, Ana! Are you crazy?"

"No" was the correct answer, the one I wanted to say, but instead what came out was "probably," then a wet, congested sound in my chest. Luka sighed and dropped a hand on my knee, and I cried the kind of suffocating sobs I hadn't since I'd been on the other side of this same road, ten years before.

III

Safe House

1

My eyes burned. The sun sat on the horizon and I walked toward it. The road forked. The main road was big and level, and the smaller road was unpaved and sloped down into the lowlands. A spiral of smoke twisted up from the valley, beckoning me with a wispy finger. The big road said nothing. I followed the smoke. It led me to the center of a village, down a rocky street lined with houses. A woman wrapped in a purple shawl was feeding leftover crusts to emaciated chickens in her yard. I felt her looking but kept walking. As I got closer, her mouth slackened at the sight of me—a tiny, blood-crusted zombie, soaked in other people's bodily fluids. She approached, called out to me. I stopped in the middle of the street.

She came to me and kneeled, asked my name, where I

was from, what had happened. I tried to determine from her accent whether or not she was a Serb, if it was safe to speak to her. I couldn't tell, and decided it didn't really matter, that I had nowhere else to go and I might as well answer. But somewhere along the way my body had taken a vow of silence; she talked and talked and I stayed quiet. She reached for my hand, and I vomited on the asphalt. In the end she grabbed my arm and led me to her house. She stood over me and rinsed the blood from my wrists. It was only cold water, but the cuts were dirty and it stung. My eyes welled up, but no tears escaped.

For the first week I sat on her kitchen floor with my back to the wall and my knees to my chest. I counted the squares in the linoleum, stared at the crack in the dining table leg, scratched at my gauze-wrapped wrists. I blinked rarely, and moved with a halting, mechanical edge. At night I slept in the same spot, curling into a knot on the floor.

The woman's son, a boy a few years older than I was, left the house early each morning and came home after dark. He stomped around in combat boots and talked incessantly of the "Safe House." It was a phrase I'd never heard before, and I assumed it was the village's bomb shelter. The boy never spoke to me, walked in wide arcs around my spot as if I had a contagious illness. I felt like I did. The woman gave me water in a tin cup and bread with butter, but it was hard to eat. Even breathing was a conscious effort. The first few times the air raid siren sounded the woman tried to coax me into going to the shelter with her, but I stayed in my corner. The explosions of that first week were inconsequential; I was anesthetized to fear.

The woman had visitors who entered under various pretenses and examined me from the corners of their eyes but spoke as if I wasn't there at all.

"Maybe she's just stupid," someone offered.

"Maybe she's mute."

"She's not stupid," said the woman, whose name these conversations revealed was Drenka. "It's not that she can't talk. She just won't. I can tell."

"Seems to me she got a shock," said one of the kinder old women. "I saw her all bloodied up when you found her."

Eventually my novelty wore off, and I became privy to the women's gossip—stories about the mixed Serb-Croat family who had lived across the street and disappeared in the middle of the night, about the next-door neighbor's daughter, who was fifteen and pregnant.

The JNA air force had crushed the village at the start of the war as part of their mission to make a Serbian path to the sea. Afterward, a small band of Četnik rebels—some of them villagers themselves—had taken control. The Četniks made alternating rounds between this village and several others along the same stretch of highway, interdicting humanitarian aid and Croatian military supplies and holding down the settlements as way stations for their own convoys. They had decided not to kill us, at least not all of us, not yet, so the UN and NATO food aid would keep coming. When they were in town, the Četniks maintained headquarters in the schoolhouse at the center of the village, the shutters lashed closed with a convoluted twist of bungee cords. From the women's screams, everybody knew what happened inside.

"Now you will give birth to a little Serb soldier," they had told the neighbor girl as they raped her. When she came to borrow flour, I stared at the stained brown shirt stretched thin over her growing stomach.

I left the house for the first time when the chickens exploded. These days the JNA bombed the village sporadically, almost as if by accident. The initial detonations resulted in predictable damage—blown-out buildings, shattered glass—but the real danger lay in the clearing smoke. As the bombs fell they released showers of tiny metal balls. The outside world called them "cluster bombs." We called them *zvončići*, jingle bells. They were not like traditional land mines or trip wires constructed to kill in combat zones. *Zvončići* clung to tree branches and roof tiles, nestled in patches of grass; they fell indiscriminately, like combustible hail. They were patient, making up for what they lacked in size with the element of surprise. They had surprised the chickens. The blast shook the floor, and I jumped up and ran out the front door. The sun hurt my eyes, and on unsteady legs I strained to keep up with Drenka and her son. Behind the house a cloud of feathers was settling, and I tried not to look.

Most of the village sat along a single street, the homes unvarying in style and size. Exposed cinder block was the prevailing façade in those mountains, chosen to say "we are sturdy and permanent." But the gray brick appeared perpetually unfinished, blurting out instead "we are poor." Now riddled with shell fragments, the pockmarked houses looked even more dismal. Beyond them, uneven plots of farmland sprawled along the valley, a collage of mottled greens and browns, singed fields of wheat and corn. At the traffic circle were the school the Četniks had commandeered and the Catholic church, which, likely because it was missing a wall, they had left alone. There was also a post office and a market, though neither functioned, not the way they should. An armored truck delivered UN flour, milk powder, and vegetable fat to the post office (no one could say for sure whether they'd seen actual Peacekeepers in person) and depending on the week—whether or not the Četniks were around—either we got it or we didn't.

In the shelter, seeing everyone at once, I noticed that the villagers had uniformed up in various shades of olive. They studied my bloodied T-shirt with equal interest. Some people had uniforms with Hungarian writing stamped on them, leftovers from their revolution decades earlier, but most just wore any combination of green they could put together. Afterward, when we returned to her house, Drenka offered me the smallest green attire she had—a T-shirt and cargo pants with a patch over the knee, which her son had outgrown.

"Now that you're going outside," she said. Reluctantly I surrendered my own clothes to her for washing. I wanted to tell her not to get rid of them. She seemed to understand, or else she didn't want to be wasteful; she didn't throw them out.

Outside, I learned about running. Not the bouncy, pleasurable kind I'd done while playing football or tag with my friends, but a streamlined, adrenaline-injected version of my normal stride. Once I started I ran everywhere—to the water pump, to the post office for UN food, to the underground shelter. When one was maneuvering from house to bomb shelter, it might at first seem logical to travel in as straight a line as possible, to take the quickest way. But I always ran in a haphazard zigzag—believing I could upset the statistical probabilities of hitting a land mine by forging an incoherent path, believing, in the egocentric mind-set of all children, that I was the main target. I was afraid one of the soldiers had seen me pretending to die in the forest and now, spotting me alive and well, was out to finish what he'd started. After a while, though, I noticed that others were running in crooked lines, too. When the Četniks climbed to the rooftop of the school and sprayed bullets along the road, it was clear we were justified in our self-centeredness. Somewhere in the dead space between house and shelter civilians became soldiers.

A few days after the chickens' demise, Drenka's son talked to me for the first time.

"I'm Damir." I'd known his name already, but this was the first time he'd addressed me directly, and I nodded as if he'd told me something new. "You can come with me if you like." He handed me a khaki sweatshirt and a camouflage cap, then walked out the door without checking to see whether I was coming. The shirt was huge and smelled sweaty, but I pulled it on anyway. Over the weeks I'd come to like Damir, the confident way he marched around the house, the excited chatter about his "safe house," which, I was piecing together, was not the same as the shelter. Could he be inviting me there? Pressing the hat down hard on my head, I followed him into the street. He ducked down an alley and through the side door of a house perforated with bullet holes.

The Safe House had once been just a regular house, though no one ever spoke of whose it was or what had happened to them. Inside, my eyes watered; the rooms were dim, shutters drawn, and the whole place was cloaked in a nicotine haze. Damir was talking to the front door guards, and I hung as close to him as I could without being a nuisance, studying the house as my vision cleared. On the walls were pictures of well-oiled topless women and the deep-browed, prominent-nosed face even I recognized as General Ante Gotovina, whose likeness was fast becoming the logo of the Croatian resistance. Ultranationalist slogans were spray-painted on every smooth surface: walls, doors, countertops—*za dom, spremni*—for the home, ready. The furniture was smashed, save for one red leather chair in the middle of the kitchen, which no one ever sat in. Gotovina's Chair, we called it.

I followed Damir up the stairs to the top floor, a single large room that seemed inexplicably bright until I realized a chunk of the roof was missing.

"Wait here," he said, and I got nervous. I watched Damir approach an ancient man with glasses so thick the lenses protruded from their frames. They spoke in low voices while I stood in the doorway. Despite the winter chill, just as noticeable inside because of the missing roof, the man wore only jeans and a sleeveless undershirt that revealed dry, scabbed arms. The man looked over at me as Damir talked, then raised a hand in my direction and motioned for me to come. I heard his knees crunch as he bent down to my eye level.

"What's your name there?" he said.

"She, uh, doesn't talk," Damir said.

"Never mind that. We're not looking for speechmakers. We need workers. I can see you're a tough guy." Behind the glasses his eyes were magnified round like an insect's, and I was doubtful about whether he could see anything at all, but I liked that he'd called me tough and I smiled a little. He tugged on the brim of my cap. "An adventurer, maybe?" I didn't know what that had to do with anything, but I wanted the captain to like me, so I nodded. He extended a knobby hand, and I tapped it in a hesitant high five. "Okay. Indiana Jones it is." He pressed himself back into a standing position and put his hand on Damir's shoulder. "Why don't you go set her up with Stallone?"

"Yes, sir," Damir said, removing an AK from its spot on a hat rack before guiding me to the back of the room, away from the windows.

The Safe House was populated by leftovers: the elderly and teenaged, men too old to be drafted, and boys like Damir technically too young to fight. The Safe Housers had replaced their given names with those of American action-movie icons. The house contained two Bruces (a Lee and a Willis), Corleone, Bronson, Snake Plissken, Scarface, Van Damme, Leonardo, Donatello (of the Turtles, not the painters, they were quick to assert), and several men from the next town over who answered to the general appellation Wolverines. Though I didn't know enough about the movies to decode the system, the nicknames were usually assigned by vote and were somewhat indicative of rank. Damir, for his valor in an operation past, had been awarded the most coveted moniker: Rambo. I was the only girl there.

In the corner we found Stallone, a boy about my age,

swathed in ammo belts and sporting an eye patch of inde-
terminate medical necessity.

"What's your name?" he said.

"She's Indiana," Damir said. "She'll be with you now."

"Indiana Jones?" He seemed impressed. "Where you
from?" I looked up at Damir, but he had already gone. "You
don't talk?" I shook my head. He raised his hands in a series
of gestures synchronous with his speech. "You deaf?" I shook
my head again. "My brother's deaf," he said. He pointed to a
gunner at the side window, the only person of regular military age in the house. "The Terminator." The floor around
Stallone was littered with bullets and cartridges. I cleared a
place beside him and sat down. "Okay," he said. "This is how
you do it."

From then on I reloaded magazines. My fingers were
small and agile, perfect for filling the clips. I sat on the floor
with Stallone amid piles of munitions, sorting and loading.
The ammo, Stallone said, was smuggled in through Hungary, too. Or Romania, or the Czech Republic—countries
who knew what it meant to overthrow a Communist government and were willing to ignore the EU embargo.

Stallone also manned the CB radio, taking in strings of
garbled code from other Safe House strongholds across the
region, and alerting the captain of JNA plane sightings or
Četnik activity in the neighboring towns. Sometimes we
picked up broadcasts from the Croatian police force, and I
took their coordinates and labeled them on a map on the

back wall. When we caught their frequency, Stallone always sent an SOS to see if they were coming to get us, but we never heard back. "Must be busy," Stallone would say and readjust his eye patch.

A rough-and-ready army unit, most of the Safe Housers went out on missions for days at a time, leaving only a skeleton crew back at headquarters to protect the town. We'd fill large sacks with ammo for the men to take on their trips, and after we finished all the packs I'd run through the house distributing new belts and collecting the empties from the rest of the gunners.

Though the house had three floors, we almost exclusively used the top one; it was better to have the higher ground, to shoot at a downward angle. The room lacked any peacetime artifacts, but the parts of the ceiling that remained were so steeply sloped it was clear we were in the attic. The best gunners got the prime real estate of the front dormer window, so I resupplied them first, then the side-window shooters, and then the door guards, who were the only people on the ground floor.

Like everywhere else in the village, the Safe House had no running water or electricity, and the shuttered-up first floor was dark as night at all hours. Besides equipping the guards, using the bathroom was the only reason to go downstairs. The shadowy lower rooms were by far the scariest parts of the house, and I approached both tasks with breakneck speed.

The actual bathroom had exploded in an air raid. It had been boarded off and replaced by an unfortunate replica in the coat closet, complete with bucket, hand-crank flashlight, and UN-issue toilet paper. Whoever got on the captain's bad side during the course of the day would be saddled with the foul duty of emptying the bucket in the evening.

Each night when we returned from the Safe House—after the second shift took over—Damir would settle opposite his mother at the kitchen table to suck down root soup and play *tač*. While we were at the Safe House I was busy, felt useful, but at night I longed for my parents, ran their final moments through my head. In that first month I wasn't quite mourning. Instead my mind felt hazy and detached, crowded with ideas I knew weren't true even as I entertained them; maybe, if I worked hard enough, I could win them back.

For days I choked down my bread and watched from my spot on the floor as Drenka and Damir fumbled in the candlelight, rushing to slap piles of dog-eared playing cards together. I felt suspended between living and dead, as if joining them would mean abandoning my own family. And yet, every evening I found myself inching closer to the table, my shadow elongated in the flickering light, until eventually I sat down to play, too. If they were surprised by my appearance there, they didn't show it. Damir made a bad joke and Drenka laughed at it anyway, and I felt a smile push its way up through me. Her brown face glowed gold in the low light.

The next night I sat at the table at dinnertime, too, and ate soup and bread with preserves. Before she blew out the candles, Drenka spread a sheet across the sofa and called me over. I felt my spine lengthen like it hadn't during the weeks of sleeping contracted on the kitchen floor, and I stretched my arms over my head and pushed myself deep into the cushions of the couch.

2

I'd been working at Safe House Headquarters for a few weeks when the girls showed up. Mostly teenagers, the girls had been on a reconnaissance mission down south but had been waylaid by a JNA battle outside Knin. Now they returned bearing updates from the surrounding towns. They stomped up to the attic, muddy and commanding attention, then reeled off a list of names from a receipt-paper scroll. From the reactions of the Safe Housers, I gleaned that it was the latest in casualties or missing persons from the front.

After the announcements, the conversation descended quickly into the realm of justs—speculations leveled at the bearer of the list:

"He'll be fine. He's just missing, not wounded?"

"Just shot, it says. Not necessarily *killed*."

"Probably only a flesh wound."

The list reader scanned her paper in an attempt to offer some affirmative responses to the barrage. I'd always assumed Damir's father was in the army, but Damir never mentioned him, and he didn't come up on the list while I was there.

When people got frantic the captain stepped in and took the paper. He folded it in a lopsided accordion and attempted to put it in his shirtfront pocket before realizing that he wasn't wearing a shirt and stuffing it in his waistband instead.

"The boys are all fine," he said firmly, and everyone dispersed back to their posts.

"Who are you?" said one of the girls when she came to get a new clip. She wore a patrol cap and long auburn hair, and fiddled with both as she talked.

"She's Indy," Stallone said, having grown accustomed to his role as my spokesperson. "Indiana Jones." He turned to me, lowering his voice. "That's Red Sonja. She's the girl boss."

There was a philosophical divide in the Safe House about whether or not the girls should take on exclusively female nicknames. Some argued that they didn't want their pick of badass characters limited on the basis of gender, while Red Sonja said there were plenty of worthy women action stars who were actually more badass than their male counterparts, given they had to fight in tighter pants.

"Indy," she said, frowning, no doubt at the gender attached to my adopted name. "Well, too late to change it. Nice job with this, though." She gestured at my latest organizational effort for munitions, bullets separated by cartridge type and stored in terra-cotta flowerpots. I gave her a thumbs-up and she tied off the braid she'd plaited during the exchange and went to reload.

Sorted munitions made the Safe House run smoother, but the older girls all had their own assault rifles, and I was getting restless. I had proven myself a good worker, I thought, and wanted to fight like everybody else. The following week during morning meetings, when weapons were issued to the new recruits from neighboring villages, I lined up with the rest, tucked my hair up under my cap, and hoped the dirt on my face covered any traces of girlhood. The captain looked me up and down and said there was not enough for everyone. But the next day we took on mortar fire that tore a new hole in the south wall. The captain made Stallone and me lie facedown on floor, and I loathed the familiar feeling of helplessness. I tried to lift my head but could only see boots. Someone fell beside me—I couldn't tell who—and his weapon discharged as he hit the floor. A hollow, wobbling tone filled my ears, then a roaring sound like rushing water. The man was bleeding in spurts from his neck, and I closed my eyes again.

Afterward, I sat up and looked around. Stallone was beside me, pressing his sleeve to a slash across his forehead, saying something I couldn't hear; my ears were still ringing. I took the gun from the dead man next to me, a Wolverine, and slipped its strap over my head. No one noticed. There were three other men on the floor, not moving. Red Sonja had me rip a bedsheet into squares, and she closed the dead men's eyes and covered their faces with the fabric. The Bruces were stacking weapons—guns and knives and brass knuckles newly available. I pushed the gun up against my back and knew from that moment it was mine.

The strongest men heaved the corpses down the stairs and laid them out behind the house, waiting for nightfall so they could transport them to the cemetery at the far end of the village. At dusk Stallone and I went out on recon and counted Četnik casualties. We kicked the bodies, searched their pockets for ammo.

Damir taught me how to fieldstrip and reassemble an AK. Forward grip, gas chamber, cleaning rod, bolt (piston first), frame, magazine.

"Function check!" It meant to cock the gun as a test, the last step in reassembly, but anyone completing the check yelled it triumphantly, a battle cry preceding the first bursts of gunfire. The fieldstrip was a protocol that never changed, and I found solace in the repetition.

The old men let me keep watch while they were eating lunch. Too short to shoot with my feet on the ground, I'd climb up and kneel in the windowsill. I shot over toward the schoolhouse at anything in camouflage moving in the windows, or outside ground-level on the other side of the street, then jumped down and ducked in case a Četnik was clear-headed enough to shoot straight back. With every round I envisioned killing the soldier with the brown teeth, the one who'd struck my father in the back of the knee and laughed. I relished the power that seemed to run through the chamber of the weapon directly up into my own veins.

Occupation under the Četniks was a delicate balance. In their state of perpetual intoxication they'd been satisfied in rape and pillage mode, their genocidal appetites satiated by picking off Safe Housers and the occasional roadside murder of travelers like my parents. The danger of killing too many of us and losing their UN meal ticket staved off any large-scale assaults. But the JNA, closing in on the area, sent reinforcements, and the reinforcements were not yet weary of the place, were not content with exchanging fire from the comfort of the schoolhouse. They had salaries, uniforms, better weapons, and a functioning chain of command. Relatively, they were sober. They were ready to attack.

I was at the attic window keeping watch with the Terminator when we spotted a band of armored vehicles, about ten it looked like, but it was hard to tell from the curve in the road. The trucks were green, not UN issue, and when I looked up at the Terminator he was gesturing frantically. I bolted across the attic to get Stallone, who, upon seeing his brother's signs, yelled, "Holy shit! The JNA! They're coming down the street!" The trucks were closer now, and I could see the red Yugoslavian stars on their doors.

"Let's move!" said the captain, and everyone who'd been without a gun lunged for the extras on the hat rack. I turned to the captain for his next instructions, but from downstairs we heard gunfire, the blowback of broken glass, and the door guards screaming.

"They're here," said Stallone.

We ran—down the uneven rear stairs and out the back door, through the packed-dirt alley by the market, and out into the wheat fields. The stalks bowed with rotting, grain-laden heads abandoned by farmers when the bombing started, but even in their hunched posture they were taller than I was, and I could see nothing but wheat in all directions. I wondered where Stallone had gone. Then, from a side row, I saw Damir darting toward me.

"You've got speed, girl," he said when he caught up. He grabbed me by the hood of my sweatshirt and yanked me to the left, hard. "No sense of direction, though." The butt of my rifle banged a bruise into the back of my leg as we ran.

A pack of JNA foot soldiers were coming from the other side of the field now; there were at least twenty of them, running in a clean, arrowlike formation. I froze, gaping as they closed the meters between us—one hundred, seventy-five, fifty—but Damir pushed me ahead of him and released a spray of gunfire on them. In the corner of my vision I saw him go down, but he yelled "Don't stop!" so I kept running, made a sharp turn into the field's middle strip. The wind hit my face fresh and hard—my nose dripped and my eyes watered. Dragging my sleeve across my face, I pumped my legs faster until I could no longer feel the ground, until gravity slithered off the treads of my sneakers.

At the center of the field I threw myself beneath a tractor and curled into a compact ball, covering my face with my hands. There was gunfire and yelling from every angle, and I tried to listen for voices I knew. I thought of Damir and waited for the familiar sadness to set in, but found only anger in its place. With one hand I felt the ground for my AK and was relieved to find it there beside me.

"Viči ako možeš!" Yell out if you can. The cry reverberated through the village as the remaining Safe Housers combed the fields for survivors.

"Viči ako možeš!" Other than the rescue call it was eerily quiet, that odd part of evening when the sun had set but it was still more light than dark. I ran my hands over my face and body, taking inventory, impossibly unharmed save for the blood on my wrists, where the last of the barbed-wire scabs had reopened when I hit the ground. I waited, listening for any definitive JNA sounds, watched for passing boots. But there was nothing, so I pulled myself on my elbows out from beneath the tractor. It occurred to me that I'd

never seen a tractor up close before, and I marveled momentarily at its size, the tire alone taller than I was, before a resurgence of the rescue call returned me to soldier mode.

I jogged back the way I'd come, looking for Damir, and found a group of Safe Housers squatting around a body I knew must be his.

"Indy!" Bruce Willis said, noticing me. "Don't—don't look. Go home and tell Drenka to make a bed for him."

"She doesn't talk," said Snake.

"Well then she'll do a goddamn charade. Just go!"

I pressed myself on tiptoe, trying to catch a glimpse of Damir's face, to see if Bruce had meant a sickbed or a dead-person one. But Damir was obscured by the men around him.

"Hey!" Bruce said, and I spun back toward them. "Hold the gun out in front of you, at least till you get out of the field." I nodded and pulled the AK up over my head, adjusting the twisted strap around my shoulder.

Damir was right—my sense of direction was terrible, and now that the men had turned me away from the path toward the Safe House, I'd lost my reference point. I walked down a row of wheat, but that only seemed to take me deeper into the field. Ahead, I thought I heard a rustling. I had practiced the fieldstrip so many times that cocking the gun was more an act of muscle memory than conscious thought. I pulled the handle back along the bolt carrier, then released it, heard a round click into the chamber. Whoever was nearby must have heard it, too, because there was rustling again, then the unmistakable sound of running in boots. I tried to call for Stallone, but nothing came out.

When he came around the corner, I froze. It was not Stallone. The man was looking over his shoulder but was headed straight for me. He wore a patchy beard and a green jacket, no JNA insignia. By the time he turned and saw me, we were so close we could have touched. He was visibly shocked by my size and my gun. I felt him look me over, trying to decide what to do, and for a moment I glimpsed his hesitation. Then it passed. He reached around for his gun, and I squeezed my eyes shut and pulled the trigger.

On the ground, the man was writhing and making a choking noise. I had hit him in the upper stomach, or maybe the ribs. He was probably only a few years older than Damir, acne pockmarks still visible along his cheekbones.

The blood was passing through his shirt and pooling beside him. But he was still awake, wide-eyed and angry and confused. He was trying to talk but his speech was slurred, and I couldn't understand until he stopped whatever he had been saying and just repeated "Please," over and over again.

I didn't know what else to do, so I stepped over him and crept through the wheat, searching for a way back to the house.

In the kitchen I called out to Drenka, but my vocal cords groaned with the vibrations of disuse. She turned and looked me over, trying to gauge whether I'd actually spoken. I saw her eyes catch on something and realized I was covered in blood, a little from my wrists, but mostly from the blowback of the soldier. I coughed and tried again to speak; my voice came stronger this time. "Damir's hurt."

She jumped from her chair. "Where is he?"

"The JNA. They got him." My throat burned. "Safe Housers are bringing him here. They said to get ready."

"Get ready? What does that mean?"

"I don't know."

Drenka instructed me to undress. I put on her nightgown as she wrung the blood from my clothes in a bucket on the kitchen floor.

Damir had been shot in the thigh, and the bullet was still inside him. It took two Safe Housers to carry him because they were trying to keep his leg straight. When they first put him on his bed, I still couldn't tell if he was alive. But when Drenka cut his pant leg off and poured alcohol on the wound, he jerked awake and began to yell.

"Thank God," I said. Bruce Willis stared at me, then tried to play off his surprise at my speaking.

The Bruces sat with us for a few hours, assuring Drenka that Damir was going to be fine. The captain was already radioing the neighboring villages to call for the doctor, they said. I thought of the soldier I had shot, wondered if he had been rescued or if he was still out in the field, bleeding to death.

Damir moaned and sweated in his sleep. Drenka and I stayed up all night staring at him and waiting for the doctor to come. He mumbled incessantly about his grandfather and watermelon, while Drenka cradled his head and poured swallows of *rakija* in his mouth.

"Listen," she said to me the next morning as I slung my gun over my shoulder and double-knotted my shoelaces. "If you tell me where you're from I can help you get back. There must be someone waiting for you." I eyed her from across the table until she resumed her pacing. I thought about what it would be like if the doctor had to cut off Damir's leg in front of us, right in his own bed. I thought of Luka knocking on the door of our flat, of his impatience and worry at the silence on the other side. The red shine of his bicycle streaked across my vision. I thought about the man I had shot, but I was not quite sorry. I went to the Safe House.

There was no one guarding the door. Inside, the house was trashed. The posters had been torn from the wall; their taped corners clung obstinately to the cement. It looked like Gotovina's Chair had been set on fire. I ran upstairs, where I found the captain warbling a distress signal into the CB. Besides the Bruces and one of the Turtles, the place was empty.

"Stallone?" I managed, my voice still clumsy. The captain looked startled but quickly regained composure.

"A lot of people are okay. They're at home, healing up for a day or two."

"Stallone?" I said again, taking note of the captain's evasion.

"Stallone is missing," he said. "His brother is out looking." I stood there frozen, the strength I'd gained over the past months gone all at once, as if it had drained out my feet. "Don't worry about that now. Tell me about Damir."

I told him Damir's leg was swollen and oozing something yellow. "He needs help," I said. "He's dreaming of his dead grandfather."

"Indy. You must go home and take care of Drenka now. The doctor will be there soon." I stood there, immobile, which the captain mistook for protest. "That's an order," he said, so I gathered myself and went.

In Damir's room the curtains were drawn, and he stirred as I sat on the edge of his bed, jamming and releasing the lever that detached the forward grip of my gun.

"Almost as good as a boy," Damir said, surfacing momentarily from the fog of fever and brandy. From him this was a compliment. But his leg was twice the size it should have been, and there was pus. I left the gun leaning against the bookshelf and returned to my corner of the kitchen floor.

I thought of telling Drenka the whole story of where I'd come from and what had happened, but she was ripping bedding for bandages and worrying. Just as I was beginning to think I'd worked up the courage to open my mouth, a pallid face appeared above me in the kitchen window. I jumped to my feet and let out a yelp.

"Psst. Indy. Open up!" the face whispered through the glass. I looked again, the magnified eyes now familiar. I unbolted the door.

"How's he doing?" the captain asked.

"He's alive," I said.

"Oh good, Josip, you're here," said Drenka from down the hall. It was the first time I'd heard anyone call the captain by another name. But her face dropped when she came round the corner. "Where's Dr. Hožić?"

The captain lowered his eyes. "We, uh, can't find him."

"What do you mean? You were supposed to—you said you were bringing a doctor."

"Last we heard he was over in Blato, but that was a few days ago now."

"Well then, he should be here soon, right?"

"Drenka." The captain sounded almost tender now. "We don't have time."

The captain pressed by us and began banging around the kitchen, neck-deep in the cabinets. When he reemerged he was holding a paring knife and salad tongs. "We need to take it out." Drenka collapsed into a nearby chair, and the captain turned to me. "Can you boil some water?" he said.

The scream that came out of Damir was not human— guttural and even more desperate than the cries in the forest. I stood in the doorway of his bedroom looking and trying not to look as Drenka held Damir's arms down against the bed and the captain bent over Damir's leg in the candlelight. I clapped my hands over my ears and ran back to the kitchen to boil more water.

The canisters were almost empty. Should I go to the pump, or wait and see if they needed me here? Soon, though, the captain came out into the kitchen. He gestured to the remaining water, and I poured it over his bloody hands in the sink. He wiped his palms on his jeans, and I stood by, staring, waiting for my next order. But the captain just rested his hand on my shoulder.

"It's all right, Indy," he said, though he was looking over my head. "You can stand down. You did good." He pushed his glasses up his nose and went out into the night.

I fell asleep on the floor and woke up cold. Turning sideways, I slipped through the door of Damir's room, where Drenka was sleeping in a chair pulled close to his bed. She looked older now, skin sallow without the warm tones of her shawl up around her face. I grazed my fingers against her arm and she jerked awake.

"Zagreb," I said, and she looked confused. "I'm from Zagreb." The name of my city felt foreign.

Drenka stood haltingly and stumbled as she led me to the couch. "Okay," she said, covering me with a blanket. "Okay."

3

News had spread about Damir, and the next day the women of the village came through the house offering help. They brought broth, towels, jam jars of *rakija*, and war cakes—flat, hard discs made with a quarter of the normal amount of yeast and no sugar. I was sitting in my corner and tried to listen for news of other Safe House casualties, but since I'd spoken Drenka had reduced herself to whispers in my presence, and the other women followed. I assumed they'd be rehashing recent events, planning what to do when the JNA came back, but instead I felt them staring at me sidelong and exchanging crinkled dinar notes.

At sundown Drenka counted the money. She took the last two hard-boiled eggs left from the chickens and packed them along with a heel of bread in a plastic sack, tying the ends of the bag tight. We were leaving. She brought me my old T-shirt, and I put it on, then pulled the sweatshirt Damir had given me back over top.

While Drenka was putting on her shoes, I slipped into Damir's room. "Thank you," I said into the darkness. Damir muttered something and moved like he was going to roll over, but they'd strapped his leg down to the bed, and he gave up without much of a fight. "Good night," I said, and closed his door.

The sky was black and wintry, smudged with smoke from an earlier raid—had it been somewhere else it might even have been pretty. Drenka held my hand, and, gazes fixed downward to calculate each footfall, we crossed through the high grass to the house next door. There was a faded blue car in the driveway, the only car I remember seeing in the village. Drenka rapped a syncopated knock on the front door, and a lantern appeared in the upstairs window. A girl a little older than I pushed open the glass and threw down a set of keys, then quickly swung the shutters closed. Drenka put the car in neutral, and we rolled out of the driveway and into the street. Headlights off, we drove out of the village. The air raid siren let out a farewell whoop as we turned back onto the big road from which I'd come, and I pulled the hood of Damir's sweatshirt up over my eyes, afraid to see my family's car, the soldiers, or the ghosts of the forest.

The bus was already at the stop, idling, puffs of exhaust

stark against the icy air. Drenka handed me the bag and led me up the steps. Inside it smelled like rancid meat, and I suppressed a gag. The exterior had looked like a regular tour bus, the same kind that ran the summertime route from Zagreb to the coast, but now I noticed the camouflage rucksacks overflowing from the first three rows of seats, the driver in partial police uniform, the assault rifle prominently affixed to the dashboard.

"She's going to Zagreb," Drenka said, handing him the first stack of dinar. "Make sure she gets the right transfer." She gave him the other stack and ran a few fingers over my cheek before she jumped back to the ground. I sat down next to a man in Croatian police uniform. The engine turned, the bus lurched forward, and Drenka stood and watched me leave, holding her shawl across her face against the swirling fumes.

As the village melted into the horizon behind me, I pressed my head to the window, feeling the vibrations of the motor that buzzed through the glass and up into my skull. I never learned the name of the place that had taken me in and tried to look in the dark for a road sign. I wondered whether, if I wanted, I could find it again, if I would recognize it by sight or some deeper feeling in my stomach.

"There are bodies in the back, you know."

"What?" I looked up at the soldier next to me. He was young, a redhead, with pimples in a line along his jaw.

"Bodies. In the backseats. Dead ones."

"Now why would you tell her that?" said the soldier across the aisle.

"It's true!"

"But she's just a little kid. A *girl*."

"She's in fatigues," he said, gesturing to Damir's clothes. "You're a Safe Houser, aren't you? I've heard about you guys."

"She's like eight!"

"Well?" said the first soldier.

"Forward grip, gas chamber, cleaning rod, bolt, frame, magazine. Function check," I said.

The soldiers' eyes widened, but the one next to me played it off. "See? Anyway"—he turned to me again—"those seats in the back are all dead guys. Hopefully we make it up north before the smell gets any worse."

"Would you stop?" said the other soldier.

"She ain't no little kid." He put his head back, feigning sleep, and ignored both of us for the rest of the night.

I woke the next morning in Zagreb with no memory of changing buses. It was an unseasonably warm day, the winter sun close and exacting. I pulled my sweatshirt off and stuffed it in Drenka's bag, stood squinting and bewildered in the bus terminal's dirty parking lot. I took the chain-link exit for authorized personnel only to avoid the crowds in the station and emerged through an alley out onto Držića Avenue.

Zagreb appeared relatively unharmed, and I was overwhelmed by its size and bustle, felt out of sync with the constant motion of the city. I noticed families walking together clad in khakis and patent leather and realized they were probably leaving church, that it was Sunday. The concept of time organized into seven-day units seemed almost foreign now, as if I'd never abided by the calendar. I wondered how long I'd been gone, whether I'd missed Christmas. I thought of school and was dismayed that everyone I knew had undoubtedly continued going there every day without me.

The city I had called my own, one I'd considered a war zone when I left it, now felt like neither. It was as if the whole of Zagreb had been repainted—Technicolor—the hues more vivid, the glass within each windowpane more burnished.

I stared at a family as they crossed the street, let my eyes linger too long, and their mother glared at my dirty T-shirt with the condescension reserved for gypsy beggars. For a second I wished I still had my rifle—just my holding it would have stopped her from looking at me like that—but immediately I felt ashamed of the thought. I needed to keep moving. I went to Luka's house.

When I rang the doorbell, Luka answered, his face lighting up with one of his rare unbridled smiles. He cleared his front steps in one jump, chattering out a flurry of where-have-you-beens and what-took-you-so-longs, and I felt my throat shrivel and close. I was afraid my voice would give me away or abandon me altogether, as it had before.

Luka continued prattling as he climbed back toward his door, but I found my feet reluctant to take orders. He spun around to hurry me along, and I saw his face change in what must have been the moment he finally looked at me. I watched the seriousness return to his eyes as he scanned the stains on my shirt.

"Ana," he said. "Where are your parents?"

"At home," I lied in my shaky voice, but he gave me a look so piercing that I burst into tears. I felt my knees soften, and he pulled my arm over his shoulders and led me up the stairs to his room, where he sat me on the edge of the bed.

"Take it off," he said, nodding at my shirt.

"No."

"Take it off!"

I yanked the shirt over my head, and, eyes averted, he held out his hand. I gave it to him, and he dropped it to the floor, then dug through his own bureau until he found a satisfactory replacement.

"Stay here," he said, and I heard him calling for his mother.

Luka returned with his mother behind him, and he took my bloody shirt from the floor and handed it to her. I hadn't cried at all in the village, but, now that I'd started, stopping proved difficult. I cried myself a nosebleed, and Luka and his mother sat beside me as I sprawled facedown on the carpet, twisting my fingers tightly through its fibers until my hands tingled. Each time someone tried to touch me I shrugged them away, but eventually I grew tired, and when Luka's mother reached out I didn't recoil. The weight of her palm steadied the small of my back, and when I ran out of tears I fell asleep.

I woke on the floor and stared at the morning through the skylight in Luka's ceiling. Luka's mother was asleep in a rocking chair, and Luka was in his bed against the opposite wall. My eyes and throat were swollen and slow to react. I stood, and Luka's mother stirred, then snapped awake when her forehead scraped against the wall. She looked at me, confused, not unfamiliarly, but unable to recall why I was standing blood-streaked and puffy in her house at six in the morning. She rubbed her temples. I followed her downstairs to the kitchen.

I sat on a stool at the counter and watched her flit between the refrigerator and the stove.

"You don't need to tell me any details." She spoke with caution. "But I'll need to know some things, so I can help. We can just try yes or no questions first?"

I nodded.

"Okay. You were going to Sarajevo?"

I nodded again.

"Did you get there?"

Nod.

"Is Rahela okay?"

I nodded and hoped it was true.

"So, on the way back?" she ventured.

I didn't move.

"Were there soldiers?"

Nod.

"Did they hurt you?"

"No," I said.

"Did they hurt your parents?"

I stared.

"Are they okay?"

Stared harder.

"Are they coming back soon?"

"No."

"Are they . . . coming back?"

I shook my head. Luka's mother sat down and made a strange throat-clearing noise.

"What do I do?" she whispered. She was asking herself, so I didn't try to answer. Moments later Luka's father descended the stairs in a hurry, straightening the pins on his uniform. His bushy eyebrows arched when he saw me.

"Been a while, girlie," he said, then, surveying my bloodied nose, he turned to his wife. "Is everything okay?"

"No," she said. "It's not."

"Do you want me to call her parents?" He reached for the phone book, but Luka's mother shot him such a pointed look that he stopped short. He sighed, then wet a napkin, and wiped the crusted blood from under my nose.

"Call Petar," he said. He fumbled for his keys and headed off to train the newest troops.

Luka's mother heated water on the stove, and I took it into the bathtub and dumped it over my head. It was warm enough, and I scrubbed myself pink until the water at my feet turned gray.

Luka stayed home from school, and we played cards on the kitchen floor. Luka's mother was on the phone all day, speaking softly and twirling the spiral cord into an even twistier knot around her finger.

"Petar's going to pick you up in the morning," she said when she hung up the phone for good before dinner.

"Can't I just stay with you?"

"You're always welcome, honey. But Petar is your godfather, so legally—"

"I know," I said, feeling bad for having asked.

Luka and I slept in his bed that night. I was glad to have him beside me, but the mattress I had been jealous of now seemed sterile and unwelcoming, and I longed for my couch. Luka threw an arm over me and said, "So?" and I spilled the most complete version of the story I could, telling it like I couldn't to his mother, like I never did to anyone else. I told him about the roadblock and the forest and my father and me tricking the soldiers, the Safe Housers, the bug-eyed captain and how he'd named me Indiana. I told him about Damir, the bus full of bodies, right up to the point where I'd shown up on his doorstep. I told him about my gun.

"Forward grip, gas chamber, cleaning rod, bolt, frame, magazine, function check," Luka repeated, mimicking my hand motions.

"You're fast."

"Did you kill anyone?"

The soldier in the field was the only thing I'd left out of my story. "I don't know," I said, which was technically the truth.

We went quiet again, but I could feel him awake, and we stayed listening to the *bura* wind like that, eyes wide and blind in the dark.

Petar had called to say he was on his way. Luka's mother was buzzing between rooms dusting and straightening, and I followed her around.

"What is it?" she said.

"I need my shirt back."

"I don't think—"

"Please."

She pulled the shirt from the bottom of her bureau drawer as if she'd known I'd ask for it.

"Maybe you shouldn't put it on, though," she said, handing it to me. I nodded and tucked it into the plastic bag with Damir's sweatshirt. By this time the shirt had been washed by several hands, but the stains remained.

Petar was fit from his stint in the army, his hair growing in from his crew cut, his arm strapped in a thick plastic brace, which I assumed was the reason he was back early. He bent to one knee to hug me, then seemed to find it difficult to stop, because he scooped me up with his good arm and held me that way until we got out to the car.

Luka's mother stood in the doorway, arms crossed against the cold.

"Thank you," Petar said to her.

"Thanks," I said.

Petar set me down in the backseat next to a small pile of my clothes, schoolbooks, and the spare keys to my flat. My bike, he said, was in the trunk, and I'd be able to ride to school from his house. He'd had to cut my bike lock but had bought a new one, the combination kind, and fiddled with it for a few moments, rolling the number columns beneath his thick thumbs before handing it over to me.

"Do you know how to do this?"

"Not really," I said.

He looked away. "Me neither."

Marina was sitting on the curb outside their building, waiting for us. She motioned me to her, and when we hugged I felt her tears on my neck.

"Don't cry," I said, which made her cry harder.

"Let's get you inside," Petar said. He handed Marina my clothes and carried me into the house.

4

At Petar and Marina's grief filled the flat, as present as a fourth person in the room. Every night for a week Petar spoke to me softly, asking what had happened, but it still felt strange to talk, and finally he got so frustrated that he grabbed me by the shoulders and shook. It wasn't painful, but it was hard enough to scare me, and afterward he backed away apologizing and cradling his bad arm.

"I'm sorry. I just need to know. I can't not know."

It hadn't occurred to me that Petar and Marina were mourning the loss of their best friends, that they felt the same pain I did, and the realization gave me a little courage. I told him about the MediMission office and the roadblock, and how I'd stayed in the valley village. I said nothing of the

Safe House, but Petar had his answer and didn't press me to account for the missing time.

I returned to school and spoke to no one except Luka. He was always serious with me; with only the occasional slip he succeeded in hiding any evidence of joy in the world that had continued on without me. Still, Petar had told my teachers what had happened, and my classmates overheard things in the hallways. Everyone knew. I had my own uncontested turn on the generator bike.

It snowed. But the excitement that normally filled the city in a storm was dulled by air raid smoke and a new set of ration restrictions. Winter had always been my favorite time of year; I loved walking in the Trg drinking mulled wine, eating kielbasa, and talking to the tent vendors selling wood carvings of boats and crucifixes. I loved New Year's Eve, when people threw Roman candles in the square and shouted songs while I sat on my father's shoulders. But the holidays had passed unnoticed in the village, and if Zagreb had mustered a celebration that year, any evidence was cleared away by the time I returned. I recall nothing about those January days except the strain of an Epiphany hymn, eerie and minor, repeating on an organ from another time.

Petar and Marina took up fighting like a hobby. I'd never seen them this way before, so quick to accuse and attack one another. Petar had stopped going to Mass and Marina went to Mass more. Petar spent hours smoking and on the phone in furtive exchanges, and Marina channeled all her nervous energy into cleaning, scouring specifically, with a focus on tile grout. She'd urge Petar to do something productive, and he'd point to the receiver and turn away, covering his phone-less ear to block her out.

Petar began interrogating me on the finer points of MediMission. I didn't know much, except that Rahela was at a hospital in Philadelphia especially for children, and that the family taking care of her had been assigned through the program. My parents had never spoken to them, and I didn't know their names.

"I don't know anything else," I said, weary of the conversations.

"Just keep thinking about it. Maybe you'll remember something that helps."

"Helps what?"

At night they were sad, which was much worse than the fighting. Marina's speech was soft and indecipherable, but Petar's raspy voice traveled easily through our shared wall.

"Bastards. I don't know what to do." Marina made a quiet reply, and the bedsprings squeaked. "Fucking hell," he said, as one of them clicked off the lamp. "What do I even pray for?"

One Saturday, Marina won out and Petar agreed to go to church, "for funeral purposes only." Besides honoring dead relatives and celebrating holidays, my family didn't go to church much, especially once Rahela got sick. I had learned the prayers and made my First Communion like nearly everyone I knew, but emotional attachment to the church had always felt just beyond me. Religion, I'd assumed, would make more sense when I grew up.

Marina, Petar, and I went to the Zagreb Katedrala and spent an hour at the back vigil candles, kneeling and clicking rosaries until I'd burned the tips of my thumbs with the cheap matches and bruised my knees on the cold tile floor.

Afterward, we walked to the Trg, where the beginnings of a makeshift memorial were laid out. The Wall was made of red bricks, each one bearing the name of a person killed or disappeared. Already it was hundreds of bricks long. I took a loose block from the pile, scrawled both my parents' names across it, wanting to keep them together, and added it to the row in progress. Marina had another candle, the votive kind meant to stay lit even outside, and left it there flickering in the dusk.

Petar began acting even stranger. He came and left unannounced and when he was home couldn't sit still, instead paced the kitchen and ran his good hand through his hair. His nervousness reminded me of the year my father bought my mother an expensive necklace for Christmas. He'd also paced the flat for a week, so excited that he eventually broke down and gave it to her three days early. She'd loved it, and when they kissed his face had flushed with her happiness.

Petar's face did not have this light, and I was increasingly unsettled as it became clear I was the subject of his anxiety. Finally, one night at dinner, while Petar was staring at me and clearing his throat, Marina banged her cup down and pushed her chair back from the table.

"Petar, for chrissakes just tell her already!"

"Tell me what?" I said.

"I don't want to tell her if I don't have all the information."

"Tell me what!"

"We tracked down Rahela and her foster family," Marina said. "They want to adopt her."

"What?"

"MediMission didn't want to tell me where she'd been placed—it's against the rules—but I found her," said Petar.

"She was supposed to come back when she was better. She's my sister."

"Well," said Marina. "There may be other options."

"What do you mean?"

"The foster family said they'd be willing to take you, too, provided we can make arrangements to get you there."

"Take me?"

"Adopt you, Ana. You could go and live with them and Rahela. In America."

I felt a rage brewing in my chest. I wanted to hit something and kicked at the bottom bar of my chair. Why were they trying to get rid of me? Dump me with some strangers on another continent?

"Why can't we just stay here with you? Don't you want us?"

Petar shook his head. "Do you really think that's a good idea? To move Rahela, sick, from America back into a fucking war zone?"

"Petar!" said Marina.

I shook my head. I hadn't thought of it like that. Marina motioned me over, and I went and sat on her lap. She stroked my hair and glared at Petar.

"I think it's what's best," she said. "For Rahela, and for you."

"I'm sorry for yelling," Petar said, gentler now. "But I know you're smart enough to understand. You understand, right?"

I nodded.

"It'll take some work to get you out of here. But I think I can do it."

Petar contacted MediMission, who offered a terse response that family reunification cases were not within the scope of their work, but that he could reapply on my behalf if I ever fell ill. Then he considered refugee status, but there wasn't an

American embassy in Croatia yet. The consulate in Belgrade was running a looping voice mail that apologized for the wait time and said, due to the high volume of inquiries, they were working through a backlog of applications at this time.

"Never mind that," said Petar. "I know someone."

The next morning Petar and I rang the buzzer of a basement apartment beneath a butcher shop in a southern part of the city where I'd never been. We waited, listening as a series of chains and dead bolts clinked on the other side of the door. It opened a sliver, enough to reveal one pale eye, then closed to allow for more unlocking.

"Security," the man said. "You know how it is." Finally the door opened a passable amount and Petar and I slipped inside. The flat was dank and smelled moldy. It was hard to make out at first, but as my eyes adjusted it was clear the single-room efficiency was home to more than just an overweight bachelor; the entirety of the counter space was lined with equipment ranging from typewriters and printing presses to what was, by my best guess, a blowtorch.

"What happened to you?" the man said, gesturing to Petar's arm.

"Shattered humerus. Shrapnel still in there." I felt bad that I'd never asked, but it had always seemed like he didn't want to talk about it, and that I could understand.

The man changed the subject. "And what can I do for you today?" He squatted down when he spoke to me. "You want a driver's license?"

"Ha ha," said Petar, and the two men executed a combination handshake-hug. The man kissed Petar three times, the Orthodox way, and I winced. "Ana," Petar said, "this is Srdjan." An indisputably Serbian name. My heartbeat quickened. "An old friend from high school. Srdjan knew your parents."

Srdjan was holding out his hand. "Yes," he said. "I'm sorry to hear."

"Go on then. Shake his hand."

"I can help you," Srdjan said. I put my hand in his. "I hear you need an American visa."

I looked up at Petar, who nodded. I nodded, too.

"Well, luckily, I happen to produce absolutely foolproof visas," Srdjan said, with a sweeping gesture at his workshop. "I even have the very same paper that the United States of America uses." He rummaged through paper-filled cabinets. "How are you going to fly?"

"Probably through Germany," Petar said. "I'm still working out the finer points."

"Germany," he said. "As long as you stay in the international terminal you'll be fine."

He flipped some levers on the printing equipment, and the machines hummed. "With this paper I can produce exact American replicas! I got it from an intern at the embassy—"

"She doesn't need to know where you got it," Petar said, predicting the course of the story.

"Tits"—Srdjan held his hands far out from his chest—
"as big as honeydew melons, I shit you not."

Petar chuckled uneasily, and Srdjan looked surprised to
find worry in his friend's face.

"What's wrong with tits? She's a girl. She's going to have
tits."

"All right! Enough with the tits."

"Fine," Srdjan said. He looked down at me. "Didn't know
he was so sensitive."

"What about a passport?"

"What do you mean? We'll just staple it in her regular
passport."

"It got . . . lost," Petar said.

"Well, you could apply for a new one."

"Not enough time. Can't you just make her one? Make
her a German one!"

"Yeah, I'll make a fake German passport and we'll send a
kid who doesn't speak any German to *Germany* with it!"
Srdjan raised the heel of his hand and smacked Petar in the
forehead, then shot me a wink. "Look out—we've got a real
genius on our hands!"

"All right, all right," said Petar. "Make her one of ours
then. Don't you need to take her picture or something?"

"Indeed." Srdjan adjusted a pair of photographer's lights
that looked like umbrellas, and I stood stoic against a white
sheet while he snapped a picture.

"I'll be back to pick it up Wednesday?" Petar handed him

an envelope, and Srdjan fingered the flap and peeked inside.
"I'll bring the rest then."

"Very well," Srdjan said, and took a dramatic bow before
walking us to the door and releasing us out into the daylight.
"Ana."

I turned back.

"Your parents. They were good."

"Thanks." I tried to think of something better to say, but
Srdjan had already shut the door, the dead bolts clicking
behind us.

Voices of my neighbors echoed in the stairwell as we climbed
the stairs to my flat; the walls there had always been thin.
Just as I'd been unsettled at the idea that my friends had
been going to school without me, I was shocked to find people were still living out normal existences here in my building, that their lives had not stalled as mine had. Petar turned
the extra key in the lock, but instead of smashing against the
wall, the door stuck to the frame, and he forced it open with
his good shoulder.

"Can you stay out here?" I said. He looked hurt but hung
back anyway.

Inside, the room was dim and the air was stale. Cuts of
sunlight slid between the blinds, revealing swirling columns
of dust. The door to my parents' bedroom was closed, and I
left it that way and moved through the kitchen. A sour smell

emanated from the refrigerator, and something small and shadowy ran alongside the baseboard and disappeared under the door of the pantry.

In the living room I ran my hand over the armrest of the couch where my father used to sit. Then I pulled my clothes from the bookshelf and shoved them into my pillowcase. From the bottom shelf I gathered a sampling of the pirated radio tapes my father and I had made. Over the piano there was a photo of the four of us, and another of me as a baby in Tiska. I took them from their adjacent places on the wall. My parents' wedding picture was hung higher up, but I couldn't reach it.

Petar called out and asked how I was doing and I jumped. Plunking my hand down on the bottom octave of the piano, I ran from the room, dragging the bulging pillowcase behind me. I thought about asking Petar to go back for the wedding picture, but as he turned in the doorway, the light revealed his reddened eyes, so I said nothing.

The night before I left, Luka appeared under my window on his bike. Petar had instructed me not to tell anyone when I was leaving or where I was going, but I had told Luka anyway, swearing him to secrecy.

"How did you—"

"I snuck out. Come down."

"Come up." I met him at the door, and we trod warily

through the kitchen and out to the fire escape. Marina and the family in the next building had strung a clothesline across the alley, and someone's bed linens crackled in the wind.

"Will you be safe there?"

"I think so. Rahela is safe."

"But you know in the movies. All those cowboys and gangsters."

"I guess all places are sort of dangerous."

"I guess." He put his hand on mine, then pulled it away.

"Will you write me?" I said. He said he would, and we sat for a while contemplating the Wild West and New York City and Philadelphia, where I might be able to see Rocky. When Luka's eyelids began to flutter, I punched him in the arm and told him he could stay the night, but he had to get home before he was discovered missing. The ladder on the fire escape was broken, so he climbed back into the flat and let himself out.

"I don't know what to say," I whispered as he swung a leg over his bicycle.

"So don't say anything. When you come back, it will be like you never left." He stood up on his bike pedals and bounced down the gravel drive, then turned the corner out of sight.

—

I woke in the dark with Petar standing over me.

"Sorry," he said. "It's time."

"I'm awake." I dressed in the only clothes I hadn't packed. I went to the bedroom to say goodbye to Marina, kissing her on the cheek.

"Be safe," she murmured. "And take care of Rahela."

"Come. Be my co-pilot," Petar said, motioning to the passenger seat. He was wearing his army uniform with the left sleeve cut off to accommodate the brace. He put a yellow envelope in my lap and backed out of the driveway. "Now this is very important. These are all your documents—ticket, passport, contact information for the family, letter of invitation, and"—he reached in his pocket and stuffed some dinar into the envelope—"something extra in case anyone gets hungry."

"Hungry?"

"Not for food," he said, tapping the envelope. "You'll find powerful men can often be persuaded. At least they can here. I don't know about America. Don't worry. You'll know if you need it. Subtlety is not the military way. Now. When you get to Germany—"

"Don't leave the international terminal," I said, remembering Srdjan's instructions.

"Good. And when you get to New York?"

I gave him a blank look. I couldn't remember any advice about America.

"Just play it cool!" he said. "They're going to meet you at the airport, so once you make it through customs, you're home free."

I leafed through the papers. I went back to the start of the pile and looked through them again. There was only one ticket.

"This says Frankfurt–New York. Where's the other half?" I'd assumed the American visa would be the hardest component to procure; I hadn't considered that getting out of this country would be a problem. But the more I thought about it, the more frightened I became. Of course no company would be stupid enough to fly commercial planes in war zone airspace.

"I've made arrangements," Petar said.

"How did you find all these people to help us?"

"I've always known people. You just didn't notice. You were young."

The airport was ringed by white vehicles: smooth-front supply trucks with covered flatbeds, fuel carrier tankers, shiny white SUVs, even a series of white tanks, all bearing UN in bold black paint. On both sides of the fence, the area was swarming with Peacekeepers, their helmets and flak jackets almost luminous in the diffuse dawn light. But Petar drove past the entrance. I waited for him to turn in to a side gate or service road. Instead he got on the highway, southbound.

"Petar. The airport?"

"We're not going there," he said.

"What do you mean?"

"Too heavily guarded. They check the planes."

"Then where are we going?"

"Otočac."

"Otočac! Do they even have an airport? Aren't there Četniks down there?"

"We're counting on it," he said. "Right now, disorder is our friend. No one will notice you."

"But—"

"But nothing," he said. The sun was red with morning, and I stared at my feet to avoid the glare. We rode in silence until I no longer recognized anything.

"We're going to get you out of here," Petar said. "When we get to Otočac, a Peacekeeper named Stanfeld will meet us."

"I'm scared," I said.

"You should be."

"What?"

"It'd be weird if you weren't."

"The UN. Why is he helping us?"

"It's a woman," Petar said. "And I saved her life."

"Is that how you hurt your arm?"

"Nah. She was on my day off." Pleased with himself, he gave way to a smile I couldn't help but return. Petar put his hand on my knee. "She'll take care of you."

After about an hour, we passed into Lika and arrived on

the outskirts of Otočac. Farmland gave way to small clusters of beige and red-clay-roofed houses along the road. Most of them had been shelled and were in varying states of disrepair.

"Shit," said Petar, and I looked ahead to see bearded men in the road. "For fuck's sake."

"What do we do?"

"Get in the back and lie on the floor and don't move until I tell you," he said. I stuffed the envelope in the waistband of my pants, climbed over the gearshift, and pressed my face against the dirty floor mat. Petar threw a blanket over me and submitted to the checkpoint.

I heard him crank down the window, then a stranger's voice, close: "Can I help you?"

"I've got a delivery," Petar said, and I heard the crinkling of paper, wondered if it was some instruction sheet or dinar to quench the "hunger" he'd mentioned.

"This road is closed. You need to turn around."

"Haven't you people heard of a cease-fire?" said Petar.

"I heard the JNA agreed to one. Luckily, I'm not in that army."

"Look, I have a delivery. Commander Stanfeld."

"There's no Stanfeld here," the soldier said, repeating the foreign last name with some difficulty.

"She's UN."

"She?" he said, amused. "There's no UN here."

"You better check your messages," said Petar. "They're at

the airport right now, and there'll be hell to pay if you make them wait."

"I don't take orders from Peacekeepers." Paper rustling again. "Hold on." A radio beeped, and the soldier asked about a delivery, the staticky reply indiscernible.

"Well, comrade. My commander doesn't know about your delivery. So I'm going to have to ask you to step out of the car."

"Sure thing," said Petar, but I could see him sliding his hand into the skinny space between seats, past his seat belt, where the glint of gunmetal caught my eye.

"Hurry up! Out!"

"Ana, count to three, then run to the center post office," he whispered.

"What?" the soldier said.

"Sorry," Petar said, and I heard him open his door. "I'm just—"

I heard the pop of gunfire and flew from the car, still clutching the blanket around my shoulders. The Četnik was on the ground holding his face, and Petar was running into the scrub across the road, distracting the other soldiers as I darted through the fields down into the town.

"Goodbye!" I yelled to Petar, though I knew he wouldn't hear. Would he be able to fight or get away with his bad arm? Maybe if I ran fast enough and found Stanfeld, the UN could send Blue Helmets to help him. The streets were potholed and gravelly from mortars, and I tried not to trip.

Compared to Zagreb, Otočac was a squat town. The houses looked the same—the familiar tan and white façades and clay roofs—but there were no tall buildings here, nothing more than a few stories, so it was hard to find the center of town. There weren't many people on the street, and no one noticed me.

"Post office?" I said to a man slumped on the corner drinking *rakija* from the bottle.

"Doesn't work," he said.

"I know, but where is it?"

"What good is it if it's closed?"

"Forget it."

"Two streets up. Next to the closed bakery and the closed bank and the closed—"

"Thanks." I ran the two blocks, but there was no one out in front of the post office and it looked dark inside. The air raid siren began to sound.

Through the alley and around the back, I found a woman in Peacekeeping uniform. She adjusted her ponytail beneath her helmet, looked at her watch. I tapped her on the arm.

"Well, what do we have here?" she said in English. She gestured to my blanket. "Are you Superwoman?" I was intimidated by her language and her uniform, but needed her to send help for Petar, so I concentrated on the words I'd learned in school and from my mother.

"Stanfeld," I said.

"Yes, how did you—Ana?"

"Petar has trouble."

"Where is he?"

"Četniks," I said. "The big road."

"Is he hurt?"

"I don't know."

"Shit." She spoke into a walkie-talkie strapped to her upper arm, a series of numbers and something I couldn't understand. Then to me she said, "Don't worry, they'll take care of him. Now let's get you on this plane."

At the airport, Peacekeepers were guarding all entrances. I handed her the envelope Petar had given me.

"Money inside," I said.

"Hopefully we won't need it." She squinted at the guard by the front. "No, not him." I followed her to the next gate. "Nope." Then, at the back gate, "That'll work." She pulled the elastic from her ponytail, and her hair came down around her shoulders in blond waves.

"Hey, you," she said, and the guard looked up, startled.

"Oh, hey, Sharon."

"Mind swiping me through? We're gonna be late for transport."

"Who's the kid?"

"She's my SFF ... AF-6. I told you about her, remember?"

"SFF—" He looked confused. "Does she have a pass?"

"Of course she does," Stanfeld said. "But I had a blond moment and left it in my luggage. If you swipe us through I could get it and show it to you."

"Well—"

"You're the best," she said. She took another step toward him, too close. He slid his pass through the scanner and let us in.

"Idiot," she said when we were out of earshot. We crouched behind a generator and she retied her hair. Before the war, the airport in Otočac had been recreational, and I could see where a chunk of runway, dirt-packed, had been added to accommodate larger aircraft. I studied the plane, a stubby green cargo transport. I'd never been on a plane before, and this one looked much too fat to take off. A Blue Helmet opened the cabin latch, a door with built-in stairs, then stepped off for a smoke. Ms. Stanfeld squeezed my hand, and we ran across the tarmac.

Inside it was not what I thought a plane would look like; there were no seats, only benches, green netting on the wall to hold on to, and stacks and stacks of boxes.

"Sit here." Ms. Stanfeld led me behind an assembly of wooden crates.

"Will Petar be okay?"

"I sent some people for him. Now don't make another sound until we're in the air."

"Then what?" But there were voices by the stairs, other

Blue Helmets boarding, and she stood abruptly, not wanting to be seen conversing with munitions.

When the plane took off my stomach roiled and my ears popped, but I stayed hidden and unmoving, eyeing the rifle clips through the slatted crates. Eventually the turbulence evened out, and, bored and emboldened by the thrum of the engine, I slid my hand through an opening and grabbed one of the magazines. I rejigged my grip until I could pull the clip out through the hole, loading and unloading it unthinkingly. The repetitive motion calmed my stomach and my nerves.

"What's that noise?" I heard someone say, and I froze.

"What noise?" Stanfeld said a little too fast.

"It sounds like it's—" The voice was closer now. "What the fuck?" I looked up at the Blue Helmet in terror, and he stared back at me with equal distress.

"It's okay. She's authorized," Stanfeld said. "Come here, Ana. Come sit by me." She dug my passport out of the envelope. "See? American visa."

The other Peacekeepers stared at her. I sat down beside her and returned to my loading and unloading of the cartridge.

"Still, I trust that you all have the sense not to— Ana! *What the hell are you doing?*"

"She's fast," one of the Blue Helmets said.

"Where did you learn how to do that?"

"I just know," I said.

She readjusted her helmet, loosening the strap around her neck. "I trust all of you have the sense not to say anything about this. For appearances' sake. Wouldn't want to get poor Johnsen in trouble for an egregious failure to complete security check protocol." Everyone looked at one of the Blue Helmets down the row.

"You fought in that village, didn't you?" Stanfeld said.

"A little."

She yanked the clip from my hand and stuffed it in her cargo pocket. No one spoke again until the landing gear protracted in a dull rumble beneath our feet.

IV

Echoed by the Trees

1

"Are you sure this is the place?" Luka said.

I fumbled with my seat belt and got out of the car. "The sandbags were right here. And they had a tree across the other side of the road." Luka got out of the car, too, and stood beside me. "My dad was driving, and the one guy with rotten teeth stuck his head in our window and he had his gun—" I touched the spot on my neck where the soldier had pressed his gun against my father.

"It's okay."

"It was my fault, you know. I made them stop for lunch. If we hadn't, we might have made it back before the block."

"You were ten. You didn't make anyone do anything. And nobody could have known."

I looked into the forest, but it was too shadowy inside to see anything.

"It's over," Luka said.

"It doesn't feel over."

We pushed into the roadside brush—scrubby ragweed, cleavers, and what looked like Christmas holly scratched my ankles. Then the bigger trees—towering pine and oak—overtook the shrubbery. Soon the canopy had filtered out most of the summer sun, and a cool mist hung in the lower branches. It smelled of earth and decomposition.

From far away I had hated this place, but now even that was blurring. The hatred was there, but there were other feelings, too: excitement, almost giddiness, and the strange calm of being close to my parents again.

The woods grew darker, then thinned, but when we reached the clearing it was not how I remembered it. The trees were all wrong, the forest floor different from the way I'd imagined it. The lush summertime green of the foliage confused me. The place was alive, almost pretty.

Across the clearing I spotted a tree stump, the clean, even slice the only evidence a human had been there. I scanned the area for traces of massacre, a concavity or rise in the earth suggesting interment. But there was nothing. Only dark clay ground, damp from the forest shade.

"I'll never find them." I ran my fingers along the tree beside me, its ashen bark ridged and fissured, a history of weathered storms on display. A beetle ran down a groove in the trunk and disappeared in the dirt.

I sat down cross-legged and raked my fingers over the ground, let the soil collect under my nails. A few acorns, still green, had fallen too early, and I took one and buried it in the furrow I'd dug.

"Where are you?" I shouted. A flock of starlings, startled by the noise, shot up from a branch and out beyond the forest.

"Ana?" I'd nearly forgotten Luka was there, and when I turned toward him I got the feeling I'd been sitting there much longer than I realized. "You all right?"

My knees cracked as I stood and wiped my hands on my shorts. "Yeah," I said. "I'm okay."

We returned to the car and I pulled a U-turn across the highway and drove back to the little road, then followed the stony path down into the valley.

The village was no longer a village—anything that had once made it deserving of the title, including residents, was long gone. Most of the buildings had been reduced to rubble, collapsed slabs of concrete. The few that were still standing were all the eerier for it; the glass was blown out, but nothing was boarded up, leaving hollow sockets where the windows had been.

We left the car in the middle of the road and continued down the main street by foot. I tried to work out which house might have been Drenka and Damir's, but it was hard to tell where one lot ended and the other began.

"Careful," Luka said. "Do you think there are *zvončići*?"

I remembered Drenka's exploded chickens and froze in my tracks. "There were."

"They say it'll take another twenty years to demine everything."

Down the street I could see a large stone building, painted black. If I was in the right place it must be the schoolhouse, but I didn't remember it being so dark.

"Walk like this," I said to Luka, high-stepping toward the school. "Gives you more time to look before you put your foot down."

When we got close enough, I could see that the building hadn't been painted at all; it was black with soot, the window glass gone and shutters burned off.

"Četnik headquarters," I said. "They raped so many women here."

Luka stuck his hands in his pockets, looking squeamish.

"I was too little," I said. "And I had a gun."

Our own headquarters should have been across the traffic circle. But what was there looked more like the surface of the moon than the Safe House, all cratered earth and broken chunks of cement. Initially I had allowed myself to think that maybe the Safe Housers had torched the school-

house and the soldiers had gotten what they deserved.
Maybe the villagers had won, or at least escaped. But now,
staring at the sunken ground, I knew it couldn't be true. I
turned back to the charred building. On the far wall a
wooden plank, unburned, poked through the overgrowth.

"What is that?" I said. Luka reached out and swiped at
the vine to reveal a placard, written in jagged lettering:

In memory of our neighbors, who were burned alive
by Serb paramilitary forces during the Croatian War
for Independence, March 1992. Count 79

"Jesus," said Luka.

I pulled away the rest of the weeds and dusted the loose
ash from the plaque until my hands were black with soot.
The carving was uneven, like it had been done by hand.

"Seventy-nine people."

"You're sure this is the town?" he said.

"Yes," I said. As sure as I could be. The grave undetect-
able, the village demolished; this was their biggest victory. I
looked out toward what must have been the wheat fields.
"And if it is, I killed a man in that field." I was headed there
before I knew what I was doing.

"Fuck, Ana, the mines!" Luka said, but I did not stop. If
the village was beyond recognition, the field was even
worse—no sign of wheat or any crops, just an expanse of
wild grass. The lack of corroborating evidence could almost

convince a person she was crazy, that she had dreamt everything up, or at least that things had not happened the way she said.

In the center of the field I slowed and Luka caught up. "Careful. You trying to get blown up?"

"I killed someone here," I said. "I mean, I think I did." I told him about the man in the field, how we'd stared at each other before I shot him.

"Maybe he didn't die."

"Luka, I killed a man. Maybe more than one—who knows what happened when I was just shooting out the window. I could have hit someone else."

"You were defending yourself."

"I'm no better than any of them."

"You were a little kid. You didn't even know what you were doing."

"No, that's the thing. When I was shooting—when I shot that guy—I liked it. I knew it was bad and I liked it. I wasn't sorry."

Luka let me stand there until the sun began to set.

"It's going to be dark soon," he said.

"I know."

"The mines and everything."

"I know."

"Come on." Squinting at the ground, we returned to the car. I threw Luka the keys, and the engine sputtered, then turned, and Luka adjusted the choke.

"Who do you think made that plaque?" I said.

"Church from a neighboring town, or some NGO. All the projects now are about counting. They call it the Book of the Dead. They want to list everyone by name."

"My parents."

"My dad reported them."

"Thank you," I said.

"If that really was the spot where your parents ... we should report it, too. They have dogs or X-ray machines or something to find the graves."

I took out the map and made a mark on the spot.

"You're not a killer," Luka said, and I tried to believe him.

As we drove farther south, billboards with a familiar face cropped up with increasing frequency; it was a while before I realized it was General Gotovina. But instead of the nationalistic slogans popular when I was young, new text rimmed the posters—*Heroj, a ne zločinac.* Hero, not criminal.

"What's that about?" I said when we passed another.

"Part of the EU entrance talks. To be considered for membership we've got to do all sorts of stuff to prove we're 'committed to peace.' The cops had to turn in their guns. And we have to give up our war criminals."

"We have war criminals?"

"So they say."

"So who says? The Četniks?"

"The UN," Luka said. "And we're not supposed to say Četniks now. It's derogatory."

"They were calling themselves Četniks. Singing those awful songs."

"And *'za dom, spremni'* was a fascist slogan first," said Luka. "Our soldiers killed Serbs in the Krajina, Bosniaks killed Serbs in Banja Luka—Bosniak and Croat armies were fighting each other, too, before we joined forces . . ."

"But the UN," I said. "They should talk. They raped more women than anyone. They *videotaped* Srebrenica. Eight thousand people in that grave, in their fucking safe zone. Even the American news caught that story." I had cut the article out of the paper and kept it in my room in Gardenville.

"I know," Luka said. I had wanted him to be outraged, too, but I knew in the end the guilt of one side did not prove the innocence of the other.

I drove into the night, pushing through the briny humidity toward the sea. Luka was asleep, and I hadn't seen a town in a long time. Across the road we passed a shack with SEXI BAR spray-painted across the front in fluorescent pink.

"Hey, wake up. Where are we going to stop?"

"Soon." He yawned and sat up. After a while he pointed

to an exit that looked like a dead end. "There it is. Wait." He pushed the gearshift into park.

"Jesus, you're gonna stall it."

"Transmission's about to drop out anyway after the number you did on it." Luka motioned a switch and climbed across the center console. In a tangle of arms and legs I dove over him into the passenger's seat. He took a harsh left down an unpaved seaside path. There weren't many private beaches in Croatia, but a fence topped with barbed wire had appeared along the docks. In the water, boats with spiral staircases and electricity bobbed and hummed.

"We're not breaking into a yacht," I said.

"We're not breaking in. We were invited. Sort of."

We pulled up to a tollbooth where a man in fake police uniform slid open his foggy Plexiglas window. "Welcome to Marina Yacht Solaris. Name and code word?" he said, readying his clipboard.

"Hello, sir," said Luka in formal conjugation. "We're friends of Danijela Babić's and we're meant to meet her at her boat." The guard shone his flashlight into the car, then thumbed again through his roster.

"She's not here yet. I can't let you in without the express permission of the owner."

There was no way this was going to work, I thought, but Luka remained composed. "She said she might be late. I know the password."

"Which is?"

"Absolut," Luka said, then, more to me than the guard, "It's the name of her dog."

"She named her dog Vodka?" I said, and Luka shushed me.

"I've got the key," he said, and held his house key up to the guard's flashlight. The guard, who was now more confused than authoritative, was checking boxes on his sheet.

"Sign here." He passed the clipboard down to Luka. Luka scribbled some illegible signature—his handwriting had always been atrocious—and handed it back through the window.

"We hope you enjoy your stay at Solaris," said the guard, sounding almost defeated. He pressed a button that rolled back the gate, and we drove through.

"Amazing, right?" said Luka. "Her family's always in Italy this time of year."

"I can't believe she named her dog Vodka."

"Oh, come on. What's your problem with her?"

"I just—" But I could not think of a reason to dislike her beyond the annoying way she touched Luka's arm when she talked, so I didn't finish the thought.

Inside the resort we parked and took the blankets from the trunk. Along a path of brick pavers we passed a restaurant with a crystal chandelier and fancy liqueurs lined up across a mirrored bar, and a wood-paneled hut labeled SAUNA. On the opposite side, yachts and boats bobbed beside the dock. Some had lights in the windows, but most were dark shadows atop the black water.

"Where'd Danijela's family get their money?" I said.

"They owned a lot of seafront property and sold it to some German investment bankers who built a hotel on it."

"Which one is her boat?"

"I don't know."

"Then where are we going to sleep?"

"Here." We came to a black wrought-iron fence encircling a swimming pool and a cluster of plastic lounge chairs, the gate padlocked shut. Luka slipped one foot between the stakes on the bottom crossbar and jumped over with ease. I handed him my blanket and followed in an unsteady copycat.

We set up camp on the chairs. I lay on my back to look at the sky, black and varnished with more stars than I'd seen in years, even more than I could see from the back field in Gardenville.

"Wow," I breathed.

"Perks of being in the middle of nowhere."

"New York doesn't really lend itself to stargazing."

"Neither does Zagreb."

"I guess not." I remembered nights Luka and I had spent on the balcony of my flat, searching relentlessly for Orion, which we'd deemed the best constellation because he had a sword. Now it seemed more likely we'd just been looking at airplanes or Russian satellites.

Luka didn't say anything for a while, and I assumed he had fallen asleep. I closed my eyes and tried to sleep, too, but I was keyed up, images of the forest and our break-in and Danijela all looping through my head. "Good night," I said.

"I would kiss you," Luka blurted.

"What?" I turned to look at him but could only see his outline in the dark.

"I'm not going to," he said. "It's not a good idea. But I thought you should know. That I would kiss you."

"Why?"

"Well, you're attractive and we're sleeping outside together under the stars—"

"I mean," I said, glad the darkness covered my blush, "why is it a bad idea?"

"Because I mess up relationships. Because you're going home at the end of the summer."

I thought of Brian and wondered if he had emailed. "*I* mess up relationships," I said. "I basically broke up with my last boyfriend because he was too nice."

I considered what it might mean to be with Luka, whether it was even something I wanted. Was the envy I felt at every mention of Danijela a sign that I had feelings for him, or simply a longing for the way things used to be, when we were young and each other's whole worlds?

We hadn't talked much about my plans beyond the summer, and in more whimsical moments I'd considered staying—I could transfer to the University of Zagreb, teach

English afterward. Deep down, though, I knew I'd return to the States to finish school, go back to my family. I let the question float out to sea, and we lay still, comfortable as we always had been in one another's silences.

"Besides," Luka said eventually, as if he'd continued weighing the pros and cons of our potential relationship in his head. "You know too much." But I couldn't help thinking as I hovered between waking and sleep, maybe that wasn't such a bad thing.

I resurfaced a few hours later; it was still dark and my feet had gone numb. Once in New York water had seeped into my snow boots and frozen between my toes, but I still couldn't remember a time when I felt this helplessly cold. Covered in gooseflesh and shivering, I unrolled the jeans I'd been using as a pillow and pulled them on over my shorts.

"Luka," I whispered. "It's so fucking cold." Luka stirred, and I hoped he'd wake up, but instead he mumbled something that to my best guess was "socks" and turned over. My thoughts felt slow, my limbs weighted. I inched my chair closer to his.

2

Hours later I felt the sun on my face, first pleasant, then hot and pulsing. *We died,* I thought. Then a jagged pain tore up the length of my leg. I sat up, shielding my eyes against the morning and saw the outline of the fake policeman, now striking Luka with his nightstick and cursing.

"Derelicts!" he yelled, along with insults about our mothers' relationships with livestock. "You tricked me! Get the hell out of here!"

"We can't walk when you're smashing us in the legs!" I said. He stopped for a moment, as if to consider the argument, and Luka and I took off over the fence, trailing the orange blankets behind us.

We pushed through thick sea grass toward the public beach. The air was salty-sweet, a seawater and pine mix that had in my childhood signaled the start of summer vacation. It was still early and there were few people on the beach. I slipped off my sandals and was met with the stabbing pain of tiny pointed rocks.

"Jesus," I said, jumping back into my shoes. "They're so sharp." I had grown used to the less spectacular but sandy coastline of south Jersey.

"Yeah, you'll have to work on your calluses."

At water's edge Luka dropped his blanket and pants and ran into the sea. "It's warm!" he called and dove beneath the surface. I stripped to my bra and underwear, then immediately felt embarrassed. I'd studied Luka's shirtless physique back in Zagreb; it was only natural that he might examine me in my adult form, with hips and breasts. I wanted him to like what he saw. I looked down at my thighs, adjusted my bra strap. I wished for a towel. Nothing to be done about it now, I thought, and ran awkwardly into the sea until I was deep enough to swim, eager to cover myself and lift my smarting feet from the rocks.

The water was calmer than I remembered, nothing like the constant fight against tide and undertow that came with swimming in the ocean. Looking down, I was surprised to see my own legs, unobscured by the swirling sediment of the mid-Atlantic. I put my head back and succumbed to the bobbing rhythm of the not-quite-waves. Just when I'd begun to wonder whether one could sleep that way, something slick and powerful gripped my ankle and pulled me down-

ward. I screeched and kicked until the thing released me and
Luka appeared beside me in hysterics.

"God, you're evil," I said.

We were treading water, and our legs brushed one another. Luka ran his hand through his hair. "Come on. We
better go if we want to get to Tiska before dark."

We jumped the fence back into Solaris to retrieve the car.
We sat on the hood and downed half a bag of muesli and a
box of UHT milk, and afterward I changed my clothes in
the backseat. The guard gave us the finger as we sped
through the exit, and we returned to the main road.

Luka drove and I lay across the back, paging through the
final segment of Rebecca West's journey and looking out
the window. The landscape was growing increasingly moun-
tainous, the highland vegetation parched a tawny hue, making the ridges look almost golden.

Luka was trying to calculate how long it would take to
forget the war.

"Maybe we're already on the way," I said. "The last five or
six years' worth of kids have been born outside of wartime.
Postwar babies."

"Everyone's still talking about it," said Luka.

"Here maybe. But talking's not the same as living through
it."

"You don't need to experience something to remember it.
You're going to have kids, and eventually they're going to
want to know where their other set of grandparents is."

"And I'll say they died."

"You should tell them the truth."

"That is the truth. They died."

"The whole story. You should tell Rahela, too. She deserves to know."

"I know," I said. I let the book fall closed in my lap. I looked out at the gilded mountains and thought of the centuries of wars and mistakes that had come together in this place. History did not get buried here. It was still being unearthed.

"What is that monstrosity you're reading?"

I told him about West and her trip through Yugoslavia. "Same shit, different war."

"Some people say the Balkans is just inherently violent. That we have to fight a war every fifty years."

"I hope that's not true," I said.

3

We arrived on the edge of Tiska a few hours later. Tiska had been a provincial outpost even by Yugoslavian standards— the electricity was spotty, phone and television lines were few, most homes didn't have hot-water heaters, and it was twenty-five minutes' drive from the nearest real town. But what it lacked in amenities it made up for in clear air and sun and a cliffside view of the Adriatic.

As a child I had taken the summers for granted— a month's vacation time was the country's standard, and nearly everyone I knew holidayed on the coast. Now I considered how insane a month off would sound to an American. Jack could barely get a week away from the computer consulting firm where he worked, and even then he was constantly hassled by pages and phone calls from needy clients.

Luka and I had been debating whether or not the EU's unified currency made economic sense, but now the sight of the vast beryl water on the horizon knocked me quiet and we let the conversation fade. Something new was burgeoning within me, a feeling different from the anxiety that had pervaded most of the trip: nostalgia, untainted by trauma, for my childhood. I'd learned how to swim in that sea, how to steer our neighbors' unwieldy motorboat, to jump from the rock ledges without cutting my feet, to catch and gut and grill a fish. At night I'd sneak down to the darkened beach and talk, in a combination of broken English and charades, with the Italian and Czech children whose families had come for an inexpensive vacation.

"I hope it's still there," I said under my breath, an incantation. We rolled down the windows and let the salty air fill the car.

Down on the deserted beach, waves lapped against the roof of a red utility truck, capsized and rusting. The driver must have been going too fast on the road above and missed a turn. My fondness for the place was again engulfed by distress and a sense of purpose. Petar and Marina were either here or dead, and I was about to find out which.

There was a point, unmarked, that the road turned into a footpath. The road, which at its widest was only big enough for one car, had no guardrail and was bordered by the unforgiving rock of the Dinaric Alps on one side and the Adriatic on the other. A few meters too far and a driver might be forced to make the trip back up the mountain entirely in reverse. I parked the car on a patch of dirt before the road narrowed completely. It used to be a crowded parking spot, but now there were only two other cars and both were so old it was difficult to tell whether they were abandoned. We shouldered our bags and followed the muggy breeze into the village.

At first it was unclear whether the place was bombed out or just dilapidated. Though I'd stayed here for months at a time, looking at it now I found it hard to believe people had lived out their whole lives along the twisted innards of the Dinara, in a place so small and in such close contact with nature.

Petar's grandfather Ante had moved to Tiska in the forties after finishing medical school in Sarajevo. He and his neighbors had built one another's houses with concrete and mules. Decades later when I visited as a child, the village behaved as if Ante was still alive and well; our address was simply "The doctor's house, Tiska, 21318," the postal code of the next town over. Communal cement mixing, too, had remained a practice in the town—my earliest memories of the place were of my father and Petar hauling buckets of concrete alongside the rest of the village men to transform the path into sets of lumpy, hand-shaped stairs. The idea was that the stairs would be easier for the old people to navigate than the dirt pathways, which were slick in the smooth spots and root-riddled in others. But it had been easier to run along the pathways, and at the time I'd resented the stairs for slowing me down.

Luka and I came to the steps, descending at a jagged pace toward sea level, obeying the curvature of the mountains like a set of intestines. They snaked past the village's single store and the stone monument to the workers of the Glorious Revolution. They swooped around the small church and to the schoolhouse, which was swathed in untamed vines. The school had been in disuse even when I was small, except where the old men had cleared the underbrush to expose the packed sand floors of bocce courts. The steps continued down toward the water, passing strips of fig trees and agave plants; the figs were soft and sugary, the agave thick and barbed, their contiguous presence a testament to the fickle soil beneath.

"It's still standing," Luka called from down the path. I sped up and stood beside him on the slanted step. Through a clearing in the fig trees I could see Petar and Marina's house, sealed up and covered in weeds. The façade was pitted with scars from shell fragments, and a chunk of the roof was gone. No one would live in a place like that.

I jumped the last few steps and reached the terrace, waded through dead leaves to the front door, and stupidly began to knock.

"Hello?"

"Ana."

"Just wait," I said, and banged harder.

"Ana, come on. Don't do that."

"Hey! Get off that property!" someone said in heavily accented English.

"Sorry," I called back in Croatian.

"Hrvatske?" the woman's voice said.

"Yeah. We're Croats." I walked in the direction of the voice. "I'm looking for the Tomićs?"

The woman appeared on the balcony of a house farther up the mountain than I expected given the clarity of the sound of her voice, an acoustic wonder of the cliffs I'd forgotten. She was wizened and swaddled in a black long-sleeved dress that made me sweat just looking at it, a red flowered head scarf tied at her chin. "Sorry," she said when we got closer. "I thought you were tourists. The kids love to break into the abandoned ones."

"Abandoned?" I said.

"They've been gone for years."

"What happened to the owners?"

"Petar was killed in the war. That's what Marina said. Did you know them?"

When she said it, it sounded true, like I had always known it, but that did not stop the feeling of loss, hard and stonelike, from dropping into my stomach. Still, she had spoken to Marina. "Marina's here?"

"Not anymore. She came down for a while after Petar

died. She was trying to get out. To Austria to live with her sister, she said."

"Do you know if she made it? Where in Austria? How can I contact her?"

The woman shook her head. "Sorry, kid. You look familiar, though. Where did you say you were from?"

"We used to come for holidays with Petar and Marina when I was small. I'm Ana. Jurić."

"Jurić. Yes," she said, adjusting her head scarf. "So you're the one."

I looked at the woman and tried to discern what she meant. "The one what?" I said finally.

"The one who lived."

"I lived."

"You look like your father."

"You knew him?"

"I knew them all."

"Baka," a small voice called from inside the house.

"I'm going to the church now. Come later, to talk."

"I will," I said, but she was gone quickly back into her house, and I stayed on her terrace staring up at the space where she had stood.

Luka broke open the back window, and I slid through into the cobwebbed darkness. The air inside was heavy, laden with years of dirt. The walls were bare, the kitchen supplies gone, and I tried to determine how much of a hurry Marina had been in when she left. The ugly auburn couch was still pressed against the wall, the table and stove next to one another in the area that, though technically part of the same room, Marina had declared the kitchen. Despite its barrenness and sour smell, the place looked the same.

"Go open the front," Luka called. "I'm too big to fit through here."

I lurched toward the door, but my presence in the house was a trip wire of disintegration; a set of blinds fell from their place in the side window and a thick beam of light penetrated the dark kitchen.

I saw my parents—summer skin, sweat-slicked and tanned. My mother stood at the kitchen sink, wringing out laundry and humming an old children's rhyme, my father rounding the corner and joining her song with a whistle. His hands crept up the folds of her dress, exploring her hip bones. The water sloshed in the sink as he spun her around and kissed her forehead. From this angle, I saw her dress clinging tight around her midriff and realized she would have been a few months pregnant with Rahela the last time we'd gone to Tiska.

I heard Luka fiddling with the front door, and soon he'd managed to break it open himself. An overwhelming glare filled the house. I blinked my parents away.

"What are you doing?" he said.

"Nothing." He opened the remaining shades and shutters and windows, then disappeared into the back bedroom, where I could hear him doing the same. A concrete box, the house had been designed as a haven from the southern sun—but now, with all the blinds up and the roof broken, it was the brightest I'd ever seen it. The breeze pushed the stale air out the windows.

Luka emerged from the bathroom with a set of brooms. Petar and Marina had always used the bathtub for storing cleaning supplies and tools; the house had no hot water, so there was no real difference between the outdoor shower and the one in the bathroom.

"Come on, then," Luka said, jabbing me with the end of a broomstick.

"How'd you know they were in there?"

"Don't you remember that summer your father and Petar were resurfacing the terrace and they kept tracking the cement dust in the house and your mom and Marina were going mental?"

"Now that you mention it."

"You and I swept for like three days straight. I'm practically traumatized."

"I'm sure that excuse goes over well with your mother."

Inside Luka swept and scoured the floor and scrubbed the countertops, and I spent the afternoon pulling the vines that choked the windows. The space between my shoulder blades got sore quickly, and I realized how little I actually moved anymore, how content I was to be hunched in a subway seat or over my desk at school. But I liked the discomfort now, a productive pain, and I moved on from the façade to the patio itself, weeding and cleaning in methodical square patches. The roots of the overgrowth were deep and clung obstinately to thick clods of soil. I threw the weeds and vines in what used to be the compost pile and set my sights on the layers of dirt and dust and sand that coated the terrace, sweeping it into piles and scooping it away with a metal dustpan and brush I remembered Petar banging out in the front yard.

Beneath a dirty patch near the front door I unearthed the handprints. In the summer my father and Petar had poured new concrete for the patio, we'd each left a handprint in the square by the door. It was my idea.

"If you're bad, I'll cover up your handprint and you'll be erased from the family!" Petar had teased whenever he wanted me to run an errand for him. Now I stood before the inlay, pressed my hand into the contours of his, and considered how easy it was to erase a family. I traced my parents' hand shapes, then my own, my nine-year-old fingertips barely reaching the first knuckles of my fingers now. At the corner of the block, a vaguely toe-shaped smudge was pressed in the cement. Jealous but too embarrassed to add his own handprint to what he deemed to be a family plot, Luka had planted his big toe in the concrete. Then, even more ashamed, he hadn't washed the cement off quickly enough, and it took days to peel from his skin.

"Hey, Luka! Come see this!"

Luka appeared, sweaty and shirtless. "What is it?"

"Your toe has stood the test of time!"

"Are those your parents'?"

"And Petar's and Marina's, yeah."

"And yours," he said.

"Yeah. And mine."

"I'm glad you have this," he said, turning back in to the house. For a minute I wondered whether he was going to try to cut the rock out of the ground, but he returned instead with my backpack, and dug through it to find my camera. "Here."

I took two pictures and set them inside on the table to develop. "Get my wallet out of there, too," I said. "Let's go to the store."

We climbed the stairs back to the upper footpath toward the village store.

"Do you think you'll go look for Marina?" Luka said. I thought of the day I escaped and wondered whether Petar had died or had gone back to the front and saved others. If he'd been caught in those woods, Marina might think I was dead, too.

"I want to. But it's harder for me to wander around Austria than it is here."

"I could go with you if you want."

"Maybe I'll try to write her somehow first."

"If she's alive, you should visit."

"Let me do it," I said.

"I will. But I won't let you wait another decade this time."

The bells on the door jingled when we made our way inside, and an ancient man glanced up from his *Dalmacija News* with disinterest. The store's main stock—bread, fatty white cheese, stamps, and cigarettes—was laid out on a card table. In the cooler nearby were mackerels and mussels the fishermen had brought in. Luka and I picked two mackerels from the case. Luka asked for olive oil, and the man wrapped the fish in newspaper, then retrieved a small cruet. He added a book of matches to the pile.

"Does the pay phone still work?" I said. The phone attached to the side of the store had been the only one in the village when I was young, and even then it was finicky.

"Sometimes," he said. "Do you want a phone card?"

"Please," I said. "For America."

He pulled a plastic card from beneath the till in the register that said NORTH AMERICA in bold lettering across the front, and added it to our total. Luka peeled a hundred-kuna note from his billfold, and the man put our food in a brown paper bag.

"Come back Wednesday, if you want," he said as we left. "Some chocolate's coming in."

"I'm going to go get a fire started," Luka said, handing me the phone card. "I'll see you back at the house."

I'd only made one other phone call from Tiska, when my mother forgot her bathing suit and let me call home to have my father bring it. She'd stood behind me, folded the cord just right, and held it above our heads like an antenna. I tried replicating her maneuver, shifting the bends in the wire until I got a tone, then hastily dialing the series of numbers on the back of the card followed by my American home number.

"Ana?"

"Can you hear me?"

"Barely! How are you? I've been so worried!"

"I'm fine. We're down the coast. No Internet and stuff. Sorry I haven't been in touch more."

"I got your email. But you should've called."

"I know. I'm sorry. Is Rah—Rachel home?"

"She's at soccer practice."

"Can I call back and leave a voice mail for her?"

"That'd be nice."

"Okay, I'll do that now."

"You're good though?" Laura said.

"Yeah, I'm good."

"Well, I'm glad. Thanks for calling. And don't—"

The line crackled, then went dead. I readjusted the cord, called back, and rang through to what I hoped was the voice mail, though the sound was more static than words. "Hi,

Rachel. I'm in Croatia at the beach and it's very beautiful. I've been taking some pictures for you. Maybe, if Mom says it's okay, you can come with me next summer. You'd like it here—" The line made a loud, unfamiliar buzzing sound. "Love you!" I yelled over the tone and hung up. Then I went back into the store and bought a postcard and an airmail stamp so I could write to Brian that night.

On my way home I knocked on the door of the old woman and waited a long time for someone to come. The lamps were unlit and there were no children playing out back.

"Tomorrow then," I said to the empty house.

I showered beneath a pipe that stood at the edge of the cliff, a place of both total exposure and unmitigated solitude. I could see the whole village, busy with the activities of dusk. Old men on the pier were pulling up their wire fishing cages. The shopkeeper turned off his lights; someone at the church turned the steeple light on. The salt from the sea had dried in visible tide lines on my body, and I rubbed them away. The wind whistled in the hollows of my ears, was sharp against my wet skin, and made the cold water from the spigot feel warm.

Luka stoked the fire in the brick grill out front, and I scrounged around in the kitchen for any utensils left behind.

Marina hadn't forgotten anything of use, and I took comfort in the fact that it looked like she'd had time to pack. I cleared off the counter, lining the Polaroids of the concrete hands and Luka and Plitvice on a ledge along the wall. I'd bring them home for Rahela, but for now they fit well here.

We cooked the fish with oil and pine branches, then laid it on the kitchen table and pulled it apart with our hands. It was gritty and salty and not altogether descaled, but the oil and pine smoke flavored it enough. For dessert we ate the peanut butter, scraping the sides of the jar clean. The last of the gulls and kittiwakes were calling to each other, nesting for the night.

"You know, you could come to America," I said.

"I don't think my English is good enough." He said it so quickly I knew he'd been thinking about it.

"Your English is fine. But come for a visit at least. Come see me in New York."

"I could do that."

Tiska was black now, and I wondered how late it was. I hadn't seen a clock all day. It was a rare pleasure afforded by the village not to be governed by time, to eat when hungry and sleep when tired. And I was tired now—my stomach full, my muscles aching, and my mind warm and blurry.

I listened to Luka wonder aloud how migrating birds found their way back each season as we spread out our blankets and lay down on the floor, the tiles cool and hard against my stiff back. Through the gash in the roof we could see the sky, and we stretched our arms upward, tracing constellations. It calmed me, just like it had when we were small and hungry and scared of dying. Around the room the moon filled the shell marks in the walls with a pallid blue light, and they looked full again, like a home.

Acknowledgments

There are many people without whom this book would not exist. Special thanks to:

My remarkable editor, David Ebershoff, who was exactly what this story needed, his assistant Caitlin McKenna, and everyone at Random House who worked to make this book a book. My agent, Kristina Moore, and the great people at Wylie. Friends and family in Zagreb and Pisak—Dubravka, Matea, Marin, Joško, Šinko, Novak, and especially Darko— for sharing their stories with me. The many professors at Emerson College and Columbia University who supported me, particularly Jon Papernick, Jonathan Aaron, and Jay Neugeboren. My MFA colleagues, for enduring my incessant talk of this project, and for their friendship. Alan, for his keen editing eye and skilled hand-holding. Zach, for never letting me take myself too seriously. My family: my mother for putting a pen in my hand, my father for teaching me how to tell a story. My grandparents for thinking I was great before I'd done anything at all. And to Aly, who read this first.

ABOUT THE TYPE

This book was set in Caslon, a typeface first designed in 1722 by William Caslon (1692–1766). Its widespread use by most English printers in the early eighteenth century soon supplanted the Dutch typefaces that had formerly prevailed. The roman is considered a "workhorse" typeface due to its pleasant, open appearance, while the italic is exceedingly decorative.

To buy any of our books and to find out
more about Abacus and Little, Brown, our authors
and titles, as well as events and book clubs,
visit our website

www.littlebrown.co.uk

and follow us on Twitter

@AbacusBooks
@LittleBrownUK

To order any Abacus titles p & p free in the UK,
please contact our mail order supplier on:

+ 44 (0)1832 737525

Customers not based in the UK should contact
the same number for appropriate postage
and packing costs.